HIGH TIDE

Andrea Fisher Rowland

Published by Chenille Books, Charlottesville, Virginia, USA
Printed in the United States of America
ISBN 978-1-931922-04-3

Hans Christian Andersen excerpts from "The Little Mermaid" [http://www.gutenberg.org/files/32572/32572-0.txt], "The Wind Tells About Waldemar Daa and his Daughters" [http://www.gutenberg.org/cache/epub/27000/pg27000.txt], "Thumbelina" [http://www.gutenberg.org/files/32571/32571-0.txt], and "The Drop of Water" [http://www.gutenberg.org/cache/epub/31103/pg31103.txt] are all from Project Gutenberg editions, and are reproduced with gratitude.

William Bradford's "Some Strange and Remarkable Passages (1634)" (quoted on p. 306) as collected in Trent and Wells, *Colonial Prose and Poetry* (1901) is available from https://www.bartleby.com/163/103.html. Shakespeare, Carroll, and biblical and liturgical excerpts are readily available.

Cover images – grass [sky grastop water-4217626 scholty1970], ocean [ocean abstract-2384_1920], and swans [swan-3692618 nidan] – as well as Swan silhouette [swans-36088] are all from Pixabay and are licensed under Creative Commons 0 (CC0) license terms, with appreciation.

The publisher wishes to thank Dorene Fisher, Noelle Beverly, Bethany Farris, Kirk Schroder, Esq., BACCA Literary, and the author's family.

CONTENTS

EDITORS' NOTE

Our dear friend Andrea wrote **High Tide** over the years, in her available moments. In a life full of work, community, family, and contemplation, Andrea returned to her novel at every opportunity. Weaving together her love of language, sensitivity to the natural environment, and a core connection to her family, the central elements of her novel parallel her life.

When she saw that her life was coming to an end, Andrea knew she needed to finish her novel. Dorene agreed to edit it, and Anne agreed to arrange to publish it, along with Andrea's poetry collection, **Family Album**, which Andrea and Anne finalized earlier in 2019.

And so in the spring of the year, while Andrea was in hospice care, Dorene sat at her bedside and read **High Tide** out loud to her, chapter by chapter, making minor edits as they went. After Andrea's passing, we both continued the process, immersing ourselves in the town of Jasper, the Baker family, and, of course, Marika's story. Strangers to each other a few months ago, we are now grateful to Andrea for our friendship.

For Andrea, as well as for us, getting this book into your hands has been a labor of love. We invite you to join Andrea in the world she created: Jasper, North Carolina at High Tide.

Anne M Carley
Dorene Fisher
Charlottesville, VA
November 2019

Cast of Characters

Marika Hansen • Former marine biologist/epidemiologist originally from Denmark. Abandoned a career as a lab scientist and spends most of her time drinking, watching waves, and drawing mysterious maps of the migration of waterfowl and the spread of human diseases.

Lynn Baker • Young single mother of Kyle Peterson, ex-wife of Kenny Peterson, and daughter of Pete Baker. Once an aspiring writer, now living in her father's house and struggling to raise her son.

Kyle Peterson • Lynn Baker's young child, twelve months old as the story begins.

Kenny Peterson • Lynn Bakers' ex-husband. A car dealer who enjoys fishing and sleeping around.

Terry Baker • A local doctor, sister of Lynn Baker and daughter of Pete Baker.

Pete Baker • Widowed mayor of Jasper, father of Lynn and Terry Baker, grandfather of Kyle Peterson.

Jeanne Dubovsky • Aunt of Lynn and Terry Baker, and sister of Cathy Dubovsky Baker, Pete's deceased wife. A masseuse, Jeanne operates a tea room out of her beach cottage. Once in love with Pete, she has withdrawn somewhat from the family.

Father Don Cathcart • Priest at Our Lady of Mercy, which includes the Bakers and the Dobbs in its congregation. From a wealthy old family in Charlottesville. Having doubts about his vocation.

Alan Hirsch • Retired divorced English professor. Friend of Don Cathcart from graduate school days in Charlottesville. Originally from Brooklyn.

Jack Brockie • Owner and manager of The Sandpiper Inn. A relatively recent resident of Buxton. Husband of Deidre Brockie and father of Shona Brockie.

Deidre Brockie • Bored and promiscuous wife of Jack Brockie and mother of Shona Brockie.

Shona Brockie • Beautiful young girl of nineteen. Daughter of Jack and Deidre Brockie, waitresses at her father's Sandpiper Inn.

Barry Anderson • Young bartender at The Cove, originally from Northern Virginia. Friend of Marika Hansen, attracted to Shona Brockie.

Drew Layman • High school and drinking buddy of Kenny Peterson, Drew works construction.

Lori Layman • Drew's wife.

Marcy • Runs the Bluebird Café.

Fred the Cat • An orange tabby who roams the beach and belongs to anyone who feeds him.

JASPER

I

Marika Hansen stands in the ocean up to her thighs. It is high tide. The October sky today is clouded in patches, and the water, reflecting it, is multicolored—blue here, green there, gray there. The sun comes and goes. One minute the world is bright and golden, the next minute, lowering and gray. She finally bought a pair of waders so that she can come out this far.

She knows she is tempting fate. The riptide here at the Outer Banks is a mean and sneaky one, perfectly capable of grabbing hold of someone standing where she is and dragging her out to sea. Feeling the pull of the undertow, it isn't hard to imagine being carried away now. Always, since she was a little girl, she has been addicted to that pull.

She stands as the waves pull out and feels the land giving way beneath her feet, sucking her down a little, down a little with each wave. Even without a riptide, the sea would pull her to the horizon eventually, or so she always imagines. It is good to have such a tangible sense of something so much stronger than herself. She supposes some people feel that way about God and can get the feeling by praying, no matter where they are. But she can only get it here.

Her other life in New York seems like another world now, and she still feels the relief of escaping its noise, though it's been almost a year since she left. She pauses every now and then to contrast the lab in New York, with its bright, sterile interior, to the wide vista before her now, and the rigid protocol of the lab to the wandering explorations that now occupy her days.

Burnt out in New York, she came down to the Outer Banks to be closer to nature and found it swarming with tourists and retirees and all their accompanying detritus. This did bring her closer to nature, though not in the romantic way she had imagined. Now she feels closer to nature, but farther from her own species.

She begins to feel a little cold and dizzy and realizes that she hasn't eaten since breakfast. Clumsily, she sloshes toward the shore and over the narrow strip of beach between the sea and the dunes. By the time she unwraps her sandwich and opens her flask of whiskey, she's shaking a little from hunger and hours of resisting the motion of the waves and tide. The sandwich is tasty, but she loses interest before it's gone and throws the rest to the gulls. The whiskey holds her attention longer, and she takes several hearty drafts of it, feeling its warmth spreading as if from her heart.

As the sun sets, spreading a yellow band of light between the gray of the cloudy sky and the gray of the sea, she leans back against a dune and nods off for a few minutes.

When the cry of a gull awakens her, the sun has set. The waves are silvered at the edges by the moon, and faint stars are appearing.

She looks up at them until she becomes dizzy. Then, closing her eyes, she sways slightly, listening to that great, deep, sighing voice in front of her. Come home.

Sometimes that's what she thinks the sea is saying to her as she lingers on the beach, listening to that sound, the breath of the world, smelling its ancient, sexual smell. Nowadays sometimes she imagines she can tell how high the tide is just by listening to the lengths of those inhalations and exhalations. She feels alone except for its enormous presence—invisible, alone, drunk and full of knowledge. Happy. She knows that whatever form this land and this ocean choose to take, whether beneath or above the waves, they will outlast the people on and around them. That knowledge, which has come to her in the last few months, has changed her from a frustrated, angry activist into a grimly happy spectator. Totally irreligious, she finds that she has something in common with the various sects that await with joy the imminent end of the world. It's all so dirty, so tangled, so out of control. It's a relief to see the signs, increasing daily, that it will all be washed away. Not that she believes in a great flood, though it would be poetically satisfying. But something will happen. Even mathematically, things can't go on as they are.

She has spent some full days exploring the flora and fauna of the Outer Banks, this flat, scrubby place in thrall to the sea. Its vegetation is tough and subtle—pine, juniper, cypress in the small remaining patch of woods, and, near the beach, sea grass, Gaillardia, prickly pear cactus—plants that can hunker down and survive the salty winds and storms. Only a bridge and a ferry connect the Outer Banks to mainland North Carolina, so wherever she goes she has the feeling that water is always just over her shoulder, the sea to the east and the sound and rivers to the west. Periodically, the sea tries to thrust its way inland, saltwater breaking down sand dunes and flooding Route 12 to join with the brackish water on the other side.

Here, between sound and sea, she feels that she is on a narrow strip of land that can't seem to make up its mind whether to become an island, rejoin the mainland, or just disappear under the waves. As Marika imagines it, while the land dithers, people settle on it, like sea birds mistaking a whale's back for a rock. They run and walk and wander along the edge of the sea, where numberless waves approach and recede from the shore, each one a different color, a different shape. Marika has gotten into the habit of watching these waves every morning and every evening. The waves move as restlessly as her dreams move at night, back and forth, over and under, revealing and concealing treasures and wrecks. She thinks about how life began at the sea's edge. Maybe we cluster around it because it reminds us of younger layers of ourselves, now sunk out of sight. A liquid world, calling to our blood, our tears, to all the warm salty liquids we still contain.

Come home.

So she walks the beach day and night. She's come across all kinds of things—dying and breeding crabs, mysterious heaps of sodden clothing, perfect, intricate shells, various humans. Now and then she stumbles on a party of good ol' boys around an illegal bonfire. Dazed by their noise, she sometimes stays and drinks with them a while, as if she's obliged to enjoy the hospitality of a savage tribe encountered in the middle of the jungle. At first, uneasy with her, they quiet down a little, but as they get used to her being there they resume their despicable little self assertions, flicking cigarette butts onto the sand, bullying the women, pissing into the sea, and she hurries on, wondering what possessed her to stop.

It's October now, though, and the beach is mostly deserted except for occasional shell-seekers and fishermen. To Marika, who has spent some time studying migration patterns, October is flying time, and she always feels particularly restless when the birds are moving. Years of watching them and thinking about them have instilled their rhythms in her. She knows, for instance, that, in their nesting grounds in the Arctic, the swans actually see time. In the long nights, the lengthening of the cold Arctic darkness, a minute or so longer each night, forms an intelligible structure to them, a curve in their minds. The curve is a signal, clear and urgent: Time to go. They unfold their wings. Their voices, like muddy trumpets, call to each other, to themselves, to the darkening sky. Time to go. They fly so high that ice crystals form on their wings. They fly for hundreds of miles, following the coastline, watching for shiny patches of inland water that the older ones remember from past flights.

But now, with the spread of strip malls and parking lots, asphalt can shine like water, the sun reflecting off the ground glass that's mixed in with it, and Marika has read about a flock of swans landing in the parking lot of a Food Lion grocery store. Reading about that made her want to rip up the parking lot with her bare hands. Now she closes her eyes and imagines the air filled with the whirring sounds of wings.

•

Just northwest of where Marika sits drinking by the sea, such a flock is winging its way southward. But the swans have lost their bearings and gone astray. Really it's not the swans but the land that's gone astray. The flock flies to the limits of exhaustion, only to see no lake where a lake was last year. The lead cob falters and circles a couple of times, the flock following him. They have flown eight hundred miles without stopping, and now, where they expected a familiar place to rest, feed, and preen, they find unknown territory.

Swampland has become farmland, and the too-small, too-muddy, too-exposed pond that the swans finally settle on doubles as a hog wallow. Some birds begin preening immediately, some dive for plants and insects for the cygnets, others waddle uneasily onto shore and search the ground like chickens. They know they will not stay here long.

But it will be long enough.

•

Stowing her flask in her small rucksack, Marika decides on one more foray into the waves. To avoid getting carried away by a riptide she reminds herself of the point, immersed about halfway up her thighs, where she should stop. She pushes her way out, feeling the welcome pressure of the water almost like an embrace, and takes a stand, closing her eyes. It is high tide, and she knows that between the grains of the sand around her, tiny desiccated forms—barnacles, gastropods, algae—are springing to life at the touch of the salty flood. It is a kind of resurrection. Immediately they begin the work of feeding and breeding. And just as immediately, their predators, whom the sea has also resurrected, suck them up and convert them to energy to breed their own young. Some of those predators in turn become prey. So, at their most alive, these creatures are also closest to their death.

Too much life can be fatal. Marika muses on this paradox as she watches the unnatural foam of sulfites bobbing on the crests of small waves. We are a disease the earth has caught, she thinks, as she has thought before. The symptoms of us are becoming more and more irritating, moving, perhaps, from low-grade chronic to acute. Her eyes move toward the invisible horizon and, as her thoughts diffuse, a line from a hymn comes, from nowhere, into her mind: "Come, Lord, come!"

2

The town of Jasper has one grocery store. Locals congregate at the Bluebird Café and at The Cove, a bar on the beach. Jeanne's Tea Room offers massages and Tarot readings along with pots of herbal blends. The town boasts one large, upscale hotel, The Sandpiper Inn, and one more modest motel, The Plover. The community is large enough for an elementary school, but the high school is in the larger town of Hatteras. There are an Episcopal church, a Baptist church, and a Catholic church. The abundance of water of various kinds makes the Outer Banks attractive to migratory birds and also to humans, and to cater to the seasonal influx of tourists, there are various generic restaurants and souvenir shops with an emphasis on seashells and plastic pirate gear. Docks and boats and tour operations serve vacationing fishermen.

The town has a mayor, Pete Baker, who once ran a successful bait shop. He is a widower with two grown daughters, one of whom, Terry, is a doctor at the nearby Family Wellness Center. The other, Lynn, is a young single mother, living in her father's house, where early in the morning she is sitting in the nursery, rocking her son, Kyle.

Leaning back in her rocking chair, Lynn focuses on the small square of green which is the nursery window. Though it's pretty much still dark outside, she imagines that she can see green because she smells the old loblolly pine out there and hears it softly scratching the side of the house as it nods in the breeze. At her breast, Kyle keeps falling asleep, and she keeps jiggling him awake, hoping he'll take enough milk to let her sleep for another two hours. She hasn't looked at the clock, but she knows it's probably somewhere around five. Leaning her head back, she tries to live in this warm moment, with the quiet baby in her lap and the old pine shushing. She tries to keep her worries at bay. It really is too early in the morning for them to come calling. The past. The present. The future. None of it really bears thinking about except this moment, with this warm baby close to her, closing the circle of her arms.

Around her, the lavender nursery walls are slowly lightening to a dreamy twilight color, and she knows that not far away a line of light has appeared on the gray horizon. Lynn's not the frou-frou type, and there's not much of it in the room. A border of fish and seaweed swims around the wall, and there is a photograph of a fierce-looking boy baby that she found in the *Utne Reader*, with a quotation from Helen Keller underneath: "Security is mostly a superstition. It does not exist in nature, nor do the children of men as a whole experience it. Avoiding danger is no safer in the long run than exposure. Life is either a daring adventure, or nothing. To keep our faces toward change and behave like free spirits in the presence of fate is strength undefeatable." Lynn cut out this picture and its versified caption while she was still pregnant, feeling, even when Kyle was still inside of her, that she would want more than anything else to protect him, and that she would have to protect him from her desire to protect him. And she wonders, now, are all the things we most desire impossible things? But the photo and the quotation make her feel better. Somehow, she'll find the resolve to help him be strong.

Now, she looks down at him and her long blonde hair spills over both of them. He stops sucking and sleeps. She jiggles him, but he's gone. Slowly, she gets up out of the rocker, holding him, carefully trying to keep his position the same so that he won't be jarred awake. She lowers him into the crib, gently extricates her hands from under his warm, sleep-heavy body, covers him with one blanket and then another, tiptoes out of the room and closes the door, pulling it shut gently, but making sure it's latched so the cat won't get in.

In the hall, she leans against the wall for a moment and watches the first streaks of morning light through the little window by the front door. She thinks of that other sunrise when she was sitting, pregnant and depressed, on a dune near Jasper Pier, and suddenly three dolphins leaped out of the water quite nearby. To her amazement, at the same moment, the baby leaped inside her, and she was filled with sudden joy, seeing that all this, the dolphins, the churning waves, the keen, cold air, would be new to him. And, feeling that the silver flash of the dolphins' backs could be her own mother's spirit signaling her from under the water, she wept with a painful happiness.

Kyle has been here with her for a year, and so far he's mostly slept and nursed and cried. No smile yet. And she hasn't been to the beach since that day. She has been reading up on hormones to try to figure out why she has been so moody lately. Something about progesterone abandoning ship once the baby is out, leaving a big wave of estrogen to wash over everything.

"I should get some sleep," she mutters, and hurries into her bedroom. But it's hard to hurry into sleep. Under the covers, the windows carefully curtained against the dawn, the darkness carefully preserved, her eyes nevertheless open.

Worries parade through her mind, some rational—How will I ever be able to leave home now?—some irrational—Is Kyle still breathing? And suddenly she is racked by sobs of exhaustion and helplessness and fear, loud sobs, more like shouting, which she buries in her pillow. She fears waking her father and sister, who, as she flounders in this sea of postpartum hormones, are trying to help her on top of their exhausting jobs and are exhausted, too. Released by her tears, she falls asleep.

In her dream, she is at a beach party, and Kenny—young, breathtakingly handsome Kenny—is standing over her and saying, "Wanna go for a walk?" She has to shade her eyes to look at him. "Where?" she asks. "Nowhere," he says. But the way he says it, nowhere sounds like a very exciting place. They walk down the beach, talking, but she can barely hear him over a roaring in her ears, which may or may not be the sound of the ocean.

Then she is on the beach carrying the baby, who is weak. Maybe he's hungry. The wind is blowing, the sky is bright, but the water is dark and thick-looking. The waves have a viscous, treacly quality. Kenny and some buddies drive by in a dune buggy, laughing and drinking beer. She shouts to them, but they don't hear her and drive by. Now the beach seems vast, and she no longer has the baby in her arms. Where he was, there's only a hollow, panicky feeling, as if the worst thing in the world is about to happen. She runs up and down the beach, looking in every hollow of the dunes. She stops passers-by and asks, "Have you seen my baby?" They shake their heads, and one of them says, in a worried, admonishing tone, "You know, the tide came in half an hour ago." She runs on, but there's no baby anywhere, no anything but the sand and the water. The waves are close now, advancing, dark and syrup-like.

Raging and sobbing, she screams at the sea, "Where is he? Where is he? Where is he?" and then she wakes up. All is still. Or is that sobbing she hears? The sound of warm air blowing through the heat ducts seems now to contain the sound of Kyle's sobbing. Sometimes, when she's in the shower she thinks she hears him, though she knows that's impossible. Now, before she can go back to sleep, she has to go and open his door a crack and listen to his quiet breathing.

•

Kyle, a big, handsome baby, stirs in his sleep but does not wake. Inside his body, messages are unfolded, decoded, and read. Nerves shaped like lightning light their way from some tangled center to the surface of his skin, which breathes gently, in and out, as he breathes, rosy and warm from his blood, which, following its own channels, nourishes him. And other creatures—various microbes and viruses—share his body, as they share the bodies of all human babies. Most of them have come to him through Lynn's milk. In a deal worked out with his ancestors long before his birth, he provides them shelter and they do various services for him, helping him digest food and warding off less friendly microbes. Kyle stirs in his milky dreams, in his young body, teeming with generations of life.

•

The next morning, Lynn, driving home from the grocery store with Kyle, sees her ex-husband Kenny coming out of The Plover Motel with an older woman in sunglasses, clearly a member of the country club. Kenny usually gets them from the club. Funny the different ways that people have standards. It's eleven-thirty in the morning, and Kenny looks miserable. She finds herself feeling sorry for him. No doubt he didn't intend to spend the night, but passed out. He's helpless after a few drinks. No one can even tell he's drunk, and yet he's a different person. The woman doesn't look too happy either.

At the red light, Lynn looks back at Kyle. He's a year old, big enough for a car seat, and growing more and more expressive each day. He is looking calmly out the window. Suddenly, she feels very lucky. She, anyway, is keeping good company.

"Sweetie-pie," she says. She smiles and Kyle smiles back with his whole being.

"You smiled!" Lynn beams back at him.

"Aaaaah," he sings, but his face is so bright that he might be singing "Hallelujah!"

The light turns green and, turning a corner, Lynn glimpses a slender woman standing on the beach near The Cove, staring out to sea. It seems to Lynn that she has seen this woman before, doing just that, at various locations up and down the shore. There is a kind of intensity in her stance, as if there were something very important out there, though Lynn sees nothing but a rather muted sunset over the waves. For a moment, Lynn envies the woman's freedom, the freedom to stare at nothing and think long thoughts.

•

As Lynn lifts Kyle out of his car seat, the hogs to the northwest watch the flock of swans with mild interest. Tame and sedentary, the pigs have harbored for generations an intestinal virus they picked up from their human keepers. The swans bring with them an aggressive respiratory virus. Sharing the water, the two species also share their viruses, which merge to form a new one, more versatile and powerful than either one alone. The pigs are off their feed for a day or two, causing their owners a few sleepless nights, but they recover. The swans show no symptoms. This new virus is wily, enterprising, and extremely adaptable. With staggering speed, it begins to spread through the swans, which take off again to fly south the next morning, forming a circle and then a V, calling to each other: Time to Go.

The hog wallow where the swans rested is uphill from a branch of the Neuse River. So are a number of new hog farms, which accounts for the draining of the swans' old resting lake. The proliferation of hog farms also accounts for the rich muckiness of the river, a muckiness that   is like a gold rush to a microscopic form of life called a "dinoflagellate," a sperm-like creature, part plant and part animal, which has been breeding there and is about to come from a state of almost invisible dormancy into fero-cious and spectacular bloom.

The next time the flock of swans lands, farther south in another pond connected to the Neuse River by various creeks, the birds shed the new virus which, finding the dinoflagellates, recognizes in them a perfect host. The dinoflagellates share some of the virus's survival strategies: They are fast, relentless breeders, but also good at hiding and biding their time. Now, though, in full bloom, they are teeming in the water, and the many members of the virus family find them and approach them, delicately, seducing them into an embrace and injecting their genes into the dino-flagellates, doing blindly what they deem best for their own survival. In an urgent and repetitive dance, pairs of creatures merge and merge and merge. Because their bodies are so permeable, their combination is more complete than a marriage or a merger. They become one creature, a microbe. It's a very lucky microbe. It now has a form that can travel by stealth through water and through bodies. Now all it needs is a generous and vulnerable host, and time and tide are flowing in its favor.

•

Standing in the cold water, Marika realizes that her legs are going numb and that she is suddenly very hungry. She wades slowly back to shore, where she trudges to the parking lot, takes off her waders, and throws them in the back of her old Volvo. Starting the car, she feels a pleasant anticipation of breakfast at the Bluebird Café, with strong coffee in a white mug.

It's too early for lunch, so there aren't many cars in the Bluebird parking lot when she pulls up. The café is in a modest converted house, and inside, sunlight streams into the small white rooms that make up the dining area. A counter with stools runs the length of one wall. Marcy, the owner, sitting at an old-fashioned cash register at one end of the counter, nods at Marika in greeting.

Marika looks around and chooses a seat by a window tucked into a little alcove. It is her favorite table, where she can cultivate the illusion of seeing but not being seen. Marcy sees her, though, and brings her a menu as soon as she has gotten settled. She gives Marika a smile of recognition, but though Marika has been a pretty steady customer in the last few months, they have not exchanged names or stories as yet.

"Coffee?" says Marcy. There is already a clean white mug on Marika's table, along with a blue-checked tablecloth, a metal caddy full of paper napkins, salt and pepper shakers, and a small bottle of hot sauce.

"Yes, please," says Marika, holding up her cup.

"Black, right?"

"Yes. And I'll have the usual, scrambled eggs and home fries."

"Comin' right up."

Marika takes a sip of coffee. Standing in the cold water and sea breeze has made her feel pleasantly lazy.

There is only one other customer, and Marika recognizes him as a regular, sitting at his usual table. He is tall and a little paunchy, with sandy hair and a thoughtful, inward look about him. Marika has seen him here in a clerical collar, meeting various people for coffee, and so supposes he is a minister of some kind. When he is with people he seems genial and outgoing, but when alone, as now, he has the unmistakable look of the introvert, taking shelter, like Marika, in this place where for the moment, he needn't interact with anyone but can still feel like he is out in the world. He is reading, drinking coffee, and eating with relish, a large and rather bumpy glazed pastry.

Marika has brought something to read as well, a small academic journal in which she is reading an article on the possible commercial uses of marine algae, and when her breakfast arrives she becomes absorbed in her food and her reading, only looking up every now and then to rest her eyes and scan the familiar scene. She hasn't felt at home anywhere for a long time, but this place does have the feel of a good temporary haven.

Eventually, she registers more customers arriving—two men, the shorter one in work clothes and the other, tall, blond and handsome, in a suit and tie, and, a few minutes later, a good-looking young couple, attentive to and awkward with each other in the way of people who have not known one another long. She glances at the newcomers and then gets back to the plankton ("*unknown kinds of interactions between microscopic marine organisms and viruses should be studied further….*") as the customers take their seats.

In the way of many patrons of restaurants and coffee shops, she glances up surreptitiously now and then at the other customers as she sips her coffee. Observing other humans, she muses, is one of the pleasures of places like this. The two men seat themselves near the door and joke familiarly with Marcy as she pours their coffee. She hears Marcy call the handsome one "Kenny." The young couple take seats farther into the café, near a window, still easily in Marika's range of vision, and they seem a little startled when Marcy brings their menus. The boy has curly hair, the girl has a lovely figure and a pretty, lightly freckled face. The attraction between them is palpable, even at a glance, so strong that they seem to have a little difficulty concentrating on their menus.

Marika gets back to her article. Every now and then, she shakes her head. Businessmen, "developers," as they call them, are on the scent of money and rushing headlong to harvest the resources of the sea, an environment that they—and scientists—do not fully understand. Not a new story. Marika is mildly irritated, but preserves an emotional detachment. Not her problem any more.

Glancing up, her eye is caught by the handsome blond man. His face is tanned. His expression is one of vague boredom and restlessness. His friend seems contentedly stolid. They have both ordered sizeable southern breakfasts—eggs, sausages, grits, and toast crowding the small table. Every now and then the taller one passes his hand over his face with the air of someone who has a workday coming up and is not looking forward to it. Some sort of salesman maybe? The two eat in the kind of comfortable silence that suggests they have known each other for a long time.

By the window, the pleasant lilt and hum of the young couple's conversation can be heard, punctuated by an occasional ring of laughter. Marcy brings them waffles covered with strawberries and whipped cream and then returns to refill Marika's cup from a steaming fresh pot. Contentedly, Marika returns to her journal and lets the sounds of the café wash around her. Sunlight moves imperceptibly across the walls as the customers come and go.

3

About three hundred miles north of Jasper, in Charlottesville, Virginia, holding the phone to his ear with one hand, Alan Hirsch absently arranges the pile of brochures in front of him on the table into a fan shape. They are real estate brochures from the Outer Banks, where he is planning to retire. Charlottesville is heavy with late snow.

His face registers surprise at something he hears on the phone, and, after a minute, he speaks. "You old Jesuit, I can't believe you've gotten an answering machine. Isn't that against some church law? What if I wanted to confess? This is your friend Hirsch, in case you haven't guessed. Listen, I called to—"

There is a sudden squawk on the phone, and an out-of-breath voice says, "Hello? Hello?"

"Yes, I'm here," says Hirsch.

"I just got in," says the voice, a pleasant, rich, but slightly nervous tenor, "and I forgot how to pick up when someone's already called."

The man catches his breath and asks, "How are you? What's up?"

"I just called to ask you if everyone at the Outer Banks is stupid," says Hirsch. He pronounces it "stoopid," with a trace of a Brooklyn accent. "Listen to this," he goes on, without waiting for a reply. "The Outer Banks is a very special place," he reads from one of the brochures, "with very unique homes."

"You've decided not to move here because of a realtor's grammar?"

"And listen to this! This strikes the nail right on the head. These people want me to live in some sort of housing development called 'Mirage.' They think this is attractive! Listen to their slogan: 'Mirage: A Vision You Can Behold'."

"Hirsch, these are realtors, not writers."

"I don't remember getting this kind of stuff when I moved to Charlottesville."

"Well, the realtors in Charlottesville probably are writers."

"Either that or it's the general decline of language skills in the United States."

"Come on Hirsch, what's the matter?"

"Oh, I don't know," says Hirsch gloomily. "I'm just wondering whether this is the right thing. I mean, now that you're moving away ...."

"But you didn't even know I lived here when you first started thinking about moving down."

"I know, but it helped tip the balance."

"You've got your boxes packed, right?"

"Yeah, pretty much," says Hirsch, glancing around his bare kitchen.

"Well, this is just what you always do. Remember the night before your wedding?"

"Yeah, but I was right."

"Oh, nonsense. You can't say that was a dead loss."

A brief silence. "No, I guess not."

"I didn't really think you were coming down because I was here, nice as it would have been to be in the same town. You're coming for the adventure. Because it's different."

Hirsch chuckles. "And because I was there once, a long time ago."

"With a girl?"

Another low chuckle, more of an exhalation. "A long time ago. I was young, Don. Remember young?"

"Sort of. Listen, I've got to go meet with a parishioner. Are we still on for Thursday?"

"Yeah. Yeah, I guess so."

"Good. See you then."

"Bye."

Hirsch hangs up and leans back in his chair, running his fingers through his short hair and looking out the small kitchen window. The view seems much broader without the plants he's fed and watered on the windowsill. Home is anywhere you live long enough, he thinks, and he's lived here—what, seven, eight years?—ever since his divorce, when he left that much more elaborate home that he and

Gwen shared. That had seemed empty, too, toward the end, though it was full of furniture and often, of friends. No children.

Taking a deep breath, Hirsch gets up for his ritual third cup of coffee and walks to a little coffeemaker standing alone on the counter. He tries to tell himself he likes this clean, empty feeling. That's what he told himself when he first moved in. But it's a lie.

•

Down in Jasper, Father Don Cathcart hangs up the phone in his office behind Our Lady of the Sea and says a brief prayer for Hirsch. May he find his way. May we all. Don glances around his office. It's not every day, or even every week, that parishioners come to talk to him about personal problems. Mostly it's elderly women on church business. Lord knows, he thinks, they probably have their problems, but for some reason I'm not the one they bring them to.

Involuntarily and absently, as he tries to make some order out of the piles of books and pamphlets that lie on every surface in his office, he goes through his list of possible reasons they don't come to him: They have other people to talk to? Unlikely in this unhappy, family-rending time. They are too self-effacing? Possible, but they're very forthcoming with some kinds of complaints, mostly about each other, or the weather, or the price of things. He just doesn't have the knack for bringing people out? Yes.

This strikes him as quite likely, and he dwells on this problem for a minute or two. Not long enough to come up with a solution, but long enough to mortify, as it were, the flesh of his ego. He keeps meaning to bring the matter to his prayers, but so many things seem in such a mess that he always forgets. Or maybe he is afraid of what the answer might be.

For instance: You have no vocation…go back where you belong. Wherever that might be.

Looking around his office, he despairs of establishing order. He's not even sure why he's trying. Perhaps it's because the woman coming to see him is his doctor, and her office is always in perfect order, without the piles of clutter that seem to grow in his. Also, he likes her and wants to help her, and has the feeling, somehow, that if she does want to confide in him, the mail and pamphlets and hymnals will distract her. Easing himself rather heavily into his chair, he picks up *As I Lay Dying* to while away the time, but has a little trouble concentrating. For the thousandth time, he wishes for a window in this flat block of an office, but takes a deep sigh and reminds himself that it shouldn't matter. Just before the knock comes on his door, he smiles, suddenly realizing that he's come to think of the cheap wall paneling and low fiberglass ceiling panels as mortifications of the flesh. How very absurd.

His doctor's knock on the door is gentle. Terry Baker comes in, small and slight, her very straight shoulder-length hair giving her an uncompromising air. But she already looks embarrassed. He rises and comes around the desk to shake her hand.

"Hello," he says, warmly, "it's good to see you." This seems only to add bewilderment to her embarrassment.

"Oh! Thank you," she says.

As he asks her to sit down, he thinks what a world of trouble it would save if people's souls could be waiting for him, naked, like patients in a doctor's office, to call "come in" when he knocks. As it is, sometimes it feels like mining hard rock even to get to the problem, which, presumably, has brought his parishioner to consult him. Of course, it doesn't help that his mind so often wanders, as it does now, so that he is only just able to grasp the tail end of her sentence as it floats by.

"—about my sister," she says. Letting her shoulder bag slip to the floor, she sits up straight and takes a deep breath. "I'm worried about her," she says, "and … I don't know what to do." Those last few words seem hard for her to speak, and he admires her for saying them.

"You have two sisters, I think," he says, "one is a physical therapist—"

"You mean—oh, no, she's my aunt. Aunt Jeanne."

"Oh, I see. And your sister is…"

"Lynn. She has a baby, and her husband—they've split up."

"Yes."

But he's still picturing the other sister; no, the aunt. She is a masseuse and an acupuncturist and has a tea shop full of New-Agey books and doo-dads that he knows he is supposed to despise, but which in fact he finds amusing and sometimes fascinating. Sometimes even inspiring. Who is to say where inspiration will come from? "The wind bloweth where it listeth, and thou hearest the sound thereof, but canst not tell whence it cometh, and whither it goeth." But again, he is lagging behind. What is the matter with him? Like a trapeze artist, he flings himself toward the gist of her last sentence and catches it at the last minute.

"It's your sister then—Lynn, is it? You're concerned about her?"

"Yes."

There is a slight lull in the conversation, during which Terry seems to be trying to formulate what she wants to say. Don usually gives people time to come out with their thoughts (assuming he is able to focus), but he breaks gently into Terry's reverie.

"She's a single mother?"

"Yes. Her son's about eighteen months old." says Terry. "And I know that can be a very difficult...I mean... I guess I don't really know what it's like."

Don feels a great sympathy for this young woman. She began her sentence as the doctor, the practitioner, and ended it as a lost soul, the helpless witness of suffering, longing to offer comfort and not knowing how. How well he knows that floundering!

In a much smaller voice than she's been using, she says, again, "I just don't know what to do!" And then bursts into tears. Of course he has a box of Kleenex on his desk and two stashed in a drawer for such occasions. Mutely, tenderly, he offers her the box. He knows better than to offer her solutions now. Even assuming he had any. He holds her hand and lets her have her cry.

4

Kenny Peterson, father of Kyle and ex-husband of Lynn, is working out. Sitting in the middle of a Universal gym that takes up a third of his bedroom, he looks strangely like a prisoner in a hellish torture device as he does ten, twenty, fifty reps of everything he can think of. He feels his blood rushing to the aid of his muscles and limbs, which are expanding and contracting, burning and cooling. Then he becomes aware of his heart, begins to feel it beating. It starts to hurt a little bit, knocking against his chest. Then he has no chest but has become his heart, beating, beating, beating itself up.

When he finally comes to rest, exhausted, he drifts into a vision of waves racing on the shore just behind his feet. His feet are small, he is running from the waves, he is a little boy. Eyes closed, he sees his son now, in the picture Lynn sent him—she still hasn't let him visit—in which Kyle looks inquiringly at the camera, as if to ask "What should I expect?" There is such clarity in his face—no fear, no hope. Just wondering.

That's me too, thinks Kenny, beginning to feel a chill as the sweat cools on his body. Just wondering. But unfortunately—he raises his body slowly up, addressing the Kyle in his mind—unfortunately, boy, by my age they expect you to know something. In the shower he leans against the wall, trying to let his bitterness pour off him with the water and swirl down the drain.

As he dries off, he decides it is time for a beer or three at The Cove.

•

The Cove is a small bar, darkly paneled, with a limited view of the water and a limited menu of bar food. It has been around for a long time and has never shown an interest in glitzing anything up for the tourist trade. Since it is a little off the beaten path, very few tourists find it, so locals feel comfortable there pretty much year round. The main bartender, Barry Anderson, is a young man who came to the Outer Banks for a camping trip after college graduation and ended up staying. He has settled into his role quite comfortably, serving with quiet efficiency. Business is slow tonight, and Barry is leaning on the bar and staring out the window at the sea. Seeing Kenny, he straightens up and nods a welcome.

"Evening, Kenny," he says, wiping the bar with a ragged cloth. "The wind's picking up a little, looks like."

"Evening, Barry. Yup, looks like it," answers Kenny. Barry's always interested in the weather. Loves to hear about storms. Not from around here.

"How's the world treating you?" asks Barry, and, before Kenny can answer, he takes a pint glass from the shelf and asks, "Usual?"

"Usual," says Kenny, nodding. "I'll have the usual, and I guess you'd say the world's treatin' me 'bout as usual."

"That's good," says Barry. "I guess. Is that good?"

"Hell if I know," says Kenny, and they both smile. Kenny takes a long, grateful pull on his beer. After breaking open some rolls of change and pouring them into the cash register, Barry turns again to the window, staring out at the sea.

"What're you lookin' for out there?" asks Kenny. "Whale watching?"

Barry smiles and shrugs. "I like to watch the waves," he says.

Baffled, Kenny turns to look out the window. "Waves? Aren't they all the same, pretty much? Come in, go out?"

Before Barry can answer, the front door slams open, and a familiar voice shouts, "Hey, barkeep!"

Kenny turns to see Drew Layman, ready for a pitcher or two to wash away his work week with the construction firm. "Pitcher of Bud here!" Drew calls out, taking the stool next to Kenny's.

"Coming up," says Barry.

"Quittin' time!" says Drew. "Comes later and later, seems like. That's 'cause I'm not my own boss, like you, Starbaby." That's what he calls Kenny, who was the quarterback in school and has the Chevy dealership now.

"Whadya say, Starbaby?" says Drew. Kenny just grunts.

But then something happens. The door opens, and a truly beautiful young girl walks in. Drew stops in his tracks with a pitcher in each hand. She breezes by him and walks over to Barry who, Kenny notices, looks both pleased and a little scared to see her. Barry is a lanky kid with curly hair, and as the girl approaches he even blushes a little. All of a sudden, it seems like the room has been asleep and now wakes up.

Drew goes back to his table and the men drink silently, their eyes glued to the girl. Her cheeks also have a blush to them, under a small scattering of freckles unexpected below such dark eyes. She wears plain but chic and expensive-looking clothes—slacks, sweater, boots. Her figure is pretty much perfect—round breasts, long waist, long legs. It's like watching the springtime walk in.

Barry watches Shona walk toward him. From their one breakfast date at the Bluebird, he now knows a few things about her. Her name is Shona, and her father runs The Sandpiper Inn a little way down Route 1 from The Cove. Now, she smiles at him, a sweet yet challenging smile that seems to act like a tractor beam, pulling him toward her. He smiles back.

"What'll it be?" he asks.

While Drew and Barry watch the girl as she sits at the bar and orders her drink, Kenny catches sight of a woman slipping unobtrusively into the room, holding the door open only wide enough for her slight body. She looks to be in her late thirties. She has long, mousy brown hair but very clear-cut features and very blue eyes. She wears a faded brown parka. No one else notices her as she looks quickly around the room.

Her eyes lighting on Barry and the girl, a slightly annoyed, slightly scornful expression crosses her face.

Well, thinks Kenny, who's that? What's her story?

Marika quickly scans the room. She sees that handsome fellow and his fishing buddy, then catches sight of Barry, but sees that he is occupied, and withdraws quickly. Outside The Cove, she climbs back into her truck and opens the glove compartment to check on the status of the scotch. Enough for tonight.

It would have been nice to drink and talk with Barry when he got off work, but of course she can't suggest it now. No doubt that silly girl would think it very strange, even if she didn't have plans for Barry herself that evening. Silly girl, though certainly bewitching. Beguiling. That's a good word. But Marika has seen the miles of green lawn that the girl's father thinks necessary to separate her from mundane existence. Green lawn on a barrier island. The kind of silliness that destroys the world.

Starting the engine, she unscrews the top of her flask and takes a short pull, to signify that the evening has begun. The evening patrol. No pupil-companion to explain things to tonight, but solitary patrol has its merits. No interrupting the voice of the sea.

•

"Everything moves in waves," says Marika, a few days later, to Barry. The afternoon of Barry's day off is waning, and a warm, almost ruddy light gilds the waves and the sand where the waves have wet it. They sit on a dune with a thermos of coffee, wave-watching.

Marika speaks. "They've hooked up electrodes to the brains of sleeping people and seen that our dreams come in waves. When spring comes, the warm air comes in waves, advancing and retreating. And the season itself is just a longer wave of light that covers and uncovers us. This beach—this whole island—is a wave of sand. Of course, this place is particularly new and shifty, but to the eye of God, all the land is moving. He sees the continents crashing against each other, breaking apart, merging. I'm not big enough to see that, but I'm willing to bet they move in waves."

There is a long silence as they watch the sea hurling itself forward in a haze of spray, sliding forward farther until it's just a silver film on the sand, and with a great inhalation, sucking its waters back into itself.

"And human relations. Our feelings for each other come in waves, though we don't seem to acknowledge it. When you marry or swear friendship, you're saying you'll always feel the same. But you don't. You feel different every day. Hell, you feel different at nine in the morning than you do at three in the afternoon."

"But waves keep coming back," says Barry.

"Yes," says Marika. "But their coming and going changes the shore so much. Who can say what they're coming back to?"

Barry nods. He has a feeling that he and Marika won't be having these talks for a while. Even now, he feels his physical impatience, his desire to be near Shona all the time. But if Marika is talking about her friendship with him, about their year of abstract yet strangely passionate conversations, he is sure that she herself doesn't know it.

As they watch the waves he thinks about their odd friendship. It began in the bar during a storm. She came in at the last minute for shelter when there was no one else there. The power went out, and he served her whiskey after whiskey in candlelight while she told him stories of storms she'd seen, heard, or read about.

"Gloria!" he remembers her saying, her blue eyes shining, "Isn't that a great name for a storm?" Her face was lit with zeal, and he could tell that she shared his slightly excessive love of storms. It was a rare experience to meet suddenly, in the dark, with a kindred spirit, and after he closed up the bar they walked on the beach together until the sun rose, talking not of themselves but of tides and winds and whales and fertilizer run-off and human greed.

When the sun rose, things got a little awkward, as it seemed they'd reached a degree of intimacy frequently followed by sex. They parted somewhat abruptly, and he didn't see her for a week or two. But then she came into the bar one night and asked if he wanted to go and count waves.

And that's how their friendship went. One day she'd just show up in the bar and they'd go for a walk, sometimes talking, sometimes in silence.

He realizes that he doesn't know a whole lot more about her now than he had that first night. She is the kind of person he hoped to meet when he came down here—someone he couldn't have met before, though he could imagine her as a college teacher, if she were a little more—what—smoothed out at the corners. More socialized. She was hard and sharp and didn't seem to care what she said to people. He wasn't sure what she lived on. But she wasn't somebody he could've known at home in Herndon or at Tech. Not that she was typical of this place either, but he'd moved down here because it was different, because for him everything had been smooth and easy and bland, and here, in spite of all the new boutiques and whatnot, it seemed a little ragged, a little rough. Anyway, different. And of course there was the ocean itself, which he'd once dreamed was washing over the smug streets of Herndon, crashing down on the faux-country houses.

He remembers how she gave him an appreciation of this place, so that at the end of his first summer he decided to stay on, and the hell with Daddy's conglomerate and being "groomed" for "management" and all that crap. Barry always called it the conglomerate because "company" sounded too human.

Of course he'd said the hell with it many times, but somehow Marika enabled him to really resist the pull of the familiar, step back, and consider what else he might do. In the meantime, tending bar at The Cove suits him fine.

"Do you think you'll ever go back?" he asks.

"Back where?"

"Back to lab work, research, whatever."

Marika shrugs. "I don't want to." There is a pause. "They've asked me to."

"Really? The lab?"

"Yup. I've gotten a couple of offers."

"You think you'll go?"

Another pause. "Not unless I have to," she says.

Barry is not sure what that means, but lets it go. "What were you working on?" he asks.

"Algae and other marine organisms," she responds. "Their nature, their dangers, their uses. Mostly their uses. They have some potential as fuel."

After a pause, she looks at the sea, cocking her head, and says, "We never have time to get to the bottom of anything—of that—" she points out to the middle distance, where the water turns darker. "It's the same story over and over again. We try to use things that we don't understand, long before it's safe, because it might make someone rich. It might be 'monetizable'." She pronounces the word with withering scorn.

Now the light on the waves is fading and, tossing her head as if to shake thoughts out of it, Marika wades out into the waves. He knows she will stay until the light is gone or the moon rises, and perhaps even after that. At a good distance, so as not to disturb her reverie, he brings out some scraps from the bar and feeds the gulls, enjoying their sharp cries of satisfaction.

5

Early in the morning, Alan Hirsch rinses and packs his coffee cup—last coffee in Charlottesville, he thinks—and drives down to Jasper, towing a big trailer of his possessions. As he drives, the land flattens out around him, bearing fields of tobacco, produce stands, lonely, well-kept brick houses, tumble-down shacks, tiny churches proclaiming "Jesus Saves."

Without the occasional climaxes of hills, the land seems to Hirsch to have a kind of desultory rhythm. After a couple of hours, motels appear, along with billboards advertising equipment for windsurfing and fishing. Theme parks.

And then, suddenly, the giant form of Neptune looms over the road. Hirsch does a double take and stops the car. It's Neptune all right, from the waist up, about two stories tall, half-immersed in asphalt as if in the ocean, holding his trident and smiling somewhat fiercely at the highway. Fascinated, Hirsch gets out of the car, looks around, and sees that he's standing at the entrance to a "Wild Water Park," empty now, a little litter blowing around on the ground. He shakes his head and walks slowly back to the car, turning around once for a last look before he gets in.

A few hours later, he is crossing the Wright Memorial Bridge—"First in flight," a plaque says—and suddenly there is water all around and a soaring feeling of lightness takes hold of him. He smiles and rubs his hand over the gray bristle of his hair. A tune comes into his mind and he hums it, remembering the words after a minute and singing them softly: "Anchors aweigh, my boys, anchors aweigh…"

But the next morning, his first as a Jasper resident, he wakes heavy with dreams of regret. They're the kind of dreams that don't seem to want to let go, so that he's even more disoriented than he might be as he looks around his motel room. The regret is centered around his marriage, though when he wakes it's from the old dream where he suddenly remembers a class that he's been forgetting to show up for all semester. There's a terrible feeling of uneasiness and guilt as he tries to figure out whether he can get the class going again and cover enough material for a respectable course before exam time.

Cutting through his sleepy thoughts, the phone rings.

"Hirsch?"

It's Don Cathcart. "How about a walk on the beach and some breakfast?"

Hirsch's face relaxes at the sound of his friend's voice. "Yeah, sounds good," says Hirsch. "Just let me grab a shower."

Twenty minutes later, the two men, Hirsch short and well-muscled, Cathcart taller and somewhat paunchy, stroll the morning beach with Cathcart's dog, a King Charles spaniel named Rose.

"I just can't get over you having a dog," says Hirsch, grinning. The dog pads sedately by her master's side, her eyes bright and clear. "But I guess it figures if you did have a dog you'd have one that's more like a cat."

"Ah," says Cathcart, shaking his head mournfully. "There'll be no cats for me after Justinian."

"Justinian! That was his name. I've been trying to remember that. He was a pretty cool cat."

"That he was."

Unconsciously, they observe a brief silence in memory of the animal who shared their graduate school housing, a modest brick house on a back street where they sometimes read under maple trees in second-hand wicker chairs.

"That name was strange enough," says Hirsch, "but why did you have to inflict 'Rose' on this poor animal?"

"It's after the river, not the flower," says Cathcart, looking out over the ocean. The water is a milky, pearly color, gleaming under a cold, cloudy sky from which sunlight comes in sudden shafts.

"The river?"

"Yes. Don't you remember the Rose?"

"Oh yeah. I think it was too low to fish the time you took me there."

Cathcart nods. "I guess you didn't see it at its best."

There is a silence then, which seems mournful to Hirsch, though he doesn't know why. He looks out over the ocean. It isn't at all as he remembers it from his college days. He remembers sky and ocean both fiercely blue. But then, it was always summer when he came down. This time he's come down early in the season to avoid the summer crowds—to stake his territory, as it were, before they come.

Now the water is gray, and there is a kind of iridescence in it that he doesn't remember from before. Dim rainbows come and go on its surface as the waves rise and fall.

Some seagulls fly overhead, and as they cry, he has a sudden, keen memory of lying in the dunes with—Lisa, that was her name— making love on a blanket at night. He was so hot for her that everything fueled his lust, even the itching of sand and the prickling of sea oats, of which there were, he's pretty sure, more back then. She had long red hair, pale skin, long legs, small, sly gray eyes. She smoked too much, but even the smell of cigarettes on her had been arousing. The memory engulfs him and then recedes like a wave, leaving him feeling lost and displaced in the present.

That's been happening a lot lately. "I'm getting old," Hirsch thinks, "and it doesn't suit me." Then, almost simultaneously, he realizes that the iridescence of the water is caused by oil. The water is oily. The world, then, is growing old too. Too much wear and tear, too many toxins. You can only make comebacks for so long. Finally, too many things have changed, and you can't ever go back. When even the sea can't purify itself—

"I love those ladders from heaven," says Don, suddenly. "And to heaven, one hopes."

Hirsch looks at the rays of the sun, slanting down in clean, straight lines from the suddenly brightened clouds, looking like the walls of some great golden tent. He puts his hands in his pockets and recites.

> The cloud-capp'd towers, the gorgeous palaces,
> The solemn temples, the great globe itself,
> Yea, all which it inherit, shall dissolve
> And, like this insubstantial pageant faded,
> Leave not a rack behind.

Don smiles at the lines. "No one will ever match that as a farewell speech."

"Although 'Adieu adieu remember me,' is pretty good," says Hirsch.

Don nods. "Or 'Into Your hands I commend my spirit,'" he says.

Lord, thinks Hirsch, this seems to be a day for elegies. Then he suddenly remembers that his friend will soon be leaving this place.

"Why did you decide to go back to Virginia, anyway?" he asks.

Don is silent for a long time, looking, longingly, it seems to Hirsch, at the gray strip of cloud that hides the horizon.

"It's hard to explain," he says.

Hirsch waits, but Don says no more. A breeze springs up, rattling the sea oats on a nearby dune. He watches a ripple of wind run through them and thinks again of Lisa and the taste of cigarettes in her hot mouth.

Then he suddenly realizes there is someone sitting on the other side of the dune, in a small hollow toward the top of it. It looks like a woman, though it's hard to tell through sea oats and shadow.

"I don't mean to be incommunicative," says Don, as they resume their walk. The woman gradually comes into view. She is slender and tan and wears khaki shorts and a faded grayish T-shirt. Her long hair is gray-brown, and altogether she looks like part of the dune. "It's just that I haven't quite figured it out myself yet," says Don.

They come into the woman's field of vision, passing right beneath her. She continues to look past them, alertly, not daydreaming, as if she's searching the waves. Her eyes, Hirsch sees, are a startling blue.

"I know what you mean," he says. "If you waited to do anything until you had things figured out, you'd be waiting until doomsday."

Having passed the woman on the dune without looking back, Hirsch rubs his face and head with the flat of his hand and says, "Where can you get a decent cup of coffee in this place?"

•

The Bluebird Cafe is filled, when Hirsch and Cathcart enter, with shafts of morning sunlight and a buzz of conversation. Hirsch looks around. It is an unassuming place, but bright and cheerful. His mood lifts. The line at the counter is long, so Hirsch claims a table in a corner, with a view of the whole place, and Cathcart stands in line to get coffee.

Don sits down with his coffee and a white paper bag from which he draws a large pastry.

"Good God, what's that?" says Hirsch.

"It's called a Plug-Ugly," says Don, beaming mischievously, "and" —reaching again into the bag—"I've brought one for you."

"It's certainly well-named," says Hirsch, eyeing it suspiciously. It is a lumpy, brown, glazed object, about the size of a large hamburger.

"They taste good after a walk on the beach, especially when it's cold," says Don, rubbing his hands together and taking a napkin from the metal container in the middle of the table. "I'll miss these," he says, happily, taking his first bite. Just then Hirsch sees the Lady of the Dunes come in and join the line for coffee at the counter. He sees that she is of medium height, slim but not small-boned, almost angular.

"But you know," says Don, "I think I'll be glad to get back to the old place."

"You're going there?" asks Hirsch, surprised. He'd always had the impression that Don didn't get along with his family.

"Yup. It's that or sell it. Daddy died in '83, and my sister is not interested. I think she's in Thailand now, but I'm not sure. She may be back in Charleston. I can't keep up. I thought I ought to at least live in the place a while before I decide whether to sell it." Don stares into the steam from his coffee.

"What kind of place do you think I should look for here?" asks Hirsch, as the Lady of the Dunes passes him, holding her coffee with both hands, and joins a young couple at their table. "I'm going out with the real estate lady tomorrow."

"Aren't you going to buy a mirage?" asks Don, grinning.

"Probably," says Hirsch. "There don't seem to be any real houses here, just those damn gray towers all over the beach."

"Lot of money in those gray towers," says Don, thinking of the struggling builder in his congregation—What's-his-name, Drew something—who has finally landed some lucrative projects.

Between the builders and the realtors, the land is disappearing. That happens all over, of course, but here it seems to be happening so fast. Well, of course, there isn't really much land here. That's what everyone seems to forget, except when there's a bad storm and the water covers it up.

"I'd say Jasper is your best bet," he says to Hirsch. "More like a real town than some of the others."

"Yeah, I think so, too," says Hirsch, "but I haven't looked it over yet." He turns his chair and leans against the wall to get a better view of the room. He sips his coffee. It's good and strong. He's beginning to enjoy himself. The place seemed kind of bleak last night when he drove the one long, straight, dark road into town. Now it seems downright cozy and brimming with possibilities. Nothing definite, though. That's nice, too.

The little room is beginning to fill up. A slight young woman with straight blonde hair whom Hirsch hadn't noticed in line comes by, carrying a to-go cup. She heads to the counter, to the cream and sugar and spoons, but then catches sight of Don. Don begins to rise, but the girl says, "Oh no, please, don't get up. I'm just on my way to the office—"

"Good morning, Father Cathcart" says a tanned man from behind Hirsch.

"Good morning to you, Mr. Baker," says Don, in what strikes Hirsch as a slightly too hearty voice. "This is my friend Alan Hirsch. Hirsch, this is Pete Baker, our esteemed mayor. And this is his daughter, Terry—I should say, one of our local doctors, Doctor Terry Baker.

Hands are shaken and smiles smiled. Baker welcomes Hirsch. Then there is a moment of awkward silence.

"Thank you for—for speaking to me," says Terry.

"Oh, not at all," says Don.

"See you soon," says Terry, waving herself out the door.

"Good to see you, Father," says Baker, shaking Don's hand again. "And good to meet you, Mr. Hirsch." And he returns to his table.

Don sits silently for a while, and then says, "It's amazing how I can embarrass people just by being."

"By being a priest, you mean?" asks Hirsch.

Don nods. "And Lord, the energy it takes to constantly be trying to put people at ease!" he says. "It wears a body down."

"Are you having second thoughts?" asks Hirsch.

Don smiles sadly. "Sounds ridiculous, doesn't it? Second thoughts after fifteen years. But yes, I guess you could say that's what I'm having. I guess I'm going home to think about it awhile."

The men sit silently for a moment, reviewing their lives amid the clatter of cups and the hum of voices.

6

In his quiet, carpeted office, with its maps and fishing trophies, Pete Baker, father of Lynn and Terry, grandfather of Kyle, widower, mayor of Jasper and occasional proprietor of Pete's Bait & Tackle, shakes his head over a proposal to tax water. He doesn't like it. Not at all. But he can't see any way around it. These damn tourists and developers are sucking the place dry. Of course, he has no objection to money, none at all, and they've brought plenty of that, but they seem to give with one hand and take away with the other. They give money, but they suck up water and take away— what, exactly? They take away what we used to be.

Struck by the mournfulness of the phrase, Pete raises his eyes from his papers, leans back, and sighs a deep, discouraged sigh. There ought to be such a thing as a secret fishing hole, an empty road, a creel full of free fish, courtesy of the Lord Almighty. People ought to be able to make love now and then at night on the dunes, not that he himself would ever leave his flanks exposed in such a manner. These are the kinds of things he thinks about when he hears the phrase "inalienable rights"—the wildness and quietness that used to be here. When you didn't have to watch every step you took because you knew damn well that someone, from somewhere, was watching it, too. When you weren't so damn alienable.

And these government people, these environmentalists. What on earth makes them think they can stop it? People know a good thing when they see it. And then, after enough of them see it, somehow it's not so good any more. That's just how it is. But that doesn't make it feel right.

He can't help thinking that if Cathy were alive she could somehow talk him out of this feeling of wrongness. But she isn't. That, of course, is part of what's wrong. The person he used to talk to lately about this kind of stuff was Kenny. Well, that's out now. What the hell did that boy do for Lynn to light out for home like that? Or is she just being skittish? She's always been sensitive. Never put up with much. Never had to. Oh well, whatever it is, neither he nor Kenny is about to have a heart-to-heart about it. They nod when they see each other, and try to make that as seldom as possible.

There is a knock on the door. Pete straightens his papers and calls, "Come in!" in his normal voice, cheerful, efficient, and friendly. His two o'clock enters. He's a sleek one. Dark hair graying at the temples, bright smile, dark eyes that won't miss a trick. Jewish? Maybe.

"Mr. Mayor, thanks for seeing me," he says, holding out his hand, speaking first. "I know how busy you must be."

"Not at all," says Pete. He almost adds, "Always glad to talk with the moneybags," but decides it might not go down too well.

"Happy to see you, Mr.—"

"Jack Brockie," says the moneybags, gripping his hand firmly but not painfully.

"Call me Pete," says Pete. "Pull up a chair. Can I offer you anything? Cup of coffee?"

"No thank you, nothing."

"You run The Sandpiper, don't you?"

"That's right," says Brockie.

"How long you been runnin' it?"

"We've been here about a year and a half."

"How do you like it?" asks Pete.

"This area is amazing," says Brockie, solemnly, "just amazing. My family and I are very happy here."

"How many children?"

"Just one daughter, Shona. Nineteen going on twenty-nine."

"Got two myself," says Pete. "And one little grandson."

"Congratulations," says Brockie.

Pete nods, but stops short of bringing out Kyle's picture. This fellow is like a lot of the Yankees who've been successful down here. He's learned to chit-chat and seems pretty calm about it, but you can tell he can't really see the point of it.

"Thank you. Now what can I do for you, Mr. Brockie?"

"Well, Mr. Baker—"

"Pete," says Pete.

"Ah, right. Jack," says Jack.

"Sorry, go on," says Pete.

"Quite all right. Pete, I've heard a rumor about a tax on water?"

"It's one of many options we're considering."

"I see." Jack nods thoughtfully. "May I ask what the others are?"

"You certainly may, Jack. Unfortunately, we're not quite prepared to answer. We've got some studies to do, some figures to project—you understand."

"Oh sure," says Jack. "As a businessman I know all about that. You've got to have the numbers, and you might have to get them fast, but that doesn't mean you have to hurry."

Pete nods, crinkling his eyes in recognition of this distinction. He reminds himself that he probably shouldn't start to like this guy.

"I'm wondering, though," says Jack, "if you've given any thought to how this might affect your tourist business."

"That's certainly one of the things we're studying."

"Well, if you want to encourage growth—"

"That 'if' is right there on our studying agenda, Jack," says Pete.

"With growth comes prosperity, Pete."

"Hell, I know that. I'll tell you up front Jack, I don't have a thing against money or people who make money. As far as I'm concerned, we've got too many regulations and too many taxes as it is."

"Glad to hear it," says Jack. "As you know, some municipalities offer tax breaks to the businesses that they want to encourage—"

"I can't see where y'all need encouragement, Jack. You seem pretty encouraged to me. You particularly, I understand, have been mighty successful. Personally, I don't know anything more encouraging than success."

Jack smiles and shakes his head. "I must say, we're doing even better than I'd hoped," he says, with a kind of innocent amazement that is most disarming. "Frankly, I doubt that a tax would hurt us too much. I just wanted to touch base with you on it, and say, 'hi'." He rose and extended his hand again. "Great talking with you, Pete."

"Likewise, Jack."

"I hope you'll come over to the hotel sometime, have a drink."

"I may do that. Thank you."

"Well, I know you're busy. See you soon, I hope." And he's out the door.

Pete feels slightly elated at first, as if he's been in a good poker game. But that wears off, and he starts to feel tired. All this back and forth, and he sometimes wonders if anyone gains an inch of ground.

•

Gaining ground: In inland North Carolina, bulldozers are tearing at the earth. They are busy clearing land to consolidate the state's position as number-two hog producer in the country. The migrating swans must drag themselves northward now while bulldozers and hogs swallow up their breeding grounds. Run-off from farming—manure, phosphorous, and nitrogen—makes its way through to the marshlands and, where the marshlands are already cleared, to the sea. In Pamlico Sound, billions of virus-infected dinoflagellates have taken the inanimate form of cysts, hunkering down like yogis deciding not to breathe for a while. But now, in this manure-rich soup, they rouse themselves, swelling and unfurling, and begin to breed. And their offspring not only thrive, but evolve. They are becoming stronger and more versatile, learning to speak the languages of hundreds of genetic codes.

7

Driving home from his meeting with Pete Baker, Jack Brockie catches a glimpse of his wife Deidre walking with a man into the courtyard cafe at Avocet Resort. He looks at his watch and makes note of the time.

He wonders where Shona is. He still isn't used to not knowing where she is. Deidre once accused him of being overbearing.

He tried to explain. "I just love my daughter. I don't want anything bad to happen to her."

"You don't want her to leave," said Deidre, in an unhappy, accusatory way that he didn't understand.

"Well, of course I don't. Do you?"

"Everybody has to grow up, Jack," she said.

Again, he didn't get what she was driving at. Was she saying he isn't grown up? She's the one, after all, who keeps having these affairs, or whatever they are.

And that's another thing. If she's having love affairs, why is she so miserable? And if they aren't making her happy, why doesn't she stop?

•

In their sanitized room, Deidre Brockie and Kenny Peterson complete their morning ablutions separately and, for the most part, silently. Once, when passing him at the sink, she touches his bare shoulder, and he gives her a pained smile. In the bathroom, she dresses and makes up very attentively. Looking respectable after a "naughty night" has always been part of the thrill for her. This guy is very unsatisfactory in the morning—disoriented, distracted, polite. Quite a hunk, though, with his green bedroom eyes and beautiful square shoulders.

Remembering their lovemaking and how he shuddered with pleasure as he lay down on top of her, she feels sad that he is so obviously embarrassed now, so detached. This is the third time they've "spent time" together. And yet, she remembers—and it makes her sadder still—that she saw him at the grocery store the other day and, until he began to look sullen and embarrassed, she couldn't quite remember who he was.

•

On that same morning, Don Cathcart sits in the massage room of Jeanne's Tea Room, his face wet, his body so light that he barely recognizes it. There is a towel around his hips and another around his shoulders, and a cup of some flowery kind of tea in his cupped hands, its steam rising up into his face. Pete Baker recommended this masseuse, Jeanne Dubovsky—who is, as near as Don can recall, Pete's sister-in-law, aunt of Lynn and Terry—and she is very good. She has a gentle, matter-of-fact way of speaking that soothed him before the massage even began. Now she is assuring him that uncontrollable weeping at one's first massage is normal, understandable, therapeutic, nothing to worry about. Soon he'll pull himself together enough to assure her that he's not worried, but grateful. Or maybe not. He feels no urgent need to talk. He's still wondering at how the tenderness of her touch released those sobs as if they'd been hungry dogs, clamoring at the gate. It is good. It is good that they should get out. What now, he doesn't know. Reassemble himself, presumably, at some point. Put his clothes on. Go somewhere and have a drink and think about it. But then he had a drink, didn't he? He looks up at the masseuse, sees her soft brown eyes on him, and takes a sip of the potion.

"It's called 'Quiet the Mind' tea," she says.

"Thanks," he says.

The name of the tea seems profound to him. Certainly there are many times he wishes he could tell his mind to shut up. Now, though, it isn't necessary. The objects in the room—the tea in his hands, Jeanne and her brown eyes, the massage table, the sunlight— are almost the same as the objects in his mind, which for once is not hurrying off after something out of sight.

Jeanne busies herself with something so that her client can just sit for a minute.

After Father Cathcart is gone, Jeanne does her noon meditation. When she opens her eyes, she lets them rest for a long time on a patch of sunlight and the warm amber of the wood floor surrounding it. Away from the claims and needs of others, she is teaching herself to take things slowly. She gets up slowly and lays out the Tarot cards.

She keeps them in a purple silk scarf which her sister Cathy gave her on her fifteenth birthday and which she used to wear to parties back when she went to parties. She is the Queen of Cups. She has no special question so as she unwraps the cards, she empties her mind to give her subconscious more room. Slowly, dreamily, she shuffles the cards, turning one upside down now and then when the fancy strikes her. She lays out the Ancient Celtic spread, putting down the Queen of Cups to signify herself. The queen sits pensively, as always, on her dolphin-shaped throne on a beach, holding a miniature ark of the covenant and gazing into it. The tranquil sea curls its waves right up to her feet.

"This is me," murmurs Jeanne. She puts one card on top of the queen, a little to the right.

"This is what covers me," she says.

The next card she lays on top of the last, but crosswise.

"This is what crosses me."

Around the pile of three are placed four more cards.

"This is what is beneath me. This is what is behind me. This is what is above me. This is what is in front of me."

Then a vertical line of four more cards to the right of the pile and circle.

"This is how I'm moving. This is my house. These are my hopes and fears. This is my future," she says to no one.

Except for the Queen, all the cards are face down. Jeanne pauses a moment before revealing their faces. She knows she has become addicted to the cards. In her dreams sometimes the figures move and speak. When she looks at the beautiful symbols—the cup, the pentacle, the sword—she feels she is hearing distant voices trying to reach her; voices that together make up all the wisdom of some submerged human history. She believes in the truthfulness of the cards and had an odd fantasy one day of sitting and reading them all the time—living her life through them, appreciating all the twists and turns as told to her by those vivid, eerie little scenes. A woman standing blindfolded among a crowd of swords. A fool about to step over a cliff. The naked lovers and the serpent. The Queen staring at her cup while waves lap at her feet. My life story as told to me by the Queen of Cups. The Universe under my hands.

She lays her hand on the first card.

"This is what covers me." Present influences and atmosphere. She turns it over. It is the five of swords, upside down. Defeat, loss, failure, slander, dishonor, mourning, sadness, affliction, trouble, destruction, degradation, dishonor. This is one of the few cards that means the same thing upside down as right side up. Hmmm. Interesting. Covers me. Am I that miserable? She considers a minute and turns over the next card.

"This is what crosses me." The forces opposing me. The four of swords. Rest. Rest from strife or often illness; relief from anxiety; quietness, solitude, retreat, abandonment, exile.

"Hmmm!" she says, aloud. This, too, bears thinking about. Quietness and solitude are what she craves now. But they are obstacles? The cards are surprising her. She takes the next card.

"This is what is beneath me." An influence that is waning. Eight of rods, reversed. Quarrels, discord. Jealousy, internal disputes, stinging conscience, marital disputes. Being jealous of your own dead sister. Waning. Good.

Jeanne pauses for a while, looking sadly, unseeingly, out the window. When she remembers the ten years or so before she moved to the cottage and opened the Tea Room, what she remembers is not the girls, Lynn and Terry, involved as she was in their crises and pleasures, but the expression on Pete's face that day, when he came out on the front porch to meet her for the first time.

Later she wondered how on earth she had gotten herself into the position of spinster aunt and surrogate mother—she who had always been the wild one, not caring where she slept or what she smoked. Well, it was love, of course. Love of Cathy, her only sister, drowned.

And it was love, too, distorted by frantic grief, that caused Pete's face to fall ever so slightly when first he saw her. Some part of his usually super-sane mind had hoped that she might be another Cathy. Later, after Jeanne sickened with love for Pete and with the guilt and anger that followed, she was haunted by that moment. She had arrived, and the light had gone out of his eyes.

The bell on the door downstairs rings. Her client is early. For once, she is glad to be interrupted. Abruptly, she leaves the cards and their brooding faces.

•

At the Wellness Center, it has been a good, busy morning for Dr. Terry Baker. A fish-hook in a shoulder, a possible meningitis, an alcohol poisoning, a couple of flus, and a nameless rash. It's two o'clock, and she hasn't had time for lunch yet, so she's stepping across to the Lucky Seven in her white coat to get a sandwich and a Coke.

She always feels better in her white coat. Probably, she muses, there is something wrong with that; as if without it she doesn't know who she is, but with it she does.

When she walks back into the waiting room, there is Don Cathcart, looking large and uncomfortable, trying to read a magazine. She stops short and says, "Hi!" and then goes into the office.

"What's Father Cathcart's problem?" she asks Kim.

"Twisted ankle," says Kim. "Whyn't you ask him, if you know him?"

"I will," says Terry.

"You want me to hold him off till you've had your lunch?" asks Kim.

"No, no. That can wait. Send him in."

"Not hard to see how you stay so skinny," says Kim, shaking her head. She herself is a stocky mother of four who occasionally mothers Terry out of habit.

Don limps into the examination room with an embarrassed smile on his face. All Terry can think is that the last time he saw her she was hysterical. But she sees that he is not embarrassed by that but, as some men are, by the fact he is injured.

"Hello, Father," she says, awkwardly. She forgets to offer to shake his hand. "Please sit down," she says. But she can't seem to act normal. She feels as if two selves she's been keeping separate have suddenly collided with each other.

"This is an odd situation," she says finally, smiling a little.

"Doctor, I have every confidence you can fix me up," says Don, with a sincerity that heartens Lynn. "It's a foolish situation is what it is," he continues, delicately shifting the ground of the conversation. "How many times, I wonder, have I gone out the door of the church office and down those three steps? Thousands, probably. And yet this time, I couldn't quite make it down."

She has him sit on the examination table and feels his ankle. It is quite swollen, about grapefruit-sized. Turning the foot gently to the right and left, she goes through the "does this hurt" routine.

He winces and nods.

"How did you get here?" she asks.

He shrugs. "It's not my driving foot," he says.

"Well, you may need crutches for a couple of weeks," she says.

"Oh great," he says. "There's nothing people like better than seeing a preacher on crutches. He who leads them on the straight and narrow path. The organ music swells, the congregation stands, a prayer is uttered, and then *ka-thunk, ka-thunk* up the aisle. As for getting into the pulpit, 'Hey, you think y'all could lend me a forklift?'"

Terry finds herself laughing. Who ever knew he had a sense of humor? Of course, the opportunity for jokes had not often arisen during their interviews.

"You'll do fine," she says, smiling. "It's the cantankerous ones like you that do the best."

"Well, thank you," says Don, smiling back. "I'll take that as a compliment."

He has never seen her smile. It completely transfigures her face, making her suddenly look like a mischievous teenager. In spite of his sometimes gloomy temperament, he has schooled himself too well in recognizing blessings to miss this one: Here they are doing each other good! He couldn't have worked it better. He says a brief thanks to God for the sprained ankle, though not without noting that it is damned inconvenient. Must go and see that sister of hers, he reminds himself with a pinch of guilt for not having done so already.

•

That evening, with a sigh of satisfaction, Alan Hirsch slips the last book, *Leaves of Grass*, into its place on the shelf. He always unpacks his books and music first. Their presence around the walls is like a second skin to him, and he feels a little flayed until they are in place. He is drinking a beer and scanning the shelves complacently when Don rattles the screen door.

"Coming," he says.

He shakes his head upon seeing Don's splint. "Man, how long do you have to have that thing on?"

"A month, six weeks," says Don, who looks tired. "Your home is wonderful, Hirsch," he adds, looking around the room, "but I must say, I'm disappointed to see no chairs."

"Yes, I can see how you might be," says Hirsch. "We'll sit on the porch," he says, leading Don through the small kitchen and out the back door. "Sure is nice and warm tonight. Hard to believe it's only April. Care for a beer?"

"Definitely," says Don, lowering himself into an Adirondack chair and tossing his crutches down with a clatter.

"I must say I envy you, being all moved in here."

"Well, hardly all moved in," says Hirsch from the kitchen, "but I'm beginning to feel like this might be home. Glass?"

"Of course."

"I must say, I'm feeling better and better about this move," says Hirsch, sitting down and pushing a footstool toward Don. "I'm glad I didn't let you talk me out of it."

Don smiles wryly. "Well this thing is going to put off my move for a while," he says, gesturing toward his foot in its splint.

"Good," says Hirsch. "You can show me the sights."

"Hmph. What makes you think I know any?"

"Oh I know you from way back, Don. You seem all vague and otherworldly, but you never miss a trick."

"Hmph."

"Now: What music shall we drink to?"

Don pauses, considering the matter seriously.

"Fletcher Henderson," he says.

"Excellent choice," says Hirsch. He bustles off to the stereo in the living room, and Don smiles after him. Hirsch seems happy here. He hopes Hirsch's move is a positive. His move, unlike Hirsch's, after all, could be called a move backwards. As Hirsch fiddles with the stereo, Don muses on his last sermon. He'd like to leave them with something to think about.

"Do you know somebody named Marika?" asks Hirsch as he comes back to the porch.

"Marika? I don't think so. Why?"

"Just someone that seems interesting."

"Aha, I see. What does she look like?"

"Oh, I don't know, slight, thirtyish, long hair, high cheekbones. Always wears an old brown windbreaker."

"Oh yes, I think I know who you mean. Don't know much about her, though. Someone said she's a biologist, but she doesn't seem to be working now. Kind of an odd one."

"Odd? How?"

"I don't know. Brusque, you might say. Likes her scotch."

"But you don't know much about her?"

"Well, all you have to do is be in the same bar with her to know that. Not that she's ever rowdy. Never heard a peep out of her."

"Where is this bar you've been in with her?"

"Not with her."

"I know, I know."

"The Cove. Near Jasper Pier."

"Hmm."

Cathcart laughs. "I've got to say, Hirsch, I admire you."

"Life in the old dog yet, you mean?"

"Something like that."

"Well, I've got to admit, I don't really feel old. The gray hair still surprises me when I look in the mirror, like someone has played a trick on me. You know what I mean?"

Don doesn't answer for a minute, seemingly abstracted by his own thoughts.

Finally, he murmurs, "And I Tiresias have foresuffered all…"

There's a long silence then, as the two men sip their beer thoughtfully, listening to the sounds of Fletcher Henderson's clarinet, so carefree, so long ago.

•

Spring is coming to Jasper. The next day is golden, the sky high and blue, a light breeze weaving through grasses and trees. Lynn opens the nursery window and holds Kyle up to see the heavenly morning.

"Look, Kylie," she says, "sunshine!" Her voice lilts. Some words feel different when she says them to Kyle. It's as if being with him opens doors in her words, so that suddenly when she says "sunshine" now she is saying to him: refraction, rainbows, truth, shadows, God; everything that light can mean. Rocking him a little, she says it again. "Sunshine, Kylie," and then, closing her eyes and rocking a little, "Do you feel the breeze? Do you feel the breeze, sweetheart?" He's in a good mood too and nestles against her, and for a moment they disappear into each other.

8

Barry the bartender and Shona Brockie, the young beauty, have met for lunch and for dinner, seen a couple of movies together, and gone for some long walks. Last night, for the first time, they made love. Now they are lying in Barry's bed. It has taken them a few minutes, as they wake, to remember where they are. Or, almost, who they are. Whose limbs are whose. It is as if, just when their bodies were being most themselves, they dissolved, lost to ordinary consciousness.

Now, as they re-enter the world, it is changed by the fact that the body of each appears in it as a landmark to the other—part of the landscape in a new way. Now he will remember her not just with his eyes, but with his hands, his shoulders, his tongue. Now she will remember him with her neck, her belly, her throat. His chest, upon which her head now leans, has become part of the world in a new way. It's a serious thing. This seriousness comes to them gradually, through the dreamy twilight of a shuttered room. He responds to it by secretly smelling her hair, trying to will the moment to continue.

She responds by getting to her knees in the tousled bed and looking at him for a long moment, during which the beauty of her light-striped body almost brings him to tears.

"Let's go swimming," she says.

•

The next day, lounging in the back seat of his Ford Bronco, Kenny listens to Drew popping beers and making dirty jokes. "It's just an easy way to feel superior," Lynn said about his friendship with Drew. When are her words going to stop ringing in his ears? And when is he going to stop seeing her face in his dreams, first eager and captivated, then disappointed and sullen? No more young girls. He can't be responsible for all those expectations.

Though Kenny runs a car dealership, he is bored with driving. Though he is athletic, he always feels that lounging is his real calling. A number of women have complimented him on how comfortable he looks in repose. He is comfortable that way, more and more. He doesn't let on, but he pretty much feels tired all the time. Occasionally he cares. Only pride and the need for conquest keep him from getting fat. He prefers company in bed, and sex helps him sleep. Besides fishing, it is his only hobby.

Fishing is what they are up to today, and he smiles at the straight-forward, uncomplicated Saturday in front of him. If he was still with Lynn, she would find some way to let him know he should be think-ing or reading or making intellectual conversation. Too damn intense, that's her problem. Like a flame that never dies down. Unnatural.

He takes another swig of his beer and looks up at the sky through the sunroof. It is a beautiful day, fair and blue with a few high clouds scudding by. He doesn't need to think about Lynn. He can look at the sky instead.

After a few beers on the shore, Kenny and Drew split up. Drew wants to check his nets. Kenny keeps a little boat here, called *Adios*, and after cleaning it up a bit, he takes it out. He sits in it for a long time. The creek is calm and glassy, and the temperature of the air is perfect. Every now and then a breeze wafts by. Kenny watches his rod and his line and their reflection in the water.

He catches a rock and a couple of channel bass and savors his beer, happy when they're biting and when they're not, remembering those long, stolen summer afternoons on the creek with his friends while Daddy wrestled with his nets and Mama tried to keep the house together.

After a while, he realizes that Drew has been gone a long time and that it's time for another beer. He has just docked the boat and is standing on the shore, stretching a little, when he sees Drew coming toward him. Right away he knows something is wrong. Something funny about the way Drew is walking and the way it takes so long for his eyes to focus on Kenny and when they do, they don't seem to recognize him.

"Drew, what's up?" Kenny calls.

Drew calls something back, but Kenny can't understand him. He sees Drew beckoning and calling. He hears "Christ" and "fish" and "dyin'."

"Drew, are you all right?" he asks, but Drew has turned around and is walking back toward the fishing hole. Kenny follows, and the men tramp in silence around a bend in the creek and then around another. They walk for a couple of minutes when a sickly-sweet smell makes them wrinkle their noses and recoil. Drew looks at Kenny with fear in his eyes and starts to say something, but can't seem to get it out. He's sweating heavily.

"What the hell?" Kenny says. For now he sees up ahead a large patch of water that's thick and brown, the color of coffee, and writhing like a corpse with maggots. The writhing comes, he sees a moment later, from dying fish, thousands and thousands of them. Occasionally, one will leap weakly out of the water, but it's clear they're all goners. Something very nasty is going on.

"Jesus Christ," says Kenny. "What the hell is it?"

"Fuck if I know," says Drew. "It wasn't here an hour ago." Then, suddenly, he sits down with a thump on the sand, hugging himself and beginning to shake.

"Come on," says Kenny. "Let's go."

Drew staggers to his feet, and the men walk back to the truck in silence, stopping every now and then to wait for Drew, who seems to get dizzy. Kenny thinks about supporting him, but shies away from touching his arms, which have broken out in a weird-looking rash that seems to outline his veins.

They drive back to town in silence except for an occasional, "How you doin', man?" from Kenny. Drew, whatever else he's forgotten, retains his manly training and answers "All right," every time. As far as Kenny can tell, he's not getting any worse. Drew stares at his arms once or twice and then, with a stoicism Kenny much admires, folds them and looks out the window for the rest of the trip.

•

When they get to the Wellness Center, Kenny groans inwardly when he sees that Terry's on call. With her quiet, dry ways she's always made him feel like a blowhard, and since he and Lynn split up…. But then they're ushered into the examination room and Terry comes in and acts friendly and calm, nodding as they blurt out the sequence of events, taking Drew's pulse quietly as they talk, and Kenny says to himself, You asshole, you're not the patient here.

Terry smells fear when she opens the door, before she even sees Drew and his sores. She knows these "ol' boys," and it won't do to show any alarm. This looks a lot like that Pfiesteria thing they found a few years back. Shouldn't be a problem, though, unless he's exposed to it repeatedly. Chances are, she thinks, Drew Layman never read that potboiler that came out about Pfiesteria a few years back— something about "blood in the water." My, but these journalists like to scare people. Anyway, best now not to put a name to it.

"Drew, I think what you've got here is some kind of bug that grows in algae, like what shows up in a red tide. This is probably as bad as it's going to get, but what I'd like for you to do is to go home, get lots of rest and keep those sores clean, and on Monday I'd like you to go over to Elizabeth City and see a specialist. Now I'm going to have to report this thing to the fisheries people and the health department, so you might see some of them pokin' 'round your fishin' hole."

She smiles as she says this, but the men's faces are long. Even with acres of dead fish, it's still their hole. Or was. She knows how they feel because Daddy would feel the same. Poor ol' boys.

Kenny drives Drew home from the Wellness Center, and when he drops him off at his house, offers to walk him in, but Drew refuses.

He walks a little stiffly to the door. Kenny can't bring himself to start up the truck until Drew shuts the door of his house behind him. Even then, he's torn between feeling like a coward for not going in and talking to Lori, Drew's wife, and not wanting to embarrass or scare Drew by seeming like a nursemaid. As he starts up the truck, he notices that darkness is falling and the wind is rising. As usual, the evening sea is cooling off and inhaling the warm land air. But the temperature out there must be dropping faster and farther than usual. By the time Kenny nears home, the old cypress outside his house is bucking like a horse trying to shake a rider off its back, and just as he pulls up, the lights in his house go out.

"Well that tops it," says Kenny. He backs out the truck and heads on down the road.

Along the highway, he speeds by patches of darkness where he knows houses ought to be. Windsocks and flags dance around in his headlight beams as if they're on fire. To Kenny, things suddenly seem to be moving too fast. He responds not by slowing down, but by trying to outrun them. Swerving every now and then from the impact of the wind from the landward side, he watches his hood greedily swallowing up the yellow line.

•

Meanwhile back at the creek, the dinoflagellates, sated, sink back down to the bottom of the river, disguising themselves again as cysts, a kind of microscopic vegetable detritus. What's left of the fish flows with remarkable swiftness out to sea, along with the water it has contaminated, pulled by the outgoing tide. The carnage disappears from the creek as if it has never been there.

•

As Kenny drives, the rising wind buffets the Banks. In Jeanne's Tea Room it brings the wind chimes clattering down on the floor of her porch; it blows over Hirsch's new geranium plant and wakes Lynn out of a nap, so that she creeps through the dark into Kyle's nursery and lies down on the floor, because she doesn't trust herself to hear him over the wind if he cries. It pushes Deidre Brockie, who is terrified of storms, into the arms of her husband, who strokes her hair and hopes the new awning over the entrance of the restaurant is intact. In The Sandpiper dining room, Shona Brockie goes from table to table lighting candles, enjoying the novelty, looking like a Rembrandt Madonna, foreseeing big tips.

•

In The Cove, Barry brings Marika a second whiskey. It seems to him that Marika's been avoiding the bar lately, and he was delighted when the storm blew her in about half an hour ago, just like the night of their first conversation. She drinks quietly, and he doesn't say much. At first they exchange factual information about wind speed and so forth, but they've talked so much about storms—here and elsewhere, factual and figurative, in relation to the air, the sea, the land and their own minds—that they enjoy this one together in a kind of contented marital silence.

Or that's how it seems to him. With Marika at the bar, he realizes now that it's restful being with someone to whom he doesn't have to pay attention every second. Marika was very exotic at first, but after a while their minds became close, and she doesn't feel strange to him emotionally, though objectively, he knows she is rather strange by many standards. Sometimes he wonders why they never slept together. Is it him or her? Is it the age thing, or is Marika just a loner?

Just after dusk, Kenny lurches into the bar, staggering from shouldering his way through the storm and his own grief and anxiety. He is grieving for his old fishing hole and worrying about Drew, but hoping that a few neat whiskeys will take care of it. Thank God the power is still on here. There is only one other customer, a woman drinking alone at the bar.

Maybe his luck is going to change, he thinks, shaking the water off his coat and wiping his boots heartily on the doormat, as if to wipe the last few hours off them. Breaking into the quiet of the bar and Barry and Marika's wordless intimacy, he sits five stools away from Marika, giving her room.

She looks at him.

"How're you doing," he says, nodding, noncommittal. Never scare them off first thing. And he can tell by her expression that she has will power. He'll just have to hope it will bend his way. She gives him a friendly nod, something like you might give to a fisherman docking his boat next to yours. Comparing hauls would not be out of the question. Oh, but what a haul he had today! His hand shakes a little around his whiskey as the sight of those desperate dying fish comes back to him. He knows the woman doesn't miss the shaking. Well, a sign of weakness isn't necessarily bad, depending on the woman.

Switching to his bartender mode, Barry wipes the counter in front of Kenny and asks, "How're you doing this evening?"

"All right," says Kenny. "Tried to go fishing today, but—" he breaks off and shakes his head.

"Your father was a fisherman here, wasn't he?" asks Barry.

Kenny pauses for a moment, sadly, and then says. "Yeah." Then he looks at Barry. "How in the world did you know that?"

Barry smiles. "You told me," he says.

"I did? I don't usually—" he breaks off again. He has always, he thought, been a quiet drunk, something for which he's often thanked his lucky stars.

"It was very late one Saturday night," says Barry. His smile is kind and companionable, with no trace of mockery. "You just mentioned it."

Kenny nods, seeing Daddy's tired, hurt expression during those last lean years. And a son too interested in partying and dreaming of escape to be much help. That mean red tide in '63 was the beginning of the end. He takes a belt of his whiskey, finishing it. Another thing not to think about.

As soon as Barry refills Kenny's glass, the phone rings and Barry goes to answer it, leaving Marika and Kenny alone on their stools. After a little while, Marika speaks.

"My father was a fisherman too," she says.

"Is that right? Whereabouts?"

"Denmark."

Kenny nods. He thought she seemed to have some kind of an accent. Denmark. That's one of the names that seemed to glow on the map of the world when he used to pore over it as a teenager, loving the way that unfolded diagram of mysterious shapes, littered with place names and surrounded by blue, made it all seem so accessible, made him feel a breeze of freedom blowing on his face. Once, just after they were married, he and Lynn looked at a map of the world together in bed, arguing happily about where they should go—Greece, Brazil, Scotland—and laughing at their own earnestness.

He sets down his empty glass. The whiskey can't seem to come fast enough.

From the phone, Barry signals he is coming to fill Kenny's glass, but Marika waves him away and pulls out her flask.

"No need to interrupt him," she says, pouring a healthy helping into Kenny's glass. Barry signals his thanks and turns his back, bowing a little, curving himself around the phone in the way that lovers do.

"A woman with her own supply!" says Kenny, smiling at Marika with sincere delight. It is a smile that is often lethal at close range,

Marika registers its force. He is a beautiful creature, she sees. High cheekbones, green eyes. From his ears and his fingers, you can tell he is probably beautiful all over. She is several whiskeys ahead of him, and she allows her gaze to linger on him, appreciating him, but not thinking of it as anything personal.

Kenny turns toward her on his stool, lounging against the bar. "So is your dad still fishing?"

"No," says Marika, gazing through him now, as if at something far away. "He got sick and died."

"I'm sorry," Kenny says.

He thinks his own Daddy would probably rather have drowned than go the way he did, seeing all his friends go broke and move away and then coughing his lungs out with emphysema. Come to think of it, he did drown—he just did it on dry land.

"How's the fishing in Denmark?" he asks, and then realizes maybe that sounds heartless, right after hearing about her father's death. But she doesn't seem to mind at all. Definitely not from around here, he thinks.

"Oh, it's about the same everywhere, I think, for small operations," she says. And then, as an afterthought, "He was a scientist, too."

When Barry hangs up the phone and returns to the bar, Marika and Kenny have moved to a booth, where they are talking intently, intimately. Barry's head snaps back with astonishment, but fortunately they don't see. Automatically, he picks up a bottle to go and freshen their drinks, but then sees that they're drinking out of Marika's flask and that they probably don't want to be disturbed. Eventually they leave, waving vaguely to him and leaving him a big tip.

9

The next day is sunny and breezy. The air, cleaned out by the storm, feels almost thin. Spring continues to advance: The snowdrops bloom, the jasmine blooms, and, in the water, the algae blooms brown, red, green, blue-green, iridescent.

Blooms, plankton, dinoflagellates, bacteria, and viruses, hopeful and young, settle and breed. Life begins—forceful, vulnerable, infinitely complicated, yet with such a gloriously simple purpose: going on. The microbe, preserving the seed of its single-hearted identity, is preparing to propagate itself over all the earth and into eternity. This is its Big Chance. A New Beginning. A Growth Opportunity.

•

The storm has cast sand over Route 158 from Jasper to Avon, and Drew Layman, moonlighting for the highway department, drives a grader up and down the road, pushing the sand back onto the dunes, undoing the storm's work. His rash has disappeared, and he has written it off as some weird allergy thing. He's tired, though, very tired, and even with the noise and lurching of the machine, he feels every now and then like he's dozing off and has to shake himself to wake up.

Drew's body is desperately trying to cleanse itself: To identify and locate the bacterial intruder, to trail it, to destroy or eliminate it. Unlike a virus, the dinoflagellate cannot usurp Drew's cells but must simply take up life in a new river—that of Drew's blood—and dodge, as best it can, the scouts of Drew's immune system, whose strength and stamina depends on so many things, some as remote as his most ancient forebears, some as immediate as unhappiness.

•

Lynn meets Don Cathcart at his office in Our Lady of the Sea. Don is glad to find that they fall quite easily into conversation.

"I don't know how you feel about praying," he says, "But have you tried it?"

"No I haven't," says Lynn, but she appears open to the possibility. Lynn, Don sees, is a beauty, whereas Terry is perhaps only pretty. In spite of her exhaustion, there is a lushness about Lynn. Her hair, the same color as Terry's, is wavy and full. Terry's eyes are bright and brown, Lynn's dreamy and blue. Terry is slight, Lynn more voluptuous. But there is a directness and intelligence about both of them which he enjoys.

"I'm not sure I believe in God," Lynn says.

"Prayer is one way of finding out," says Don.

Lynn nods. There is a brief but comfortable silence—comfortable, Don feels, because both of them are thinking, rather than waiting for each other to speak. It's nice to be with someone who thinks.

"I understand you're a writer," says Don.

Lynn looks a little startled, but pleased. She shrugs.

"I've written some," she says.

"Are you working on something now?"

Lynn massages her forehead with her fingertips, seeming to crumple briefly, though without tears.

"It's hard to concentrate. It's hard to find time," she says. "It's hard to complete a thought."

Don waits silently. After a pause, Lynn smiles, an inward, whimsical smile and leans back in her chair.

"I read an article the other day about 'eutrophication'," she says. "Isn't that a great word? Kind of like 'beautification' or 'gentrification'."

"Yes," says Don, "but I can't remember what it means."

"Oh, it's when algae gets such rich nutrients that it takes oxygen away from the other creatures in the water and chokes them. It just seems like such a wonderful image of what the outlanders and developers are doing here."

Don is surprised to hear someone so young using the terms "outlanders," but then he remembers that her father's family was one of the original families here, shipwrecked in the eighteenth century, living hard and lonely on shellfish, homemade wine, and whatever they could scavenge from those who were shipwrecked after them. Who knows, they may have been the very ones who hit upon the idea of leading a horse with a lantern around its neck along the beach, luring ships to break up on the shore and salvaging the goods of the drowned. Now those families that have held onto their land are growing rich selling it—Pete Baker among them—but many seem to be in a permanent state of shock at the consequences.

"Thank you for asking, Father," says Lynn, smiling at him now. Then, after a pause, she surprises him by saying

"I wonder—would you be willing to baptize my son? I haven't been to church in a while, but—"

"I'd be delighted," says Don. And he notices that he actually is.

•

The day before Kyle's baptism, Lynn invites Terry out for shopping and drinks in Hatteras.

"Thanks for suggesting this," says Terry, as they sit in Dan's Pub drinking margaritas. "This was a great idea."

"Definitely," says Lynn, licking her straw.

They've been shopping for new outfits for the baptism. Now they're finishing their second round of drinks after a lunch of fresh fried oysters and cole slaw. Terry is relaxed. It's an unfamiliar, rather dizzy feeling.

"So why'd you suddenly decide to do it, anyway?" she asks.

"Do what?" asks Lynn, as myriad possibilities leap to her mind. Marry Kenny? Have Kyle? Move back in with Daddy?

"Have him baptized…at this age. He's almost two. I mean, I'm glad you did—I got a new outfit out of it—but I was just wondering."

"I don't know," says Lynn, breaking up the ice in her margarita with her straw. She sucks it for a moment and then says "I wanted him to have life abundantly. I didn't want to leave anything out."

Terry nods, considering this, then shakes her head. "I still can't believe that Aunt Jeanne wouldn't be godmother."

Lynn shrugs. "Well, at least she's coming. And she is already a relative."

"Is that why she didn't want to do it?"

"Well no. She said she couldn't do it 'in conscience'," so I guess she has some New Agey objection."

Both girls grimace.

"But, let's face it, she's just not into this. She's never come to see Kyle."

They both shake their heads sadly.

"You'd think she'd have at least come once, just for show," says Terry, angrily. "I don't know what we did—"

"We didn't do anything," says Lynn. "She's just a flake."

"She didn't used to be."

"Well, she is now."

"Maybe we laughed at her too much when she took up with all this stuff."

"Maybe. But she didn't have to take it like that. It's not our fault, Terry."

"Maybe if Daddy—"

"No, it's not even Daddy's fault. Face it, T, she flaked out on us."

Terry shrugs and sips her drink. She can't say to Lynn what she wants to say, which is "I miss her."

Lynn looks directly at Terry. "I invited Kenny," she says.

Terry nods, and there is a pause.

"That's good," she says. "I think that's good. I understand why you didn't want to get them together, but a boy should have a chance to know his daddy."

"Yeah," says Lynn. "That's what I figured."

•

Kenny spends the night before his son's baptism with Marika. Though he hasn't seen her all that much, she has become his favorite companion. She is never there when he wakes up in the morning. Nor does she think to leave him a note or other little token to commemorate their night together and leave the way open for next time. So he never has to talk to her in the morning. Big plus. In fact, they don't talk much about anything.

She never asks about what he does and all that, which is fine because that bores the shit out of him. She never asks what he's thinking, thank Jesus. In spite of that, or maybe because of it, she is the only person he's confided in about the fishing hole and Drew—about how upsetting it was.

He hasn't mentioned, though, in the weeks since then, that Drew still isn't the same. That's partly because Drew won't admit it or let anybody talk about it. He bites your head off. So somehow Kenny feels obligated to pretend everything's okay. But he does tell Marika about the fish. She seems to understand. Maybe being a fisherman's daughter.

That's pretty much all he knows about her—she's from Denmark, and she's a fisherman's daughter. She dodges the few questions he asks her. An awfully quiet woman. She never compliments him on his lovemaking. She seems to enjoy herself, but it never seems to occur to her to attribute this to him. She is strikingly different from other women her age, even in the way she moves her lean, angular body. She never seems to worry about it. She doesn't try to pose or drape herself to advantage. She doesn't care if the lights are on or off. The one time he attempted a compliment, she looked down at herself as if surprised to see her body there, shrugged, and said, "It works." She appreciates his body, though. He knows this not because of anything she's said, but because of the way she looks at him.

Altogether, she is completely different from any woman he's known. He realizes now that he's mostly known women who were in a constant argument with themselves over whether or not they were desirable, so that however they might pretend, they had little attention to give to actual desire. Lynn wasn't that way, but then, Lynn was young and beautiful. Hard to know how she'd turn out later. She had no older females around as examples except, for a while, that spooky Aunt Jeanne, and he couldn't imagine Lynn turning out like her. Lynn's too down-to-earth in spite of that writing thing.

As he waits in The Cove on the off-chance that Marika might show up, he realizes that he is getting tired of never seeing Lynn or Pete. After all, their families have known each other for generations. Okay, so he's not husband material, and he's made a mistake and left her holding the bag, but can't they tolerate him as a friend? At least talk to him, for Chrissake? He doesn't notice Barry's slightly stiff behavior toward him.

Marika comes in, and after a while, she and Kenny leave together. Fuming, Barry mops up the puddles of condensation from their drinks. Once, yes, he can see a one-night stand, but why does she keep leaving with this chowderhead?

Just yesterday evening, his frustration led him to do something very unusual. A short, muscular, intelligent-looking guy in his fifties, a retired professor, had been coming in lately and discreetly staring at Marika. Yesterday, he finally worked up to asking Barry a few questions about her, and Barry surprised himself by saying, "She's a good friend of mine. I think you'd get along. I don't think she'd mind me giving you her phone number. Tell her you want to know more about the Outer Banks. She's brilliant."

Then, still reeling with shock at his own indiscretion, he wrote the number down on a napkin and handed it to this stranger.

•

After Kenny and Marika make love, around 11:30, Marika says, "It's high tide. Let's go and walk on the beach."

"But you can't see anything out there," says Kenny.

"We'll listen," says Marika.

Well, thinks Kenny, here it is, the fly in the ointment. Every woman's kooky about something. But he can't tell her that lying in the warm cocoon of an occupied bed is one of the main things he likes about sex, and he feels he's earned his cocoon tonight; so he jumps out of bed, and, with feigned heartiness, says, "Let's do it!"

Stumbling after her on the beach, getting sand in his shoes, he notices for the first time that she always wears boots or high-topped sneakers.

"Christ, there's not even a moon," he says.

Dimly, he sees her sit on a dune and motion him to join her. He puts his arm around her and leans over to kiss her, but she pushes him away.

"No, no," she says, impatiently. "Listen."

Kenny doesn't know what to say. It's like being with Lynn. How can you just sit there, she would say. Don't you have anything to say?

He tries.

"Very romantic," he says.

Marika looks at him uncomprehendingly. When they trudge back to the motel, she picks up the books she was going to read in bed while Kenny slept and kisses Kenny on both cheeks.

"Good luck," she says, and leaves.

Kenny stares at the door for a minute. Then he turns back the blankets, makes a woman out of pillows to lie beside him, undresses, gets into bed, turns on a late movie with the sound low, and drifts off to sleep, aware intermittently, of his suit for tomorrow's ceremony flapping its empty sleeves in the breeze of the air conditioning.

10

The moon rises late on the eve of Kyle Peterson's baptism. Lynn sees it resting on the crest of the old pine outside his nursery window as she's sitting by his crib. The window is open, the air is mild, Kyle is content. Suddenly, and for no reason, she feels peaceful and good. Another hormonal mood swing, she thinks ruefully. But there's more to it than that. It's happened a few times before in her life that suddenly, for no reason, she had a perfect day. She'd know it, as if recognizing a friend, the moment she woke up.

This time she feels her muscles suddenly soften, her thoughts become lucid, her very breathing freer, on catching sight of that moon, so perfectly round, with its faintly flawed white face glowing tenderly at her. These days she knows she can't hope for a perfect day—there's hardly such a thing as a day any more, only segments of time divided by Kyle's needs—but she's having a perfect moment.

She wraps her arms around herself, turns to Kyle for a minute to include his sleeping face in the perfection, and thinks, I'll take it.

The next morning she is irritable again. Trying to keep Kyle's schedule—eating, sleeping, diaper change—in mind while dressing him up and packing his bag—big-boy diapers, sweater, teddy bear, change of clothes—and dressing herself up and getting them both breakfast. Once again it all seems too much, but she's aware that she could be depressed and stuck, and this morning, at least, she has somewhere to go. She comforts herself with that and slips into her old green dress as she couldn't find anything else she liked when she went shopping with T. This looks fine, especially with Mama's pearls.

•

The Bakers wait in the narthex of Our Lady of the Sea for the baptism to begin. The Bakers have opted to have the ceremony without the rest of the congregation and to have a brief run-through before the actual ceremony. The church surrounds them with its solid, blond paneling. Tall windows behind the modest altar look out on the big, old cypresses and loblolly pines of the cemetery. The trees sway in the breeze, moving sunlight back and forth.

Kenny is late. Lynn fingers Mama's pearls. She is angry at Kenny, but she can't get up much steam behind it. She's feeling weary and out of control and wondering why she's brought all these people together. Kyle is sitting on her lap, watching everything. He's being good so far—that's something. Daddy's on the phone somewhere, as usual. A door slams and Kenny comes in, looking dazed and nervous. He doesn't attempt to join the rehearsal, but sits down in a chair near the door. Father Cathcart makes no move to include him. When they are finished, Kenny walks hesitantly over to Lynn and Kyle. Lynn greets him with as much courtesy as she can muster, which isn't much.

"Hello, Kenny."

Kenny, who has been looking at her apprehensively, looks down at Kyle. His eyes widen. He stands very still, reminding Lynn of a deer caught in the headlights. What is he so afraid of? Then she realizes: He is falling in love. He remains frozen until she speaks.

"Kyle, this is your Daddy," Kyle stares up at Kenny with wide blue eyes.

"Would you like to hold him?" asks Lynn.

He looks at her, then back to Kyle, smiles a little, and holds out his arms.

Lynn gives Kyle to him, tenderly, and Kyle reaches out his hand, curiously, to touch Kenny's face.

"Hey, little guy," says Kenny, softly. "Glad to meet you."

And suddenly, Lynn is swamped by a feeling of relief so strong that she almost cries. She sits down in the chair in front of Kenny's and stares at the two of them, who continue to stare at each other.

What she's thinking is: Kyle has a father. She's been thinking of him as fatherless, thinking that if Kenny really wanted to see Kyle he'd make more of a fuss over her refusing to let him. She's not really sure how much she can ever rely on Kenny, but somehow just seeing him smitten by this unreasoning, overwhelming emotion—seeing him fall before Kyle's power, as she has, comforts her beyond words, and makes her feel less crazy. And then it occurs to her why she's brought these people here: She wants to see other people worshiping Kyle, so she won't feel so crazy worshiping him. Or anyway, paying him extremely close attention. Sometimes she feels she can't sleep because Kyle's face is imprinted on the inside of her eyelids, and his presence, even when he's asleep in the other room, conveys an almost suffocating urgency to her. It's as if she's living in some kind of state of emergency. Under siege.

Just then, Jeanne walks in wearing a gauzy turquoise dress and dangling silver earrings and carrying an armful of stuffed animals.

"I got a little carried away," she says, sheepishly. "Besides, these are overdue."

"Wow!" says Lynn. "Look, Kylie!"

From his father's arms, Kyle does look, wide-eyed, and reaches out for the animals. Without looking at Kenny, Jeanne puts a plush starfish into the child's hand, which closes and waves the toy around triumphantly.

Pete comes in just then, and his face relaxes into a smile. He stands there for a minute, smiling, and they all smile back, even Jeanne. Pete crosses to Kenny and, unable to shake his hand over Kyle, grabs his shoulder for a minute, nodding and saying only, "Kenny."

Kenny nods back. "Sir," he says, though before he's always called him Pete.

Pete crosses to Jeanne.

"Good to see you Jeanne," he says, and kisses her on the cheek. But that's a mistake. He shouldn't come so close, he shouldn't touch her. When he steps back she doesn't look up. Everyone pretends not to notice. Pete takes comfort, as they all do, from Kyle.

"Hey, young 'un," he says, giving Kyle his finger. He is rewarded by a flicker of recognition, a thrashing of limbs, a cooing sound.

"Yeah, you know your granddaddy, don't you? Don't you? He knows you too, feller. You bein' good for your mama?"

Taking his place behind his lectern, Don Cathcart calls out, "Ladies and gentlemen, I think we're all here. If you'd like to take your places, we'll begin the ceremony."

"Friends," he begins, once everyone's where they should be, "Welcome to this baptismal ceremony for Kyle Joshua Peterson. Though it's not customary, I'd like to say a few words before we begin about the significance of this ceremony. The church recommends that baptisms be performed, when possible, in the spring, near Easter. This is because, like Easter, baptism is a celebration of renewal. A baby is already born into the world, and through baptism, he is born again into the love of Jesus Christ and the Kingdom of God."

Jeanne folds her arms, thinking, "Once isn't enough. Men need to get in on the act. If he's not consecrated by a male God, he doesn't exist. What nonsense."

"But the birth of a baby," Don continues, "like the ceremony of baptism, is also a chance for each of us to renew ourselves—to be born anew. For us adults, life has dished up disappointments. We have disappointed each other, others have disappointed us, and we have disappointed ourselves."

Kenny shifts his weight in his chair, sinking down a little. He's sure this is directed at him.

"Each of these disappointments is a little death, and if we suffer enough of them, we can begin to feel that we are less alive than we once were. But when we look at a baby—at little Kyle—and when he looks back at us, we can feel his life renewing us just as spring renews the earth; just as Jesus Christ came that we might all be made new. I'm very happy to be celebrating that renewal with you here today."

Jeanne feels like the wicked fairy at the christening. These are sweet words, but where in this situation is renewal for her? There are only old ties, demands she can no longer meet, rage, guilt, spoilt loves. Kyle is certainly a treat—though still a little squishy, he shows signs of inheriting his parents' beauty—but to be renewed by him she'd have to love him, to be involved with him, to babysit, to worry, to give him a slice of her life. And she can't seem to do that. She doesn't feel like she has that much to spare now.

But Kenny sits up straight now, pierced by the priest's words. Yes, he understands now. Kyle is his chance. He doesn't know how, but Kyle will take away this feeling he has of having screwed everything up and lost his chance at life. Suddenly, he has a vision of Kyle and himself in a canoe, rowing down the Amazon River. Then it's just Kyle, after Kenny is too old, Kyle a famous archaeologist like Indiana Jones, rowing deep into the jungle to discover ancient Mayan civilizations. He shakes his head a little, wondering where this fantasy came from, but he dwells on it, in it, anyway, listening to the fantastic chatter of monkeys and birds and watching a few scattered spirals of sunlight twist their way through the jungle darkness.

Meanwhile, to calm herself, Jeanne thinks about Don Cathcart's body—his sloping shoulders, his flat feet, the way he always murmurs with pleasure when she smooths the furrows on his brow. Somehow it dissipates her anger when she remembers the burdens of flesh that people carry. She feels compassion for them then and respect.

"What dost thou ask of the Church of God?" asks Don.

"Faith," say Lynn, Terry, and Pete.

"What does Faith bestow on thee?" asks Don.

"Life everlasting," say Lynn, Terry, and Pete.

Don Cathcart thanks God for the blessing of water and anoints Kyle's forehead. Kyle's arm jerks out in surprise, and he makes his "hallellujah" noise, but doesn't cry. In fact, he smiles at Lynn, who looks lovingly down at him. A little shiver of fear runs through her. How vulnerable it makes you, to feel that anything is this important! She's pretty sure you can't feel this kind of passion without paying for it. Well, all right then. This is life. And suddenly she remembers standing in her communion dress, Mama's bright brown eyes on her, shining with pride and love. How unabashed Mama was in her loving! How happy it made her! Lynn knows she herself takes after Pete—stubborn and guarded—but she resolves to be more like Mama. Throw your love away with both hands. If you hold onto it, what is it?

Pete too is thinking of Cathy, of how happy and funny she would have been with little Kyle. She would've done parodies of herself as an indulgent grandmother. She would've played with Kyle for hours, making him squeal with delight. Just by being in a room, she would have made everyone in it feel part of something. The tears stand in his eyes and sting. He wants to be alone so he can talk to Cathy. Last night he dreamed that she was laughing at him for screwing up with Jeannie. She was explaining how simply things could be put right, but she was explaining in French, even though he kept telling her he took Spanish in school.

•

After the baptism, Don Cathcart removes his vestments slowly. He's in no hurry to get to the celebratory brunch, though he knows he has to put in an appearance. He feels the combination of exhaustion and exhilaration that he usually feels after baptisms and weddings. People are shining with joy, nervousness, apprehension, wound up tight, expecting perfection in spite of themselves. At funerals they seem mute, hooded, bowed down. Strangely, after funerals he generally feels calm and content. Often he goes home and takes a nap. Now, sighing, he runs his finger around the inside of his collar and puts on his old tweed jacket. His ankle throbbed a little during the ceremony and feels naked without the splint. It's starting to feel numb now. That's what happens, he thinks. Pieces of you die, but you have to go on using them anyway. Wincing at the morbidness of this thought, he charges out the door, shutting it too hard behind him.

The brunch is in the dining room of The Sandpiper Inn, Jack Brockie's place. A wall of sound hits Cathcart as soon as he enters, and he hardly registers Jack Brockie and Pete Baker shaking his hand, smiling and flushed with good fellowship and Champagne. The old familiar panic creeps up on him. Except at a few places, like the Bluebird, where he's a regular, he has always felt lost in crowds, at parties—any gathering over four—and sometimes the feeling has almost amounted to a phobia. The pulpit, a little apart from everybody, is his compromise between loneliness and agoraphobia, "fear of the marketplace." Fear of the brunch, he thinks wryly, adjusting his collar again.

He sees they have seated him beside the lady who sold Hirsch his house—oh God, what was her name? But she's deep in conversation with Pete Baker who, having greeted Don, has sat down beside her. Everyone at the long table seems to be glowing with the light that often emanates from families at these times, when briefly, they seem to become one big, powerful self. Terry is holding Kyle, who has fallen asleep, and she is talking to the massaging sister, no, aunt—the sight of whom causes Cathcart to blush in spite of himself. He has occasionally thought about her, her wise hands and gentle eyes, when he was falling asleep at night. Looking around, though, he sees that he can get himself a cup of coffee, congratulate a few people and leave. That's what he'd better do.

In spite of his painful sense of being at once exposed and irrelevant, he forces himself to say a word to everyone, even the ne'er-do-well father. As he shakes Kenny's hand, he's surprised to see his expression of urgent earnestness, and even more surprised, after he says, "Your son is a fine boy," to see Kenny's eyes well up with tears. Too much Champagne, perhaps, but you never know, he reminds himself, striding out purposefully as if he has somewhere to go, escaping from the glare of all that togetherness. Maybe I converted him. He smiles. Not for a minute does he believe that might be true.

•

After the brunch, Jeanne goes home and takes out an old photograph album. She hasn't looked at it for years, but now she's looking for a particular picture of Cathy, one she loved when she was a little girl—here it is—her sister at about seventeen, standing on a fallen log, sunlight filtering through a dense thicket behind her, her face and body dappled with light and shade. A patch of light falls across her brown eyes, so that they glow, bright and warm, amid the cool shadows of the leaves. When she was twelve, Jeanne remembers, she put this picture on her bureau in a little silver frame. It reminded her of fairies, elves, tree spirits. Secretly she had always thought of Cathy as a kind of whimsical good fairy. But now Jeanne is forty-six, and she looks at her sister, in this picture with new eyes. She remembers Cathy's body—how her long toes wiggled when she read in the hammock; how, when she was about fifteen, acne appeared on her shoulders and Jeanne was always coming upon her twisting in front of the mirror in her room, trying to see the full extent of the blemish. Her allergies in the spring, when the whole house would resound with her sneezes. How she loved to wash her face and then dab it all over with witch hazel, leaving fragrant little wads of cotton in the wastebasket.

Jeanne stares at the picture. Cathy may have been a tree spirit. She may now, as Jeanne has many times imagined, be a water spirit. But somewhere in there, she was a person, too, with a body. A body that drowned. And suddenly, Jeanne is folded double by a shocking wave of grief, which pulls out of her throat deep, hoarse sobs of pain and protest. She cries for a long time until sleep engulfs her, and she dreams of a baby made of water, looking out from his mother's arms with all the stunning openness of a baby's expression somehow there on his transparent face. The mother is made of water, too, but her face is hidden.

||

I n June, the tourist season that started with a trickle down Route 1 turns into a flood. Families return to their beach houses, fishermen rent shacks by the beach and charter boats, couples check into The Sandpiper, or camp in the Jasper Woods. Shell-seekers and surfers get up early to pick up their cast-off treasures or test their mettle. By afternoon, the beach is criss-crossed with the tracks of pickups and dune buggies.

In its own time, the tide comes in and washes them away. Most people have a good time. At the least they relax, at most they experience a kind of rebirth from breathing the sea's breath and hearing its voice. They are nourished by its profound, salty presence. And they keep coming and coming and coming. As they commune and eat and spend and excrete, they create an atmosphere of great richness that, in its turn, attracts microbial tourists in swarms.

At the beginning of the summer the human locals, who've been bored and restless and short of cash, are excited to see the vacationers when they come. By the end, they are tired and resentful. The Cove and The Sandpiper are busy, and Barry and Shona work long hours and then fall into bed together, smoke pot, watch movies, and sleep in the wee hours. Sometimes they talk about their customers in their smoke-filled love nest, and their comments become more and more bitter.

"I think I can top your disgusting drunk for this evening," says Shona.

"Oh yeah?" says Barry. He sucks smoke up the bong, watching the water at the bottom bubble furiously, then listens to Shona with artificially bated breath.

"Yeah, oh my God, this guy did it all. He complained, he made a pass while complaining, he made me taste his margarita to show me there was salt in it—there wasn't—and then he grabbed my hand and cried all over it."

"Brutal," says Barry, smoke sliding from his mouth and curling toward the ceiling. "No one's ever cried on my hand. They've cried, but never—"

"And then, while I'm standing there trying to get my hand back, I notice he's got this rash all over his arms. So I think, great, he's crazy, he's drunk, he's got leprosy, and he's at my table."

"Was he alone?"

"Yes, amazingly enough, he was dining unaccompanied."

They both laugh, but Shona's laugh turns into a wail. "Barry, what's wrong with us? How'd we get so mean? I mean, the poor guy was sick!"

Barry nods, one part of his mind contemplating this, the other filled by the pot with puffy little clouds.

"Too damned many of the suckers, that's all," he replies. "You know how everybody goes gaga and stays glued to their sets when a little boy falls down a well. But when two thousand people get offed by some earthquake in Tibet, you forget it by the next morning. And some of those Tibetans were probably cute little boys."

"Yeah," says Shona, nodding sadly.

"It's like there's a limit to how many people you can care about," says Barry, flicking his lighter on and off. "One refugee, a hero. One-hundred refugees, a nuisance. One-thousand refugees, a threat. It's like our minds have borders."

"Thanks, Nostradamus," says Shona. "I'm sorry I asked." She takes the bong from Barry and lays her head in his lap.

"Anyway, it's just us now," she says.

He strokes her hair, thinking that he wouldn't mind burying his face in it and shedding a few tears himself. He's been feeling low lately. Too much pot, maybe. Too many drunks.

•

The next evening, Barry listens to Marika, who is nursing a drink in The Cove and propounding to him her theory that the earth, in its much slower and more comprehensive way, is like our minds. Faced with too many people, it becomes stressed out, hostile, poisonous. She doesn't realize, as she speaks, that, partly from exhaustion and sore feet, he's feeling pretty poisonous toward her. Hunched over her drink, glowering, she looks to him like some kind of female Scrooge. He used to think she looked like Greta Garbo when she was in this mood, but now she seems self-centered. She doesn't see him when she's like this, she doesn't see anybody—just her own obsessions.

Behind her, he sees a big table of college kids starting to get rowdy. A pitcher turns over. A yell goes up. A boy picks up a squealing girl and stands her on a chair. Sighing, Barry goes over to try to calm them down. When he gets back to the bar, Marika is gone. He wipes the bar and pockets her tip and searches the face of the clock for a sign of closing time.

•

The day after, the weather is hot and sticky, and the ocean breezes are not making it in as far inland as the Family Wellness Center and the strip mall beside it. Ducking into Food Lion on her lunch hour, Terry Baker runs into Drew Layman's wife, Lori Layman, whom she knew in high school. In Lori's family's better days, they were the Bakers' neighbors, and the two girls played kick the can in the back-yard, or on hot, lazy days watched traffic go by from their front steps, idly swatting mosquitoes and poking holes in the ground with sticks. They shared time back when there was some. In high school, Lori was a pretty, languid girl, with an easy blush. She was startled and flattered by Drew Layman, who fell head over heels in love with her.

Now, in the Food Lion, Lori looks pale, sad and puffy, like someone who drinks too much or cries too much, or perhaps doesn't cry enough. Must be the latter, Terry figures, because when she enquires about Drew, Lori bursts into tears with her anxious smile still frozen on her face, and she looks as surprised as Terry feels.

"You wanna go somewhere and talk?" asks Terry. "C'mon, let's go to my office. It's just down the road. Of course. Everything's just down the road here," and, babbling on nervously in that vein, she takes Lori by the elbow and steers her around the checkout line. Lori keeps her eyes cast down until she's in Terry's car, where she lights a cigarette and smokes it with trembling fingers. In the office, Terry sits her down in an easy chair and says, "Now what's up, Lori?"

Lori stubs out her cigarette and makes as if to speak, but bursts into tears again. "I'm sorry," she says. "This is ridiculous."

"No, Lori, I'm sure it's not. I've known you for a long time, and you never were a crybaby. Now what is it? Is it Drew?"

Sobbing, Lori nods, and after a time, chokes out. "I think he's losing his mind. I think he's sick—I mean, not crazy but, you know, really sick! But every time I mention it, he—"

And she breaks down again, leaving the rest to Terry's imagination. "Well Lori, didn't Drew ever go to that specialist in Elizabeth? I told him to go, and I've been waiting for that report."

Lori shakes her head. "He says we can't afford it."

"Well, won't insurance—"

Again, sadly, Lori shakes her head.

"No insurance?"

"Nope. Drew's company got bought. They—the new bosses—cut benefits. You know his mom's in the nursing home, so he said—we've always been pretty healthy—"

"So no insurance."

Terry takes a deep breath, feeling a familiar anger. The dreaded helplessness washes over her. More and more, medical and health insurance costs seem to be colluding with disease, preventing her patients from seeking treatment until it's too late. She doesn't cry about it any more—not that she'd cry in front of a patient anyway—but the feeling of helplessness still appears unexpectedly, frequently, like sludge in her veins poisoning her resolve. Now, she makes herself move, at least to do something, hugging Lori instead of curing her, offering her a cup of coffee, turning on the coffee machine, tearing the filter with angry fingers.

•

"I don't want to be an alarmist," says Terry, breakfasting with her father the next morning at the Bluebird, "but—"

"That's right," says Pete. "Lord knows there's no shortage of alarms these days."

Pete pronounces "alarms" with mock alarm, widening his eyes, raising his hands. Jack Brockie, sitting next to him, laughs quietly. Terry envies the relaxation in Brockie's dark, handsome face. She's seen him around town, and he always seems to be in his element. Is that possible? Wearily, she closes her eyes, sore and heavy from lack of sleep and scrolling through various Medscapes on the computer. Her father continues.

"And you've always been very intelligent that way," he says, patting her hand proudly and congratulating himself on refraining, at the last minute, from calling her "sensible." He dimly remembers that she objected to that word once. Something about Lynn always being the pretty one. Of course, that was a long time ago when Terry had braces.

"You doctors must see it all," he continues. "I read somewhere that most things just go away by themselves if you wait about two weeks."

Terry looks a little strained.

"Of course," says Pete, "you can't take that chance."

"Oh, no," echoes Jack.

"You've got to follow up," says Pete, as Jack nods solemnly.

"It's just that nobody wants another Pfiesteria hysteria."

Both men shake their heads, smiling a little at the uproar over a few dead fish and a few drunk people losing their tempers and their memories.

Terry feels herself fading. Not enough sleep. Sleep, and then she'll know what to do next. And it probably won't be talk to Daddy and his new friend with the nice suit. To them now, she just says, "I don't think it's Pfiesteria." And sucks up the rest of her Coke while Pete recalls dead fish he's seen which did not, as he puts it, "bring on the Apocalypse."

●

But the microbe is busy finding other bodies. It coats its protein envelope with carbohydrate and becomes a virus in bacterial clothing, disguising its intention from the host cells of a particularly attractive human body, whispering sweet nothings so the cells will lower their defenses. I'm from out of town and you look good to me. And the body, distracted, perhaps, by keeping up with the breathing, the moving, the thinking, the speaking, the eating, the excreting, adjusting to temperature and the presence of other bodies, lets the disguised virus in.

12

Don Cathcart is working on his farewell sermon when Adele McCue knocks on his office door. He's quite pleased with the twist he has just introduced into it. He likes a sermon with a twist in the middle. He'll start out by decrying the way that modern mobility has decreased people's appreciation of where they are at any given moment. If you always have a sense that you are "just passing through," then you might be tempted to assume that the problems of the place you are in any given moment are someone else's concern. You pollute and move on. Everyone, he knows, will think of the tourists as he says this.

He might even say that when you are able to "Be still and know that God is God," you tend to want to take care of the place where you have experienced the stillness. He would gesture at the clean, gleaming wood of the church, at the bright new altar hangings and offer the beauty and orderliness of this place as an example. People would beam with complacency.

Then the twist.

But, he would say, we also know that in a larger sense we are all "passing through." We are passing through this visible world. In fact, we are all visitors. Here he might pause, hoping that one or two of them might look around at the sanctuary again, but in a different way now. Perhaps the high-ceilinged room might take on some of the consistency of the sunlight pouring in the window and spilling lavishly over the altar. Things might appear, for a moment, slightly transparent, quivering on the verge of dissolution. Though most of the congregation, of course, will be half-asleep or thinking about dinner.

Then, after the pause, he would propose that though we must always keep moving, if not from place to place then from one phase of our lives to the next, we must do the best we can to be responsible where we are.

Another pause here.

What does this mean? It means that as visitors, we are responsible to take care of the place we are visiting while we're here. Clean up after ourselves. Maybe even plant something, a tree or stand of sea oats, even though we may leave and never see what we've planted grow to fruition. And it means, too, that we must take care of each other, even though we're just visiting. Even if you've been married to your husband or wife for thirty, forty years, and it seems like he or she has been there forever (the congregation is mostly retired couples, and he expects a little laugh here), in fact, you're just visiting. Chances are one of you will stay and one of you will go. Enjoy your visit while you can.

And this goes for all the people you meet, however briefly. Maybe it feels like you stand still and they come through so fast they're just a blur. You clean up your town and they come through and throw trash on it. But in fact, you're both in different stages of the same journey. You're fellow travelers. You need to look out for each other.

This is as far as he's gotten when the knock comes on the door. Hastily, he makes a note ("end with farewell") and calls, "Come in!"

Adele McCue enters—a tiny, hesitant woman with a backbone of steel. He knew a few such women in his youth, friends of his grandmother's, self-effacing, sweet, correct to the death, outliving everybody. Lives full of difficulties—deaths, illnesses, wayward children, reversals of fortune—that were borne unflinchingly and never allowed to interfere with a smooth coiffeur, an unwrinkled blouse, a mannerly greeting. He fancies that southern women of that generation still bear, on behalf of their parents, the loser's burden: to maintain dignity in the face of annihilation.

She's a very active member, but he hasn't gotten to know her that well. She's not one of the complainers, thank God, but he always finds her forbearance a little off-putting, as if she would only allow their conversation to flow through selected channels.

"Please come in, Miz McCue," he says, heartily. She is dressed in her best, wearing a little gray suit over a pink blouse, and even a matching gray hat with tiny pink feathers. Her faded cheeks are lightly rouged, and Don smiles. She's a pretty sight.

"Am I disturbing you?" she asks, taking a small step backwards.

"No, no, not at all. It's always a pleasure to see you," says Don, ushering her in. "Please sit down. Can I offer you some tea or coffee?"

"Oh no, no, no thank you," says Mrs. McCue. She sits on the edge of her chair, hands in her lap, smiling shyly, and clears her throat.

"Father Cathcart," she says, "I've come to thank you for all you've done for us in your time here." Don winces and begins to demur, but she continues. He realizes she has prepared a little speech, and he will have to sit through it, even though he knows—and she must know—that his relationship with the congregation has not been a very happy one. He visited the sick and dying, but could think of little to say. He counseled and married young couples, but felt awkward and hypocritical—what did he really know about that kind of intimacy? When a storm blew a man's roof off, he had little to offer except feeble consolation, knowing that the minister over at Liberty Baptist could roll up his sleeves and lead a team in putting on a new roof, and the rector at St. Peter's Episcopal could hector his congregation into setting up a fund to help parishioners through such emergencies. Don is best at the parts of being a priest that he himself thinks are least important—the ritual, the liturgy, and, sometimes, the sermon.

"I'm sure that the congregation as a whole will want to give you something," says Mrs. McCue, and Don groans inwardly at the thought. "But I'd like to give you something just…just from me." And, leaning down to reach into her large purse, she brings out an object wrapped in many layers of tissue paper and, hesitating a moment, hands it over the desk.

"Mrs. McCue, this is so sweet of you, but you really shouldn't have."

"I wanted to," says Mrs. McCue, firmly.

So, under her eager gaze, he unwraps the paper layer by layer and reveals an exquisite porcelain Madonna. He stares at it for a minute in silence. He can tell immediately that it's very valuable. The workmanship is inspired. The gold of her crown, the blue of her gown, the soft look of her skin. And her expression. What is it? Infinite wisdom. She looks as if she knows everything—or everything that's important. Infinite love. Her arms are slightly bent, her palms facing slightly upward, beckoning the supplicant closer. She looks at Don as if she completely and utterly accepts him and approves of him. And moreover, she looks, somehow, as if she's right to do so. As if she knows something.

Finally, he looks up to Mrs. McCue, who is smiling radiantly, waiting for him to speak.

"Mrs. McCue," he says, "what have you given me?"

"She's from Portugal," says Mrs. McCue. "My mother gave her to me."

"But—but—you must want her," stammers Don. "She must be so precious to you—"

"No." says Mrs. McCue firmly. "My children don't want her. I think she needs to be given to someone. I want you to have her."

Don lapses back into staring, until he hears Mrs. McCue rise to go. "Oh, I'm sorry," he says, leaping to his feet, "it's just that I'm so overwhelmed—"

To his surprise, Mrs. McCue darts forward and takes his hand.

"I'm glad you like her," she says.

"Yes," says Don, "Oh yes—" and he shakes her hand, holding onto it, until she gently extricates it and backs out the door, saying "Well, I'll let you get back to your sermon, Father. And thank you again for everything."

Don sits down at his desk, his head whirling. He picks up the Madonna and stares at it. He turns it over in his hands, not so much to examine it as to conceal and reveal the face that shines on him like a lighthouse beacon.

After a long moment, he puts her gently down and leans back, staring at the wall. Then he picks up the draft of his sermon, tears it smartly into two pieces, and drops the pieces into the wastebasket. He paces around his office for a while and then gets the ripped sermon out of the trash. It might still make a good introduction. But by itself, it's the wrong way to say goodbye. He stands still for a minute with the torn pieces in his hands and thanks God for saving him, in the nick of time, from being stupid. He still feels a little shaky from the force of his revelation. It's always a little frightening to suddenly feel that God has an interest in you.

The next morning is Sunday morning. Walking up the aisle of Our Lady of the Sea, Don sweats heavily. It's the most nervous he's ever been before a sermon, not because it's his last, but because, for him, it will be the most difficult.

But the message of the Madonna, with her beautiful open hands and radiant eyes, was quite clear: Don Cathcart, you must do the thing which is hard. You must do the hard thing. And so here he is, carrying his unwilling body up the aisle, barely able to form the prayer in his mind: "May the words of my mouth be acceptable in your sight, oh my Strength and my Redeemer." Please let me get through this and do it right.

His text is the parable of the Good Samaritan. Gripping his lectern as if it might get away from him, he thanks God inwardly for his voice, which seems unaffected by his nerves. It rings out clearly, smooth and sonorous, and he thinks maybe these words are acceptable.

He sketches the parable for them. The man asks Christ what he must do to get into heaven. Christ patiently repeats the words of the prophets and then introduces his own new twist: You must love your neighbor as yourself.

"And the man asks," Don continues, beginning to trust his voice and loosening his grip on the lectern, "and the man asks an intelligent question: Who is my neighbor? Who is this that you're asking me to give as much love as I give myself? Because, let's face it, for most of us, that's a lot of love. How many people am I expected to give all that love to?

"And to this intelligent question, Jesus answers, indirectly, brilliantly, as he so often does, with a story. What he doesn't do, you'll notice, is come right out and say Everybody! Everybody is your neighbor, even though that's the truth—the great truth, springing from the love of God, that He came to bring us. But He knows that if He just tells this man that he's got to love everybody, the man will be overwhelmed. Think about it—it's hard enough to love the people you're related to, let alone unknown numbers of people you don't know. Likely as not, the man would have said 'Uh-huh,' walked away, thought about it for a while and given up. He wouldn't have said 'this is too hard.' He just would've forgotten about it, because the idea is too big and wouldn't sink in.

"So instead of overwhelming him, Jesus tells the simple story of the outcast by the roadside who was helped by a man who just happened to be passing by. Even though the Samaritan might never see the man again, he helps him.

"After the parable, Jesus allows the man to draw the conclusion for himself: those two strangers were neighbors. Neighbors are people who help one another."

Here Don pauses, and a blinding wave of panic almost knocks him down. He got caught up in his story and forgot that the hard part of the sermon is still to come. He looks down at the lectern for a minute, focusing on the river-like grain of varnished wood and prays: "Please, if it's what you want me to say, help me to say it."

He straightens his notes. He steps back a bit from the lectern and drinks some water, thinking, Why is this so hard? He'd known it would be, but he didn't understand why—has never understood why, and still doesn't. Without looking at them, he feels the expectation of the congregation like heat on his averted face, gulps, and begins.

"As you have no doubt perceived, I am a shy man. I'm afraid that I may not have responded to the gestures of friendship and support that you have made to me over the years—in—in such a way that— as to make you feel that your efforts were welcome." He is looking down at his lectern again now, hoping that his voice will do what his eyes cannot.

"I want you to know that they were. They were welcome, every last one of them, welcome as water in the desert. From my first arrival here, when Amy Tolliver greeted me with that wonderful dessert party" (here he looks at Amy, a pretty, wan young woman with three sons and a bad-tempered husband who gives her no peace) not that I'm particularly fond of sweets (here his listeners laugh heartily, remembering the cake after cake and pie after pie he sampled at that party, grateful to have this way of gratifying, briefly, the hungry eyes of the women who baked them). "From those desserts to the priceless organizational skills that Miz Betty Sue has brought to my occasionally less than pristine office" (another laugh, which he allows to crest before looking at Betty Sue, her eyes alight, her face ravaged by fifty years of alcoholism which have left her skin deeply furrowed but, somehow, her mind and her jackhammer laughter intact). "Thank you Betty Sue. God bless you." Her laughing eyes fill with tears.

"And then there's Bob Atkins. What can you say about Bob? If my ministry has left any mark on this parish, the credit goes to Bob and his extraordinary Storm Ministry."

He looks at Bob and then, lightening his tone, says,

"And if this building is still standing, it's also due —"

And here he's interrupted by a wave of laughter, not only because everyone knows that Bob, a quiet, gentle bachelor, fixes everything from leaky toilets to broken gutters, but because the congregation has been suffused with a warm approval of itself. And that's how it should be. A shepherd doesn't point the way his flock should go and then head off to Charlottesville.

He continues:

"Among the many others who work quietly to make this church a place of beauty and of spiritual sustenance in life and in death are the Laymans."

Everyone turns to look at Drew and Lori who haven't been coming much lately. Drew is looking at his feet, and Lori blushing furiously.

"The job of sexton is one that requires brains, tact, organization, and, sometimes, a little muscle. Drew is just the man to fill that ticket. And Lori makes sure, week after week, that the altar is not only immaculate, but a beautiful center for our worship. We are lucky to have them."

The faces of the congregation are glowing. And now, as it comes time to wrap up, it's Don's eyes that fill with tears. He feels as if he's kindled a little fire on a frigid day by striking flint on stone. He looks at Bob Atkins, who lives alone, and wonders about his loneliness and whether he feels, at this moment, as Don does, a rare sense of con-nectedness that is almost too much to bear. Bob Atkins smiles and blushes and looks down at his shoes.

Don wants to say to them all, "I feel I have not served you as you deserve," but that would redirect attention to him, and this is not meant to be about him. Looking down, he wills his tears to slide back into his eyes. Of course they disobey, but, as he wipes them discreetly away, no more follow, and he is able to say, "This is a wonderful group of people sitting here in this church. I hope you appreciate yourselves, and I hope you appreciate each other. I know you will welcome and support your new priest, Father Brookner, as you did me. And, God willing, he will see what a blessing he has in you. Amen."

And with that, thank God, thank God, it is done. It remains only for him to eat a few pastries, make a few jokes, shake a few hands, and he can take off these heavy robes.

•

It's misty when Hirsch drives Don to the Greyhound station in Kitty Hawk, and a light rain falls, on and off, as they travel Route 1, a road that Don has always privately called "the straight and narrow." When the rain lets up and the mist rises a little, they look over the scrub for glimpses of the sound on their left and the sea on their right, rolling down the windows to smell the spice of wax myrtle and bayberry mingling with the salt of the breeze from the sea. Don feels some excitement, some apprehension, but mostly a kind of grateful emptying out. It is a relief to feel his identity slipping away from him, like taking off his collar after a long day. The rain begins again, the mist descends, and both men roll up their windows in silence.

At the bus station, they stand together awkwardly for a while. The journey ahead, Don's abandonment of his "vocation" and return to his childhood home, all seem a little too momentous to talk about when they may be interrupted at any minute by the snorting bus and the bustle of arrival and departure.

When the bus pulls in, they shake hands and promise to stay in touch. Don climbs onto the bus. His suitcase is stowed, Rose is stowed (he feels a little guilty about that, imagines he hears her barking), the Madonna is in her own special suitcase with all his towels wrapped around her. The engine begins its roar, and the smell of exhaust fumes mingles with the smell of upholstery and stale air conditioning. Don feels a momentary stab of panic, but it passes quickly, and he relaxes into a pleasant sense of emptiness, between two lives, unmoored, unvexed.

•

The next day, Hirsch breaks the ice with Marika when he least expects to. He didn't use the phone number Barry gave him—he's never been too fond of the phone. Doing some exploring, he comes around a bend in the Neuse River and sees her squatting beside it, gazing at the water with a map on the ground. Is that all she does, he thinks bemusedly, look at the water and drink?

She picks up the map and, standing up, peers at it.

"So where are we?" asks Hirsch.

She turns and looks at him, shading her eyes. She smiles. Apparently this lack of opening formalities appeals to her. Good.

"Who knows," she says, shrugging. Then she shifts her weight onto one hip and stares at him, still smiling a little, as if waiting to see what he'll do next. Her eyes are so blue and piercing that he almost wishes she would look back at the water.

His hand itches for the beer he'd like to offer her, but it's back in the cooler in the car, and to go back and get it would look too designing. What next? Then, miraculously, a gust of wind blows the map out of her hands and in his direction.

"Damn," she says, and springs after it. She pounces on it so fast that he doesn't have a chance to reach for it, but they're close together now, and shaking her hair back from her face, she holds the map out for him to see.

"Actually, we're right about here," she says.

They bend their heads together over the map. It's that easy, like a dream. Almost too fast for Hirsch, but the boat's launched, and he jumps on board. Doesn't want it to leave without him. It's a little dizzying after all these years, but not as hard as he might have thought.

He looks at her. For some reason she's explaining the pattern of water flow on the map. He can't quite focus on what she's saying. He had meant to come to the river in the morning, but he ran into traffic, and it's about noon to judge from the sun. Her face is itself a map of light and shadow, the bright parts almost too bright to see.

They talk about the map longer than is strictly necessary to orient them. Neither moves away. Marika mentions the heat of the day.

"I've got beer in the car," Hirsch says, surprising himself.

She looks at him. Yes. She is thirsty. She is weary of searching for Kenny's fish graveyard and thinking dark thoughts.

She asks, "What kind?" She looks up from the map. She's seen him around. She likes his face. Intelligent. And she likes his shoulders and his upright way of carrying himself.

"A good kind," says Hirsch, smiling broadly.

Marika folds up her map.

"Let's go get some," she says.

Smiling, they clamber over the rocks, a warm friendly wind at their backs. As they climb into the car, the bright river continues its course to the sea.

THE FLOOD

13

"Have you been under a lot of stress lately?" asks Terry.

Barry snorts scornfully. He can vividly imagine his father's response to the idea that he might be "under stress." Barry has been thinking a lot about his father lately. Involuntarily. Now, he shrugs.

"No," he says. "I'm a bartender."

Terry smiles. "Well, sometimes that can be—"

But Barry dismisses her with a gesture. "No," he says, buttoning his cuff. The rash he had a few days ago has faded. "Brain surgeons are under stress. Bartenders pour beer."

"Well," says Terry, "I'll run a few tests, but I don't see anything obvious. Might be mono. Might be low iron. Are you a vegetarian?"

It takes Barry a minute to answer. How slow his thoughts sometimes are these days. And what a feeling of anguish floats around them, like a fog.

"Hm? Oh—no, I eat meat. Now and then."

Terry nods noncommittally, but knows it's time to commit herself. "You seem pretty down," she says, reserving the word "depressed" in case she needs it.

Barry looks at her. He's clearly thought of this.

"I don't know what it would be about," he says, shrugging. His closed expression opens a little, as if he's half hoping she'll be able to tell him what's wrong.

"Have you considered counseling?"

"Well…not really. I can't imagine…I can't imagine it helping."

"Have you suffered from depression before?"

"No."

There is a silence. This is about as far as Terry wants to go.

"Well, I'll call you about those tests," she says. "In the meantime, as my daddy used to say, 'Get a little sun, have a little fun'."

Barry wants only, and rather desperately, to get home and away from this doctor's well-meaning face. Saying a few disconnected words, he flees, perspiring with the effort of—of what? He doesn't know. In his car, he focuses on driving. At his apartment, he focuses on getting his key in the keyhole, closing the blinds, walking to his bedroom and sprawling on his bed. But a scream wrenches him from oblivion. Or an alarm. No. The phone. He picks it up mechanically and grimaces at the sound of Shona's worried voice.

"Barry? Are you there?"

"Yeah."

"What did the doctor say?"

"Nothing."

There's a pause as Shona waits patiently for him to say something more.

"She's going to run some tests," he manages to say.

"For what?"

"I don't know."

"She didn't say?"

"Uh…no."

Another pause. "Did I wake you up, hon?"

"Uh…yeah."

"Oh. Sorry. I'll call you later."

"Yeah."

"Okay. Bye."

"Bye."

Barry hangs up and rushes into sleep, away from the mysterious intensity of his anger at Shona. Her solicitude enrages him, and his rage frightens him. It's all too much.

Shona hangs up and mourns, worried and sad and beginning to get angry. Does he love her at all? What's wrong with him? She's been counting on the doctor to tell him he has some kind of bug, like mono or—what's that new one—the yuppie disease—"Epstein-Barr." She grins for a minute, thinking how pissed Barry would be if he were accused of having a "yuppie disease." Well, maybe the doctor will still come up with something. She checks her watch. Time to meet Dee Dee at the Bluebird. What's gotten into her Shona can't make out, with all these little mother-daughter dates, but they seem harmless, and the timing is good, what with Barry going nuts and all. She checks herself in the mirror to make sure she's passable, grabs her keys and heads out the door.

•

Deidre Brockie sucks a drop of leftover lemonade from her straw. She'll order another one when Shona comes. She leans back and stares absently at the bright, almost metallic blue sky beyond the restaurant's porch railings. Behind her, the voices of other customers ordering burritos and coffee and Plug-Uglies meld into a soothing blur. She sits comfortably, feeling a sense of calm that's utterly new to her. Where does it come from? She doesn't really care.

Curiosity requires a certain dissatisfaction—a dissatisfaction with not knowing—and she can't muster it right now. She's been feeling this way for a couple of weeks. A wisp of hair falls across her face, and after a second or two, she brushes it back. She's wearing her hair pulled back in a ponytail—hasn't been to the hairdresser in a while—and an old denim shirt and jeans. She hasn't even tucked her shirt in. Today Jack looked askance at her when she left the house. He didn't say anything, but she knows he will, especially if she doesn't look right at work. A slightly ferocious smile spreads across her face as she pictures herself, hair unwashed, no bra, bare feet, showing people to their tables and taking their money, and she almost giggles at the phrase, *Sudden Slattern!*, which flashes across her mind in slanted, orange letters, like the title of a romance novel. Silly, silly, silly. Lightly, she bites her straw. And it occurs to her why she's been enjoying Shona's company so much lately—she can be silly with Shona, and Shona will be silly back. No matter how much small-talk Jack might make, the bottom line is never far from his mind. And the other men—well, when it comes to sex, they tend to be either serious, or stupid, or both. No women friends any more.

Deidre stretches lazily. Where's Shona? She's starting to feel like she could use a nap.

•

Deidre's languid mood is caused by a furor of activity in her blood. The energy that usually fuels her charm, her exactitude, her promiscuity, her unhappiness has in large part been diverted to preparing a response to the strange new creature which has entered her blood. Special cells in her lymph nodes have made a picture—something like a wanted poster—of the intruder. Vigilante cells are reading and replicating the poster and rushing to every outpost of Deidre's body by the millions and millions. So, while she registers a slight headache and decides on some iced coffee mocha, her body is on red alert.

14

October 5

Dear Hirsch:

Do you still write letters? I realize that not many do these days, but after a couple of weeks at the Homeplace I feel a need for correspondence. (I don't much care for the "e" version).

Maybe I came back here to deal with old ghosts, but that doesn't mean I have to spend all my time with them!

On the way here I was struck by how much the country changes in just four hours. I found myself waxing nostalgic about that smell of holly and cedar and myrtle, mixed with salt and sand, that comes through the window as you drive along Route One. And it's so flat and open there. Just after you cross the line into Virginia, the land—as if aware that it starts to go by a different name there—rears up into these familiar green hills.

So here I am.

And you? Are you settling in? Is everybody still stupid down there? Drop me a line if you find time.

Don

•

October 8

Don:

Any leaves turning yet up there? This is about the time, as I recall. Except for a few windy days and a slight thinning of the tourist horde, it could be midsummer here. But fortunately, in answer to your sarcastic question (I know you think I should suffer fools less crankily), not everyone here is stupid. In particular, that woman I mentioned to you—you may or may not remember—Marika Hansen—thinks quite a lot. The good part is that she's in a field I know nothing about—biology—and she knows nothing about literature, so we can learn from each other instead of splitting tedious theoretical hairs—so far, at least. We're spending a fair bit of time together. I guess you could say we've "hooked up," though there's certainly nothing formal or official about it.

And how are you settling in? Just because you once called a place home doesn't mean you feel at home there. Am I right?

Cheers,

Hirsch

•

October 13

Hirsch:

You have put your finger on it exactly. Please take it off.

I am going, slowly, through my parents' old papers, and, more swiftly, Dad's old scotch. Enabling me to become more like the lilies of the field.

And yes, the leaves are beginning to turn. The dogwood and poison ivy are blood red and the old maple by the stable is yellow at all its edges.

I don't think you ever saw the old place. I'd be curious to know what you think of it. Or what I think of it, for that matter. Why don't you head up here some weekend? Better hurry if you want any scotch.

Don

•

As Don lays down his pen, a horse chestnut falls onto the arm of the wicker chair where he sits with a large mug of coffee beside him. He starts and looks up at the big tree that spreads over the porch. Even with the slight breeze that is blowing, he can't quite figure out the trajectory the thing could have followed to fall on the arm of his chair. But soon he gives up trying to trace it and resumes staring into space. It's four o'clock, and the shadows of oaks and magnolias are long on the lawn. This little porch off the east wing, "Mama's porch," as he thinks of it, gets the morning sun full on, so, with a flannel shirt and cap, he can sit out on it as she did, in her little boiled wool jacket, in all seasons.

Some professor or other in seminary, he remembers, said something about sin coming from a root word that means "separation" and that all sin was a form of separation from God. Don was unable ever to find confirmation for this etymology, but it rang and rings, true to him. This morning, he found himself unable to give thanks. He knows he is in trouble. A period of heavy drinking has been followed by a period of abstinence, and none of it has done any good.

Last-night he watched a TV show in which some woman went "back home" after her parents died. There she was in the old house, looking over old letters, occasionally smiling. After she read them for a while, the voice-over supplying the text to the viewer, she dissolved into a flashback which led to some crucial insights and a coming-to-terms with her past.

Last night in his father's study, he caught an unexpected whiff of Dad's pipe tobacco. How that smell survived all these years is a mystery. And, looking around at Daddy's leather-bound books, hunting trophies and engravings, he realizes that his father is not all that much more absent now than he was during his life. These things were pretty much what he knew of him then. How can I miss you if you won't go away? How can I miss you if you were never here? As for Don, the longer he's been home, the more his identity seems to dissolve. In this place that presumably made him who he is, he feels more unformed than ever, and it's a frightening feeling, as if, as Alice in Wonderland said, he is in danger of becoming whatever the flame of a candle is after the flame has gone out.

He's been thinking about Alice a lot lately. *Alice's Adventures Underground.* It was a favorite of mother's in her early, charming days. She even had a small but valuable collection of Alice-related texts and artifacts.

On the east porch, surrounded by fallen horse chestnuts, Don closes his eyes.

> It'll be no good their putting their heads down and saying, 'Come up again, dear.' I shall only look up and say, 'Who am I then? Tell me that first, and then, if I like being that person, I'll come up: if not, I'll stay down here till I'm somebody else.

In his mind, an image of his mother accompanies these words, as they ring a little flatly (because in this depression nothing has much resonance) in his mind: About forty-five, peering at herself in the big round mirror of her "vanity," looking very pretty, dressed in silk and pearls and powder, but scared stiff because she's been allowed to attend whatever party she's primping for only on the condition that she will not take a drink.

Don drinks deeply from his coffee mug as this image fades from his mind. So pathetic, Alice's next words, said with a sudden burst of tears:

—but, oh dear!…I do wish they would put their heads down! I am so very tired of being all alone here!

And he is just recalling the Dormouse's story about the three little sisters who lived at the bottom of a well (" 'What did they live on?' asked Alice. 'Treacle,' said the Dormouse. 'But they'd have been ill,' remarked Alice. 'So they were,' said the Dormouse, 'very ill'."), and thinking that perhaps he'll go mad and perhaps that will feel better than this life at the bottom of a treacle well, when the phone rings, and it's Hirsch.

"Don," he says, brusquely. "The invitation for Thanksgiving still on?"

"Yes, yes of course," says Don, without the vaguest memory of any invitation.

"Good. I'll be there around two."

"Wonderful," says Don.

"See you then," says Hirsch, and hangs up.

Good, thinks Don. Hirsch is coming. Something to look forward to. I must have invited him up for Thanksgiving. I'll book at the C&O. Good.

•

Back at Jasper Pier, Kenny has his first outing alone with Kyle. He parks his pickup near the pier and extricates Kyle from his car seat, wondering if he'll be able to get him back into that convoluted assortment of straps and buckles. Lifting him up, he's overwhelmed all over again by his son's lightness and warmth. Is he imagining it, or does he feel Kyle's pulse through his clothes? His whole little body seems to pulse, as if he were one big heart covered with skin, nestled into Kenny's arms. Kenny's heart. For a minute Kenny closes his eyes and rests in the feeling that he has with Kyle when they're together— that they're the center of the world. But Kyle, the explorer, is restless. He wriggles and strains toward the dunes. Kenny keeps ahold of him until they reach the crest of the sand, and the sea spreads out before them, blue-green and frothy today, the air crisp but not too windy. There Kyle wriggles more violently, and Kenny releases him, on guard in case he runs toward the sea.

Kenny can picture vividly Kyle's flight, running after him, calling him back, the sea wind blowing his words away. But in fact Kyle doesn't seem to notice the sea. Instead, he squats down on the crest of the dune and starts playing with the sand. Picking up a handful, he cups his hand and then opens it, so that the sand runs through his fingers. He does this many times, so many that Kenny stops shifting his weight and waiting to walk on and sits down beside Kyle, prepared to enjoy the mild breeze. At that moment, Kyle suddenly throws a handful of sand down the ocean side of the dune and lurches down after it. "Hey, hey, there," calls Kenny, struggling to his feet. But Kyle has stopped after a few steps, and appears to be searching for the sand he just threw. Kenny smiles, bemused. "All gone, son," he says, spreading his hands wide, "all gone."

Kyle looks at him gravely, as if weighing this possibility. Then he picks up another handful, throws it down the dune and lurches after it again. It's a large dune, and by the time they get to the bottom, Kyle has repeated his experiment five times. Finally, at the bottom, he spreads his hands in a precise imitation of Kenny, and says, "Aw Gon!" Then he brushes the sand off his hands in a gesture so adult-looking that Kenny figures Lynn must have taught it to him.

A flock of seagulls wheels overhead. "Looky-there, Kyle," says Kenny, pointing to the sky. Kyle looks up and raises his hand with a sweeping kind of gesture.

"Aaaaaah," he says, then looks at Kenny for clarification.

"Seagulls," says Kenny.

But Kyle is tottering off again now, over to where the sand is wet. Kenny follows him closely, his boots making huge indentations around Kyle's footsteps, which are barely dents. When Kyle stops short, Kenny almost tumbles over him, then watches with a strange mixture of irritation and fascination as Kyle picks up a fistful of the wet sand. Here we go again, thinks Kenny. There's no chance of getting comfortable here—no place to sit down. For some time, Kyle squeezes the sand and watches it ooze through his fingers. Kenny thinks about the wipes in the bag that Lynn gave him, which is back in the truck. Damn thing is bigger than his gym bag—he wasn't going to be lugging that all over the beach.

Kyle brings the oozy muck toward his mouth, looking at Kenny.

"No-no, son, don't eat that stuff," says Kenny, pushing Kyle's hand down. Again, watching Kenny, Kyle brings his hand to his mouth. "I said no!" says Kenny, raising his voice.

Immediately he regrets this, but Kyle merely gazes at him for a minute, and scooping up another handful, throws it as far as he can, which is surprisingly far.

"Good arm, boy," says Kenny. But Kyle has followed his throw and is looking at the little pile of wet sand where it landed. Squatting down, he pokes the sand with his finger and then looks at Kenny, who, understanding, beams.

"That's right, son. That sand is not all gone. That's 'cause it's wet. It'll sink down in a minute."

Kyle studies the sand for a moment and then, suddenly, a flush rises on his face and he seems to stop breathing.

"What's wrong? Are you all right, son?" asks, Kenny, panicked, kneeling down beside him. Kyle doesn't look at him, and Kenny is desperately trying to remember the steps of CPR when Kyle relaxes, his face goes back to normal, and a rich aroma floats to Kenny's nostrils on the sea breeze.

"Ohhhh," says Kenny. Is that all? You 'bout gave me a heart attack! Just a little poop!"

Relieved, he scoops Kyle into his arms and heads toward the dunes. "Let's get you a clean one, boy," he says, concealing his apprehension.

This will be his first diaper change.

Lynn explained to him that Kyle, at two, has been a little slow with toilet-training, but that this was to be expected in an active boy whose parents had separated. Lynn talked Kenny through the diapering business, but still…and as if picking up on his uncertainty, Kyle begins to struggle.

By the time Kenny gets him back to the truck he is letting out a series of loud moans in which the spirit of protest is clear. Holding him under one arm, Kenny gets the diaper bag from the cab. Unsure about the spreading power of the poop, he decides to do the changing in the back of the truck—easier to hose down. As soon as he hoists Kyle into the back, the boy starts screaming in earnest and tries to climb out. Kenny sees that he thinks he's in some new, primitive kind of playpen.

"Hang on there, dammit," he says.

With one arm he makes sure Kyle doesn't get out, with the other he fumbles in the diaper bag. Finding the diaper, he realizes that it's going to be mighty hard to get it on without Kyle's cooperation. He puts his hands on both of his son's shoulders.

"Now look," he says but then stops.

How do you give a pep talk to a sobbing toddler? Just then, though, Kyle's sobs are suspended, and he seems to catch sight of something behind Kenny. Turning, Kenny sees a beautiful, young, dark-eyed girl wearing a red wool hat covered with multi-colored zigzags. She's looking at Kyle.

"You like my hat? She asks him, with that smiling voice women use on little children. "You wanna see it?" she asks, taking it off and holding it out.

Kyle reaches for it, and she gives it to him.

Kenny looks sidelong at the girl and says, in an undertone, "Thanks!"

Quickly and carefully, he pulls down the gate of the truck bed and eases Kyle into a lying-down position. Kyle continues to stare at the hat, shaking it a little to see the zigzags dance. He seems, somewhat disdainfully, to have left the matter of his troublesome nether regions to Kenny. With a few missteps, Kenny manages to clean him up, get a clean diaper on him and dispose of the old one in a plastic bag. He is keenly aware of the girl standing behind him, but he feels he must concentrate. Kyle is due home soon, and he'll be damned if Lynn will have a chance to reproach him, or even laugh at him for an incompetent diapering job.

When he's done, he pulls up Kyle's pants, picks him up and turns to the girl, unable to avoid a proud smile. The girl smiles at him, too, looking amused and interested. She reaches out her hand for her hat, but Kyle shrinks away, holding it tighter. After a few attempts, it becomes clear that he won't give it up without a fight. So they stroll together to the Bluebird, where the girl says she was headed when she came upon them. Once there, she distracts Kyle with a sugar packet and reclaims her hat. Before Kenny leaves to take Kyle back to Lynn, he shakes hands with the girl and they exchange names. Hers, he learns, is Shona Brockie.

•

The next morning, Hirsch lies next to Marika in her narrow bed, wanting to laugh out loud for sheer joy. His body is warm, satisfied, cleansed, and there's a certain hilarity in the ease of it, the feeling of completeness after all these lonely years. It seems funny to see

Marika—this attractive, inscrutable woman—lying beside him and to know that if he reached out and closed his fingers over hers she would not demur; would perhaps stir and smile a little in her sleep. He doesn't try it, though, in case she in fact furrows her brow and turns away or starts awake and doesn't remember where she is. After all, it's still early days. But just the possibility of intimacy, of contentment, keeps Hirsch lying still a few more minutes than he normally does when he wakes. Still with wonderment. When he was young he probably would have taken all this for granted, however much he enjoyed it. But the emptiness he's felt since his divorce has sharpened his appetite for—for all this. This feast. Luxuriously, he stretches. Without thinking, he curls his fingers over Marika's, which lie on the pillow next to him. She turns on her back, stretches, then looks at him with those startling blue eyes and smiles a little smile.

"Good morning," she says.

They spend the day together, reading, eating, walking on the beach. Sizing each other up. She invites him to stay over again. He makes a joke about bringing a toothbrush.

Late that night, he wakes to see a light on beyond a doorway. He gazes at the light for a minute, still half asleep, until a silhouette crosses the doorway, and it occurs to him to wonder where he is. In the next second, he remembers that he's in Marika's narrow bed, that she's not beside him, that she's the silhouette in the lighted room, which is her kitchen and that perhaps she has insomnia, which she's mentioned she sometimes has.

He puts on his pants, goes to the doorway, and leans on the jamb. She is standing at her big pine table, ironing. Ironing? He blinks. Has he become involved with a woman who irons in the middle of the night? Then he sees that she is ironing a long sheet of wax paper. A towel is under the wax paper to protect the table. She looks up and sees him in the doorway, but doesn't seem to register him for a minute, staring at him with a faraway look. Then she puts down the iron and wipes her hands on her T-shirt which, with a pair of underpants, is all she's wearing.

"It fixes the colors," she says.

"Aren't your feet cold?" asks Hirsch, whose own feet seem to be longing for the blankets he left. He sees that she's been doodling on napkins. Next to an empty glass he sees sketches of what look like microscopic creatures. On another sheet is a kind of chart with series of animals on it leading to the names of diseases: flea, rat, human, plague, malaria, typhoid.

She shakes her head, smiling a little smile with care, but also with a bit of a flourish, like a magician, she pulls the wax paper up to reveal what seems to be a complicated map.

"Wow," says Hirsch, forgetting his feet. He comes around the table to look over her shoulder. She has used very fine-point pens in every color of the rainbow for most of the map. He recognizes the general outline of the Outer Banks but doesn't at first understand the significance of the myriad different colored lines that run inland, north, south, and out to sea, some of them curving around and reversing direction, some of them tipped with arrows. Nor does he understand the shading, all in different colors, some portions intersecting and changing colors as they combine. Then he sees that there is a key at the bottom with tiny, precise pictures of waterfowl. Blue is for swans, green for ibis, orange for ducks, black for geese. Another key assigns colors to types of water: fresh, brackish, salt.

"It's beautiful," says Hirsch, though, even with the keys, he doesn't completely understand it.

"There are different colors for different seasons," says Marika, "and for different directions." And he sees that the map is not really designed to be understood by anyone but Marika. Most of the key must be in her head. Still, its beauty is easy to comprehend. He gazes at it in silence, thinking it's beautiful like her, and, like her, a little scary.

Carefully, she places clean coffee cups on each corner of the map. Somehow the quiet skill of her fingers conjures up in Hirsch a sudden avalanche of lust. He can barely wait until she puts the last cup down.

He embraces her from behind. Her taut body is chilly. She lets her head fall back onto his chest. Then, turning around and kissing him, she steps onto his feet. Kissing, they walk back to the bed.

15

It is October again, and because of the scarcity of resting places, there are more migrating swans than usual this year at the Pea Island Bird Sanctuary, about an hour north of Jasper. They come down at night, so when light begins to spread over the sanctuary they are already there except for a few latecomers. These arrive after the human watchers, who walk stealthily, so as not to disturb them. There are two pairs: Marika and Hirsch, and further along the shore of the lake, Pete and Lynn Baker. Each couple is somewhat annoyed to note the presence of the other, but politely ignore each other and keep their distance as they walk along the trail and choose separate observation platforms.

The trail and platforms are a decent distance from the lake, and the swans are in a clear majority, so they don't take much notice of the human movement on the shore beyond a flick of a wing or a slight start in the midst of preening. It's been a long, lonely journey from the Arctic, and they are relieved to be on water, feeling, through its ripples and undulations, the presence of one another, of the flock.

The quiet morning becomes noisy with the crescendo of their satisfaction in feeding. The lake is teeming with herons, ibises, coots, and ducks who, until the swans came, were having a party of their own, eating grasshoppers, flies, and beetles, who in turn ate diatoms, algae, dinoflagellates. The humans, however, for the moment, feast only with their eyes.

The grace of the swans is continuous. When a swan raises one wing to preen its feathers it's as if an exotic flower has suddenly unfurled. If a swan raises and flaps both wings, to challenge or to fly, it is an event like a burst of fireworks. Wings folded, their swimming, their gliding, appears so smooth as to defy the laws of friction. Ripples spread out around them like thoughts round an idea. Yet of course they're beasts, not ideas. When they curve their lovely necks as if daydreaming, they are really searching for food in the water. They fight, copulate, defecate, make mistakes, won't listen to reason, mate, reproduce, sicken, grow old, die. And still, there is that irrevocable beauty. The humans watch, wondering what to do with it.

A swan drifts toward shore near Hirsch and Marika's platform. Its black-masked face gives it an air of mystery. All its expressiveness seems to be in its wings and neck, yet Hirsch being human, looks for expression in the face, which remains mysterious. The dawn light strikes the lake beneath the swan, and for a moment the swan's form seems to be a continuation of the zigzagging lines of light on the water.

Hirsch and Marika see this and turn to each other. Hirsch is startled by the open delight on Marika's face, and only then realizes how guarded she usually looks when she looks at him. Like the swans: sidelong, with face averted.

The cool dawn light and the shimmering water mesmerize the humans and the swans are quiet too, for a while, busy feeding. But as the sun rises, the swans begin to converse in a raucous way, breaking the spell.

•

Farther along the path around the lake, father and daughter share a rare, quiet moment watching the water.

"How is Terry?" Lynn asks Pete.

"Worried about some mystery disease," says Pete.

"Mystery disease?"

"Yeah. Kept asking me about rashes. Had I seen any strange rashes around town." Pete chuckles. "That girl would work in her sleep if she could," says Pete.

Lynn says nothing. Kyle is with Kenny, giving Lynn a break, and she is still unaccustomed to being without him, finding that even as she enjoys freedom and Pete's company, Kyle is always in the back of her mind.

•

After a while, Hirsch and Marika walk away from the observation platform, through the tangled tunnel of squat live oaks that leads toward the sanctuary parking lot. Hirsch takes Marika's hand. She feels a sudden sweet peace, a relaxation of muscles in her shoulders and face that she didn't know were tense

She walks a few steps more, holding Hirsch's hand, and then a dizzy feeling of panic grips her stomach. She wants to throw herself into Hirsch's arms, but she also wants to run away. She wants a drink.

By the time they get to the car, she feels bad enough to be almost telling the truth when she tells him she's sick, begs off spending the afternoon with him, and asks him to take her home.

Once home, she sits still for a very long time, paralyzed and numb. She cannot move even to avail herself of her usual consolations—whiskey, her maps, a walk by the sea. She paces around her small, dark living room, scanning her shelves for a book to read, but none of them interest her until her eye falls on some old family albums buried under a pile of other books. It's been years since she's looked at them. She works to unearth them, roughly at first and then, as she feels how loose the spines are, more gently. The covers are of faded maroon leather.

Her mother, she remembers, was fond of these albums and would spend hours in the evenings arranging the photos and mementos. Marika used to think it a rather pathetic way of dealing with Papa's absences, with her loneliness. But now she looks at every page, sitting cross-legged on the floor, turning back sometimes to look again at a picture or a pressed leaf. The album seems at the same time to console and to sear her with a kind of medicinal pain. When she has looked at all the albums, she very uncharacteristically crawls into bed and falls asleep.

She dreams that she is walking down an empty street in Copenhagen. It is a summer evening, slow twilight approaching. Some people, vaguely familiar, come toward her and break into smiles of welcome like old friends. She sees that it is her first lab team, back in Denmark, with Sjoerd, her lab partner, at the front, opening his arms for an embrace. She feels an infusion of warm, simple happiness, a kind of relaxing of her spirit. But then she sees that her friends are not greeting her but another group of people behind her. As they pass her, one of them speaks from the group, without turning toward her: "You left."

As Marika watches them go, loneliness reasserts itself around her like ice with a tightening grip. Fortunately, she thinks grimly, she did not greet her old friends. She has given nothing away. And, keeping her expression fixed, she passes them as they exclaim over each other, not changing her expression at all. The street narrows and grows dark.

16

October is drawing to a close. This Hallowe'en there seems to be a little more decoration than usual around Jasper, in the Bluebird, in the grocery store, in the various shops selling knick-knacks and coral. There are garlands of autumn leaves, the beautiful colors of decay preserved in plastic. Haunted birdhouses. Hands holding eyeballs. Witches' brooms for sweeping the sky. In the past few years, people have come to realize that with a little effort there is serious money to be made in October and even in November if the fishermen that come down so faithfully for bluefish and marlin can be persuaded to bring their families. Partly this realization has dawned gradually, but it's been helped along by Pete in his thousands of brief, genial chats hither and yon, at the barbershop, the drugstore, The Cove.

Pete in turn has been influenced by Jack Brockie, who, after dinner on the thirty-first, helps Deidre string artificial cobwebs from the wall sconces in The Sandpiper's dining room and then settles down for a drink with Pete.

"We've got to get them to bring their wives and girlfriends," says Jack, over scotch and water. Around them, a few pirates and wenches carry trays and drinks. A masquerade party will soon begin, and the staff has been encouraged to dress up.

"Both at the same time?" asks Pete, raising his eyebrows, and they share a quiet laugh. They have another drink, Glenfiddich on the rocks. Pete's a beer man ordinarily, but Jack's been working, pretty successfully, to convert him—and Pete continues. "And here's a question: What do we do about the fact that most of these guys are coming down here to get away from their families?"

Jack's eyes crinkle. "Yes, I have thought of that. But I'm sure there's a way to convince the men that they can keep the women happy here without necessarily being with them all the time."

They lean back, ice clinking, and think this over in their different ways.

•

While Deidre hangs cobwebs at The Sandpiper, Jeanne Dubovsky, in the Tea Room, lights candles with her front door open, performing the old Samhain rite, inviting the dead to enter, to visit, and then to leave. She burns incense, smokes a little pot, and lights more and more candles until she's sitting in what, to her bleary eyes, seems a shimmering web of light. At midnight she eats an entire pan of roasted potatoes, fragrant with rosemary for remembrance and drinks some white wine. Then she stretches like a tabby cat, blows out the candles, undresses and goes upstairs to bed, dreaming that she is covered by a miraculous patchwork quilt on which scenes of her life are constantly woven and rewoven. People who have never met each other wander into each other's squares and chat. The Ace of Swords spars with the

Ace of Wands. The Empress embraces the bag boy from the Food Lion. The Food Lion plays with an orange tabby cat who lies in the lap of the Queen of Cups. Terry and Lynn, in beautiful white dresses, take Communion from King Neptune. Pete and Cathy, the Lovers, take shelter under Jeanne, the apple tree. Lynn and little Kyle ride on a donkey led by Bob Dylan, whose song, comes visibly from his mouth in hand-written lines: "I'll Be Your Baby Tonight."

The quilt becomes more and more complex, with more squares and more intricate patterns, though it stays the same size. There is a whole dream Jasper, populated by people she's massaged, people she doesn't know but would like to, people she's caught glimpses of and never seen again. It is beautiful beyond anything. There has been a threat looming over her, some kind of danger, but somehow the intricacy of the quilt will save her.

•

And this may be true.

The microbe has found a way into Jeanne and into many others along this shore. Like the sea that glows outside in the moonlight, like the sleeping Jeanne and her human brethren, the microbe's power and influence grow out of its ability to change. Or, to put it another way, to accommodate change, to seize a constant form from ever-changing elements.

We turn rushing water into a lighted city. The microbe rearranges its own DNA like interchangeable beads on a necklace, taking beads from other necklaces and threading them into the pattern. "Come and be me," it says, welcoming microbial passersby. "I'll be you. We'll combine forces and see what else we can eat, what else we can become."

As the mutating microbe enters Jeanne, her cells scramble to form a response, and she dreams of a teeming patchwork quilt.

•

At The Sandpiper, the Hallowe'en party is beginning to take off. There are certainly more men than women, but the discrepancy is energizing the men, and the women are enjoying the charged atmosphere. Jack observes the mix carefully. Few of the fishermen have brought women. Most of the women seem to be locals. It's a good party, though, and people seem to be hooking up. That's fine, thinks Jack—families or hook-ups, either way the party will rock and money will be spent. He relaxes a little, scanning the crowd. Shona's brought her new boyfriend, a big blond guy who seems okay so far. Chugging down the booze, Jack notices, but holding it all right. Looks big enough to protect her, anyway, if necessary.

Some time passes. Jack loses a few minutes, maybe half an hour, and realizes he's been putting it away pretty quickly himself. Through the crowd, he sees Deidre and Shona making their way toward him. They look very glamorous in their gauzy Fleetwood-Mac-type raggedy fairy costumes, with sparkles in their hair. They're giggling behind their hands at something. When they get to his table, they smile, and he sees with an unpleasant shock that they each have several teeth missing. They burst into cackles of laughter, and he realizes that they've blackened the teeth out. Some kind of joke. He remains shocked, as if they've suddenly turned into witches. The more he sits there, not laughing, the more they laugh, until finally he decides it's time to break it up and gets up to walk unsteadily to the can, the laughter behind him swallowed up in the noise of the rock band he's hired singing "Smoke On The Water." Deep Purple, indeed.

Kenny and Shona have danced quite a few dances when Barry arrives in a lull between songs. He's in the middle of the dance floor before he is noticed. It is a shock to see him, even for people who don't know him. He looks like a derelict, confused, red-eyed, unsteady on his feet. In fact, he is feverish enough to have imagined he was well enough to come to this party and frightened enough to make the effort to be out among people. But the people he's among are not ready to see someone who looks like him.

Shona hesitates to go over to Barry, wondering if he's on drugs, or if he's angry. He has seemed so angry and withdrawn lately. It's been a few weeks since she stopped going to see him, being pretty sure she was unwelcome. She's worried about him occasionally, but figured she'd done everything she could to help, and started thinking about this new guy, Kenny. But Barry is standing in the middle of the floor now, swaying, looking around slowly, as if he can barely see. Before Shona can reach him he suddenly crumples and falls forward, falls gently, almost as if there are no bones in him, as if he's just a bunch of old clothes.

Kenny and Deidre are the first at his side with Shona following close behind Kenny.

"Mom, is he okay?"

At the word *Mom*, Kenny looks at Deidre, shocked, but recovers quickly. Deidre looks from him to Shona, raises her eyebrows and then returns to taking Barry's pulse, which is racing. He's burning hot to the touch.

"Must have the flu or something," says Deidre. "Let's get him into the lounge." She and Kenny carry him out of the party room as the band, following Jack's instructions, keeps playing and singing, "Wastin' away again in Margaritaville." Shona follows Kenny and Deidre. In the lounge they lay Barry on a couch.

As the party resumes, Hirsch orders a drink from Jack, who is helping out at the bar. "I think I know that kid," says Hirsch. "Friend of a friend," remembering that the boy is a friend of Marika's and once offered him her phone number. Only now does it occur to Hirsch to wonder if the boy had done that before. He is disturbed by the boy's collapse but forces his attention back to the party. Nothing he can do, after all.

In the lounge, Deidre feels Barry's forehead. "Shona, go wet some towels with cold water," she says, closing the door to the party room to block out the noise.

Shona hurries off, glad to be doing something. There's a brief silence after she leaves. Deidre feels Barry's pulse. Then she looks squarely at Kenny.

"She's nineteen," she says.

Kenny feels himself sobering up.

"Yes'm," he says.

Shona returns with the towels, and as Deidre mops Barry's forehead, he begins to stir. He looks around for a second, squinting, then closes his eyes again.

"Barry?" says Shona. Again, his eyes flicker. "Barry, are you okay?"

Barry turns his head away.

"Barry, should we call a doctor or something?"

Barry shakes his head ever so slightly. "Sleep," he says, waving them weakly away.

They stand watching him for a minute.

"Did you see if he was drinking?" asks Deidre. The other two shrug and shake their heads.

"He just got here," says Shona.

"Well, maybe he just has the flu and had too much to drink. Let's get him some water."

Kenny goes for water.

"What happened between you two anyway?" asks Deidre.

"Who?"

Deidre indicates Barry.

"Oh, I don't know. He just suddenly started acting really weird. Like he was tired all the time, and he didn't seem to want me around."

Deidre nods. Her head hurts.

"Depressed, maybe."

Then Kenny comes back with a bottle of water. Deidre puts it against Barry's lips, and he sips a little.

"Well, he's conscious," says Deidre. "What say we just let him sleep and check on him every half-hour or so?"

The other two are agreeable to this suggestion, and the three return to the party. A half-hour later, Shona tiptoes in and puts a tablecloth over Barry like a blanket. His eyes, she notices, are moving under his eyelids, and beads of sweat stand on his forehead. She tiptoes out and then the party roars on by, and no one comes in. They've all drunk too much, even Deidre, who is usually a light drinker. Jack has pissed her off by suggesting that she's lowering the tone of the party by blacking out her teeth, and her response has been a full-blown, murderous rage which she is trying to drown in daiquiris and vodka gimlets. Kill all the men, she thinks. Jack first. Then maybe that blond lug over there. She could see Shona and Kenny talking in a corner, with Shona working her wiles on him. What are the chances of him resisting? Zip. Kill them all.

Deidre puts her head down on the table. Jack sees her there, and his mouth tightens. A minute or so later one of the barmaids comes over, whispers to her and helps her to her feet. Jack watches as the barmaid puts her arm around Deidre's waist and leads her gently out of the room, nodding at whatever Deidre keeps saying. He shakes his head and dispatches someone to empty the ashtrays. The first barmaid takes Deidre out the back way, so they don't walk through the lounge where Barry lies, struggling with death. It is clear the next day, though, that he is very sick, and Deidre goes through his pockets, finds his parents' number, and calls them.

●

We are highly organized beings, simultaneously performing multiple functions of staggering complexity even when we sleep. Viruses, doing the one thing, namely furiously and sloppily mutating, are not highly organized, and in fact, they teeter on the edge of chaos. Nevertheless, with the help of its viral nature, our microbe has managed to slip past the part of Barry that says to interlopers "I am me, and you are not me."

Rather like a terrorist roaming anonymously in the city of the enemy, it makes up for a lack of organization with an utter singleness of purpose.

Terrorist cells have taken over Barry's body, his life, his consciousness. He is breaking down.

Deidre, on the other hand, is sleeping soundly. Her cells are dehydrated from too many vodka gimlets, but, for the moment, the virus is lying low. Why does it thrive in one and not another? More microbe-eating acid, perhaps, in Deidre's stomach when the microbe first tried to invade? The virus less "virulent" because of the long lag between hosts? An inborn lack of genetic "chemistry" between Deidre and the disease? Why one and not another?

•

Soon, or sometime in the eternity to which his pain and fever have introduced him, Barry sees many mothers leaning over him with worried faces, hears many fathers asking questions, trying to establish facts. He hears the word, "fever," and the words, "how long?" and each utterance seems to echo infinitely. His body aches, his tongue is dry and swollen. Something cool is laid on his forehead. He's lifted and carried. He sleeps, wakes, moans, sleeps again. His mind, used to roaming far and wide, has shrunk in this emergency, and occupies only those parts of his brain that either maintain his life or fight to defend it.

The self he's shrunk down to, the basic life support system, is not the self he's used to being, and the basic core of life he's defending is one that he, in his youth and strength, has barely been aware of before, busy as he has been with music, bartending, reading, pondering, complaining, loving, and watching waves. He's hiding in his bomb shelter—an important part of the city in wartime, but bewilderingly constricted, to one accustomed to space and peace. Unfamiliar as a permanent dwelling. Home and yet not home. His body, now a receptacle for pain, weakness, heat and cold, is unfamiliar when he wakes in the middle of the night. Only in the occasional hallucination does he find a temporary, uneasy release. In hallucination he roams freely in time, now arguing with his father in the kitchen of the old house in Reston, now facing down a belligerent drunk at The Cove, now caressing Shona or Fred the cat, now a hero, as he's always meant to be someday, fighting in a battle where the cause is purely just.

In his final delirium, as the microbe invades his nervous system, his speech becomes oddly clear, and those around him perceive that he believes he's directing some kind of a rescue mission. Sometimes he's rescuing a girl, sometimes a ship at sea. Once he seems to be evacuating a Vietnamese village, at which point his father, Jay, stands abruptly and excuses himself. He goes to the men's room and just stands for a while, breathing heavily. Some of his son's hallucinations are based on his own past life, and Jay has a powerful, irrational desire to enter the hallucinations—to stand shoulder to shoulder with Barry so that, for once, they can fight on the same side. He wraps Barry in a blanket and carries him to the car to drive him to the emergency room.

At a rest stop, when he turns off the engine, Barry's harsh, laboring breaths become audible from the back seat. When his parents turn to look at him they see that his skin is blue-pale and there is no expression on his face to match the anguished sound of his breathing. Jay calls 911 on his cell phone and after a minute of hemming and hawing, reverts to his military training, giving only the facts, as tersely and impressively as he can, impressing the dispatcher with a sense of emergency.

"He's just too sick, Jay," says Barry's mother. "I'm scared."

The helicopter arrives swiftly, but Barry dies on the way.

Hovering helplessly above the earth, his father is shocked by an intense anger. He feels as if he has been deliberately misled and betrayed into catastrophic failure. He cannot keep his mind from racing after a solution. After they land at the hospital, as his wife weeps over Barry's body and nurses and social workers come and go with forms to sign and cups of tea, Jay goes over every detail of the past few days, searching for the ones he can change to make this come out right.

After a day of paperwork and a sleepless night in a motel, they drive home slowly. Sometimes the rain is so heavy that they can barely see through the windshield, but they don't stop. Every now and then they make a comment about how to arrange the funeral service. Barry's body is being "shipped" to a funeral home near their church in Alexandria. He has been torn away from the world, and his parents, silent, bleed freely in the places inside them from which he has been torn.

As they drive, Barry's mother grows quiet. But she sees Jay's jaw flex and his hands tighten on the wheel. He's planning something, some sort of action. But what could it possibly be? Complaints to the authorities? Parlay with the Almighty? When they arrive home, he goes right to the computer, and when she brings him coffee, she sees that he's googling Barry's symptoms. He wants to find out what Barry had. One could want to know that, she supposes.

She herself wants nothing. She is ashamed of this, but can't see what to do about it. She goes to bed and pulls the covers over her head to get as much nothing as she possibly can. At dinnertime she gets up, makes a toasted cheese sandwich and brings it to Jay, who is still at the computer.

"I can't get anyone who knows anything!" he says, taking a huge bite out of the sandwich.

She nods, feeling herself pulled strongly back to bed. She sees that he is looking at the web page of the Centers for Disease Control in Atlanta. He will work his way up the chain, and he will get answers. Such as they are. For her answers, she will have to wait until she can get to church, and even then she's not sure what they'll be or if they will seem different from the nothing that now surrounds her.

17

It's Thanksgiving Day, and in Charlottesville, at the C&O Restaurant, Don orders a potent red wine. He inhales deeply, closing his eyes, when the waiter presents it to him. Like an old-fashioned rose, the fragrance of the wine seems to tell a story, with a beginning, a meandering middle, and a satisfying conclusion. This, he thinks, bodes well for the evening.

Hirsch is restless and can't seem to find a comfortable position in his seat until Don pours a hefty glass for him and raises his own for a toast.

"Happy Thanksgiving," he says quietly.

They clink glasses and sip their wine, which, living up to its promise, is very, very good. Hirsch looks at Don curiously. Without his clerical collar, he looks more like the friend Hirsch remembers from graduate school days—a little paunchier, the rings under his eyes a little deeper, but the same dreamy expression—sad, diffident, honorable, uncompromising.

"You can say grace if you like," says Hirsch. "I mean, if that's what you'd like to do."

"Maybe later," says Don.

They sip the wine, which warms them, a warmth starting at the throat and spreading quickly through the blood. Alcohol and men, thinks Don. How odd we are. We talk about "pouring out" feelings, but more often we seem to be pouring them in.

"Well, this place has changed," says Hirsch.

"In some ways," agrees Don.

"Do you miss the Banks, or are you just glad you left all that behind?" asks Hirsch.

Don leans back and considers this question. He thinks of Neptune rising out of asphalt by Route 1, of the cold boil of a gray winter sea, sand, wind, traffic, and of waves of sunlight streaming into the tall windows of Our Lady of the Sea.

"Most of it seems like a dream now," he muses. "But then, so does this." He indicates the room around them, but he means the present—life here and now. Hirsch regards him somewhat quizzically. Don rubs his face with the flat of his hand like a tired reader. The worst of one's personal demons, he thinks, is that they're so God-awful boring.

"What about you?" he asks. "Is the place still suiting you?"

"It's all right."

"I remember a letter about a lady friend and a letter about a storm," says Don.

"Ha! Not much difference between the two," says Hirsch.

Now it's Don's turn to look slightly quizzical. The arrival of the first course saves Hirsch from elaborating. Funny, thinks Don, how these good restaurants always seem to synchronize the service with the conversation.

The waiter puts lobster bisque in front of Hirsch and peanut soup in front of Don and tops up their glasses. The soup is hot and rich and gives the men courage to continue.

"A stormy relationship?" Don ventures.

"I don't know," says Hirsch. He takes a sip of bisque and a sip of wine. "I must be stupid."

Don smiles. There's that "stoopid," again. The only remaining trace of Hirsch's Brooklyn roots.

"I mean, I'd like to find some other explanation, I really would. But it happened all over again. I find a great woman. I think everything is fine. But in fact, as becomes suddenly apparent, everything sucks. Were there signs? There must have been signs. But—" with the spoon still in his hand, Hirsch shrugs.

Don nods, eyes downcast, waiting to think of something to say. But after another sip of bisque, Hirsch looks at him mischievously.

"So how's your love life?"

The silence is deafening. A paralysis of embarrassment creeps over both men. There's nothing for it, though, short of bolting from the table, and they've known each other too long for that. Don takes a long draught of wine. The soup is almost gone.

"There's a gay bar in town now," he says.

The waiter comes to clear away the soup. Now it's Hirsch's turn to nod and wonder what to say. But the wine is getting to him.

"Did you go?" he asks.

Don is moving very slowly now, like a sloth or some cold-blooded lizard in the shade. Faintly, he nods. "Mm-hm."

The waiter brings the salads. Really, thinks Don, his timing is extraordinary. Big tip brewing here. Both men say yes to fresh-ground pepper. The waiter heaves an enormous pepper mill over their plates and grinds. The men watch solemnly.

"That's fine," they say, when there's enough.

"And?" Hirsch says, when the waiter leaves.

"Well," Don chews his salad thoughtfully and swallows. "Apparently," he says, "celibacy was the right choice after all."

Hirsch nods.

"At least," continues Don, "that was the opinion of the gentleman I met there. He was very kind. He said I was well out of it, and he was thinking of celibacy himself."

"Well, there's something to that," Hirsch agrees, nodding and starting on his salad. "Right now I can see the attraction of celibacy."

But much later, at Krispy Kreme, over coffee and a honey bun for Don, looking out at a windy November night, traffic lights changing and swaying, a flurry of early snow, Hirsch says, "Dammit, she owes me more than this. She at least owes me an explanation."

"Do you think she'll give you one?"

"I don't know. But I'm going to ask her."

Don wipes his honey-stained fingers on a napkin and, for emphasis, throws it down on the table.

"Good for you," he says.

•

A few days later, Hirsch stands at Marika's door. The air is heavy and thick, and it seems to Hirsch that there is an almost uncanny stillness in the air. The windsock on Marika's porch is hanging straight down. Finally he knocks. She opens it before he has finished knocking.

"Hi," he says.

"I was just on my way to The Cove." She doesn't invite him to come along. She has a slightly wild look, like a deer about to run. Words that Hirsch has prepared stick in his throat. Absurdly, he tries to make conversation.

"How's that bartender?"

"Which one?"

"Uh…your friend. Bruce? Barry?"

"Barry? Fine, I guess. I haven't seen him in a while."

"I saw him pass out at a party. Not drunk. He looked pretty sick."

"When?"

"Hallowe'en."

Marika considers this. "Yes, he hasn't been in since then. Did he seem feverish? Disoriented?"

"Yeah," says Hirsch. "Pretty sick."

Marika nods, grimly. "He won't be the last," she says.

Anger seems to thump Hirsch between the eyes. "That's it?" he asks.

"What?"

"That's all you have to say about it?"

Marika looks at him poisonously for a second. "I need a drink," she says.

"You're already drunk."

"That's right, I'm a pickled Dane," she says, folding her arms and leaning against the house.

He hates the flatness of her eyes. "You know something about what he has, don't you? It has something to do with those maps you drew."

Marika doesn't speak for a moment. "Maybe it's not so bad if something winnows out our numbers," she says, quietly.

Hirsch looks at her for a minute. "Is that how you see it? Given up on the species, have you? Do you really think we're worse than any other species would be, given our opportunities?"

She considers this for a moment and seems about to reply, when he bursts out, "You know what? That's not even the problem. This isn't an intellectual thing. You're just scared. You're too damn scared to be human!"

"Thank you, professor," she says, mockingly.

But there's a spark in her eyes now, and a wave of love almost knocks him down. For a minute he watches some sea oats in the yard whipping around in a sudden gust of wind. Then he looks straight at her.

"Don't give up on us, Meeka," he says, huskily. And then, meeting her eyes, "Don't give up on me."

Her eyes widen, and she seems to flinch as if he's slapped her.

"I need to go," she says, and shoulders past him.

He grabs her roughly by the arm.

"No!" he shouts. You don't run away!"

They look at each other, shocked. His shout seems to hang in the humid air. Then he lets go her arm and steps back. This isn't the way.

"Sorry," he mumbles.

For what seems a long time the two of them look down at the floorboards of the porch. Outside, the wind picks up and a few drops of rain fall. A seagull lets out a piercing cry and then falls silent. Then, noiselessly, she steps into his arms.

•

"My father was a fisherman," says Marika, staring into her drink.

She and Hirsch are sitting at The Cove.

For three days they have barely left Marika's house. Most of that time they spent in bed. She made love to him with such intensity that he could barely keep up.

They didn't talk much, limiting themselves to noises of profound satisfaction as they coupled and more, of a different kind, when they finally remembered to eat. It was as if Marika could only let him back in by reverting to some primal level.

She drank fairly heavily but never lost control. She's switched, he notices, from whiskey to gin. She stares at the clear, water-like liquid now, as she speaks.

"My father was a fisherman," she says, "until the seals began to die. I still believe, irrationally, that I saw the first sick seal, at least on our beach. I used to go down to watch them every day." She spreads a napkin out in front of her and smooths it with her hands, gazing at it as if she sees something there. "There was a place where I sat every day before dinner, after I'd done my housework, when Moder was napping. I just sat watching, not expecting anything. Later I found out that that's what all naturalists try to do, watch quietly with no expectations.

"It was a very good spot. It took me a few weeks of exploring to find it. Because of the placement of scrub and rocks, I could climb down a cliff, lowering myself hand under hand, and slip right out of view. That was very nice: to feel—invisible."

She closes her eyes for a minute, then sips her gin and tonic and continues. "The seals were often there on the beach below, sunning themselves, mating, sometimes fighting. I could tell one from the other after a time; got to know their different personalities. They always came together. The land was not really their medium—they were awkward there, and it wasn't safe for them except in numbers. Of course, even numbers wouldn't protect them from hunters, but there was no hunting on our beach."

She pauses here and takes a large sip of her drink, wincing at some bitterness, perhaps in the gin. "There was a kind of informal agree-ment—my father was studying the seals there for the—what do you call them here?—the 'fisheries'? Such a funny word. I think they were trying to discover at what age a seal should be killed for maximum profit—how many seasons the average seal should be allowed to live, considering breeding potential and so forth. Naturally, I didn't know that then. I was young and naïve. It never occurred to me to wonder why my colony—I thought of it as mine—was so peaceful."

Hirsch can hardly bear the pain in Marika's face. He wants to hold her hand, as if she were giving birth or having something amputated. He almost interrupts her and suggests that they defer the rest for another time, but would there be another time? How often can she do this? And he has to admit, he's asked for this, and he still wants it.

"Probably," Marika continues, "it wasn't that long that I visited the seals. Not as long as it seems to me now. A month or two. But it was the only place where I could—" She stops, and her eyes refocus, for a minute, from the past to Hirsch, sitting beside her.

"I suppose I need to tell you about all that too," she says.

She leans back, rubs her face and passes her hands through her hair. Outside there's a sudden shrieking gust of wind, and something slams against the outside of the bar. Inside, the patrons are startled but soon get back to their conversations. A waiter goes out to investigate.

"Something blowing up," says Marika, looking toward the window, smiling slightly.

That kinship she feels with storms, thinks Hirsch. Odd, for a fisherman's daughter. She leans her head back against the wood of the booth and closes her eyes.

"My father had always been away a lot. Fishermen are, but he was especially…absent. This was true even before he started doing the study, but afterward, we didn't see him for months on end. There were several different beaches he was keeping track of up and down the Jutland coast. Even when he was home he was usually either exhausted or preoccupied.

"I was considered to be very…like him. I looked like him. Sometimes my mother would stop in the middle of what she was doing and suddenly stare at me, and I knew I had done something— made a certain gesture or spoken with a certain tone—that was like him. She found it funny and fascinating. But my father was not even mildly interested. In me, or in any of us, I suppose. A month or two before I discovered the seals—I'd like another, please."

She holds out her glass to Hirsch without opening her eyes. He takes it and holds it up for the barman, who nods. As the barman makes the drink, they sit in silence. We're resting, thinks Hirsch, as if we've been beating our way through a jungle. When the waitress brings the drink, Marika takes a sip and opens her eyes, keeping them averted and downcast.

"It was syphilis my mother had, but I didn't know that until quite a bit later. All I knew was that she was going out of her mind, flying into rages—"

Suddenly a tear splashes down Marika's cheek. Her eyes open for a minute in surprise, and she bites her lip. She looks very frightened.

"It's all right, Marika," says Hirsch.

She looks at him, blue eyes dimmed, lost, as if struggling to believe what he says. Then she nods several times and resumes.

"She'd been faithful to my father, if you're wondering, though he had the nerve—" She compresses her lips, for a moment, into a tight line, and then continues. "I don't think he really believed she'd been unfaithful. It was just his way of justifying—not desertion, exactly, but—let's just say he made no alteration in his schedule. And he could have. He could have."

"I don't understand. Syphilis was curable by then, wasn't it?"

"Penicillin. They discovered it around 1947," says Marika. "They were using it on soldiers. Fader was a scientist. He probably knew about it, could have gotten treatment, but he would have had to admit he had it. That didn't suit him. Apparently."

"Were you an only child?"

"No, I had—I have—a brother, Soren. I think he's a banker now. I haven't seen him in years. But he was away at school when Moder was—"

There is a pause, during which Marika blinks several times, defying tears to surprise her again.

"So you took care of her by yourself?"

Marika doesn't answer, but stares out the window. For a moment, Hirsch's own mother flashes into his mind; in the nursing home, yellow with jaundice, liver cancer it was, at the end. He remembers her holding his hand, smiling at him, an oddly dazzling smile, between bouts of pain he could not imagine.

"Fader got sick, too, eventually," says Marika.

"At first it was assumed I would nurse him, too, as I had nursed Moder. But Soren had finished school, and I insisted that it was my turn to go. In the process of insisting, I said a few things which apparently impressed Fader that I would not be the best nurse for him. Not the best 'Sister of Mercy'." Marika smiles now, a dry little smile, and finishes her gin.

"So Soren took care of him. But he died quickly. I had been in America less than a year when Soren wrote to me. He had scattered Fader's ashes on that same beach where the seals once died. No one ever discovered what they died of; they died so fast, and there was no one to carry on the research. I have some idea now, I think. There were other seal epidemics later, in the Mediterranean and the Netherlands, and they were studied in more depth. They turned up a new virus, something like distemper, something like measles, which originally came to humans, you know, from wolves and dogs, when we first began keeping company with them. But with our seals, there was something else…I'm sure there was something else. There seemed to be two distinct phases to the disease. The first one would disappear and then the second one would…and the thing is, it all started after an algae bloom. What they call a 'red tide'."

"That was your specialty, wasn't it? Diseases of marine mammals?"

Marika nods, with a faraway look. "At that time, yes. But the grants dried up. There was more money in algae. Biofuels."

There is a long silence. Marika looks at the window, where rain is beginning to whip against the glass.

"I dream about that beach sometimes," she says. "Actually… dream is too weak a word. Sometimes I am still there."

Outside the bar, the wind suddenly shoves the door like a storm-trooper, and the power goes out.

Marika laughs, a sound Hirsch doesn't remember hearing before. Someone behind the bar curses and turns on a flashlight. By the time the waiter lights a candle on their table, Marika is in Hirsch's arms, leaning her head on his shoulder, almost asleep. Gently, he wakes her and drives her home.

•

Up and down the Banks, the tide rises in earnest. The wind toys with the works of men, slamming a gate here, overturning a trashcan there. Fred the cat lowers his head, fur bristling, and sniffs the buffeting air. With tail thrashing, he creeps under the pilings of a house not far from The Cove, where he still checks regularly, though no one feeds him there any more. He backs into the smallest space he can find, a hollow place between a piling and a dune, and eyes the incoming waves with hostility.

The storm dies down around dinnertime, but that night, in the wee hours, it becomes furious again; a serious nor'easter. Like a bomb, the storm explodes while the Bakers are in the deepest part of their sleep, and it enters their dreams.

18

Pete Baker, sleeping, hears the storm as a woman shrieking the same thing over and over at him. The woman is very angry and alarmed about something, and no matter what he says to try to reassure her, she just keeps shrieking.

Kenny hears a crowd roaring at a football game and flails around in his sleep, doing a victory dance to celebrate his touchdown.

Lynn, of course, hears Kyle, and her sleep is broken by frequent trips to his room, until she finally gives up and takes him into her bed.

In Marika's dream, she is a mermaid. She is dancing at night on the rocks by the sea to get rid of her tail. In the darkness, she makes no sound except for the tail's scraping and splashing. She grits her teeth against the pain and waits for the ordeal to be over. But she becomes aware of a strange, unearthly sound, a kind of moaning scream, and feels strange shapes writhing around her, jostling against her. Peering around, she sees by moonlight round dark eyes shining, rolling in pain. With a spurt of horror, she realizes that all around her seals are dancing, too, emulating her, trying to become human, crying and crying.

Then Hirsch is holding her hand, telling her it's all right, that in some way she can't understand now, it will be all right. She tries with all her might to believe him. She concentrates on the rough warmth of his hand.

When she wakes, she is holding tight to the blanket, and Hirsch is not there. She lurches out of bed in search of him then remembers, in the kitchen, that she asked for a night to herself. Out the kitchen window, sees a wave crashing over the deck. Her gut wrenches as if she's suddenly seen a monster—her first impulse is to strike at it, but already, she's running to the closet and pulling on her waders and jacket over her pajamas. A wave slaps like a fat flipper against the French doors to the deck. She grabs her map portfolio and puts it into a trash bag, winding the bag around itself several times. Almost out the door, she pauses, runs to the bookcase, grabs the family album and a tiny, ragged book, stows them, and winds the bag up again.

Outside, it's early dawn, gray and cold. For once she doesn't look out to the horizon. The horizon has come, shockingly, wrongly, to her. Slowly, she wades down the steps, into the water, holding on to the railing, gauging the water's force. It's up to her hips, but the current doesn't seem too strong. There's no wind. She lets go the railing and pushes her way down into the water. It's slow going, the water offering more resistance than buoyancy, and as her thighs and back begin to ache, she feels mired again in the world of her dream. Shaking her head, resting her bundle on her shoulders, she realizes that she needs a plan. When she comes around to the sound side of the house, she sees an ocean world, the tops of houses standing stiff and absurd in the water's mocking embrace. The sea has cut through to the sound, and as far as Marika can tell, Route 1 is gone. But, she reminds herself, there could be as little as an inch of water on the road. Can't tell in this gray light. She strains her eyes, but sees nothing moving up there. High Ground, she thinks, High Ground, and heads for what she can see of what's left of the dunes, a soft curve here and there above the dark water. But she's getting very cold.

All around her the water begins to seem immense and ravenous, and she's beginning to feel very small and tired. It's early, she reminds herself, and soon, others will wake. It occurs to her that she should wake them. But her neighbors are not close, and she can't think of anything to yell that would be understood, even if it were heard. "Storm?" "Water?" "Watch Out?" None of those would work. "Help?" They might understand that. But she can't bring herself to shout for help. She's not ready.

She smiles wryly, pushing through the water. She can see the headline: *Biologist Drowns—Afraid of Sound of Own Voice*. Then, suddenly, she's assailed by doubts. Why didn't she try the phone before she left? Or the radio? Maybe she should go back to her cottage and climb up on the roof. Ahead, the sun struggles briefly through the clouds, lighting a writhing patch of water. Somewhere a church bell is ringing, over and over. Tolling. She'll make it to that patch of light. Then there'll be another one somewhere. Keep walking. Plenty of time. "So much time," Moder whispers in her ear. "You have so much time, and you are so brave…go on, go on, girl…."

When the water reaches the bottom of her rib cage and begins to lift her feet from the ground, Marika begins to say goodbye to Soren, to Hirsch, to the seals, and when an empty boat called *Adios* suddenly nudges her shoulder, it seems all part of the same thing, even as she throws in her bundle and hauls herself aboard.

"Adios," she thinks, only barely able to feel the relief in her muscles as she slumps against the seat and ceases her struggle.

•

On that flooded morning, Kenny becomes aware of Jack Brockie banging on the outside of the pool house door and of Shona hopping around the room half-dressed, trying to put on several items of clothing simultaneously and hissing, "Kenny, Kenny, get up!" in a stage whisper to him across the room.

They had been pretty drunk the night before, particularly Kenny, and though he is able to galvanize his body into action now by something like instinct, his mind is playing absurd tricks on him while he pulls on his pants and buckles his belt, such as suggesting that his impotence last night is somehow behind Shona hopping around telling him to get up and also behind the father's voice at the door calling Shona in urgent tones. What are you doing in there with a man who can't get it up, he imagines Jack saying. As he buttons his shirt, Kenny shakes his head vigorously, in spite of the pain he knows will ensue. That's probably not what her father is thinking. He hands Shona a sandal and tosses the covers over the bed.

"Coming, Daddy," calls Shona, throwing a packet of condoms into a drawer. As soon as she opens the door, Jack bursts in.

"Goddammit, Shona, do you have to lock that door?"

From behind him, Deidre's voice cuts in with unusual sharpness: "Jack, there's no time for this."

Jack nods. Then he gives Kenny a quick, assessing look.

"There's flooding," he says. "I could use some help over at the Inn. Shona, you and Mom stay here."

Kenny nods and the two men leave with remarkable speed. The women look at each other briefly with startled eyes.

Then Deidre opens the blinds and looks out. "Still dry here," she says. "Let's make some coffee."

·

The men have loaded sandbags for about a half hour, without speaking or even grunting, when Kenny straightens up to wipe sweat off his forehead and freezes. Jack looks at him and then follows his gaze and sees what he sees: a river where there wasn't one before, flowing from the ocean toward the road, between the men and the pool house. The dune must have just broken, because the water is flowing fast, and there's a lot of it. Kenny barely has time to register this before Jack is running toward the new inlet, clearly intending to ford or swim it. Kenny bolts after him, tackling him before he reaches the water. Jack gets up cursing. Kenny anticipates his swing and blocks it mildly with his forearm.

"Shona's over there!" Jack yells, and Kenny sees that the man is literally wild with pain at the thought of his child in danger.

"The water is too deep to cross here, and it's nowhere near the pool house!" yells Kenny, pointing. Jack looks and sees that Kenny is right. Breathing heavily, he masters himself, nodding once.

"We need to go get her," he says, curtly, a little truculently, as if afraid that Kenny will disagree with him.

"Okay," says Kenny. "Let's see if there's a good place to ford."

•

In the pool house, they find the women looking out separate windows. They see the alarm in their own faces reflected in the faces of the women, and immediately, but still a hair too late, assume a nonchalant air.

"What is it?" asks Shona.

"Some water has broken through the dunes," says Jack. Kenny is surprised and impressed by the calmness of his voice.

"Where?" asks Deidre.

"It's all right," says Jack, "it's a ways away, but I'm thinking we should clear out."

Kenny notices that Jack is still looking at Shona, though Deidre asked the question, and looking at Deidre himself, he suddenly feels a sharp apprehension of the pain in her, as if he's almost become her for a second, and her sadness is so real to him that he feels a brief, startling urge to take her in his arms and comfort her, only until the pain is at least softened at the edges. And before he has time to wonder at this strange feeling, he glances at Jack, who's looking at Shona, and Kenny feels her father's anxious, unwieldy love for his child. Kenny turns his eyes to Shona's face, which seems now incredibly young, so young that he seems to see traces of baby fat in her cheeks, and he thinks of his unprecedented impotence with her, and then, suddenly, he thinks of Kyle, and everything else is blotted out.

Kyle. Of course he's with Lynn, and he's all right. But only if she's all right. If a cold finger of water has not reached obscenely through the dunes and tapped her on the shoulder. Kenny pictures a watery, cartoon-like Grim Reaper, finger outstretched, and once again, heedless of the cost, he shakes his head. Did someone, he wonders, slip some acid into his tequila last night? Coffee, he thinks, coffee. But then, no, adrenaline should do it. After all, there's an invasion going on here. Don't let the water get the womenfolk.

Then Deidre's voice cuts through his thoughts, saying safe deposit box, insurance papers, birth certificates, Things To Be Saved, and he hears himself interrupt her in an authoritative tone saying, "I don't think the water's coming any farther, but leave the stuff and let's get to higher ground."

Oddly, they listen to him and quietly prepare to leave. Somewhere inland, Kenny thinks, Kyle is safe, dry, and happy. But he needs to see him.

•

What used to be an alley behind the Baker house has become a good-sized creek, but Lynn and Pete are still surprised to see an empty boat floating down the street, and still more surprised when a woman slowly sits up in it. She has no oars, but does not look distressed.

Pete runs outside, slamming the screen door.

"Need a hand?" he shouts, cupping his hands around his mouth. The woman in the approaching boat peers at him but makes no reply.

Odd, thinks Pete, and then he starts. That looks like Kenny's boat—the red letters *A D I* come into view. It is! Without thinking, he runs to the creek, wades in, and grabs hold of the side of the vessel.

"Where's Kenny?"

The strange woman looks at him, uncomprehending. "Kenny Peterson—you know him?"

She appears to be considering the question.

"This is his boat!" shouts Pete, exasperated by her slowness. She shakes her head, and seeming to make an effort of memory, says faintly, "It was just the boat…"

Involuntarily, Pete looks back at the window where Lynn was standing. It is open, but Terry is there now.

"Bring her in, Dad," she calls, "she's soaking wet!"

Pete sees that this is true, and hastens to help the woman, who, he sees now is in some kind of shock, out of the boat.

The woman's body is lean and hard under her jacket; she's trembling violently. Now Lynn is coming out of the house with a blanket. Quickly, Pete turns the woman over to Lynn and pulling with surprising strength, wrestles the boat up onto the small patch of lawn in the yard that remains unflooded. Lynn is already leading the woman in—Pete doesn't think she's recognized the boat—and he sees there's a coil of rope under the seat and crudely ties the *Adios* up to the pilings. If Kenny is alive, he's going to want his boat.

Working hurriedly, the girls strip Marika and wrap her in a down comforter. Terry opens the cupboard for tea but then remembers that the power is out. Lynn goes in search of sterno. The door to Kyle's room is ajar, and she sees he's still napping. When he wakes she must remember to prepare him for the sight of high water.

After two cups of tea, Marika's shivering subsides. For a minute she seems about to nod off, but then she suddenly sits upright.

"My maps!" she says. Her voice is faint.

"What?"

"My maps!" says Marika more loudly. "In a bag, a plastic bag."

Terry looks among Marika's wet clothes, but finds nothing. Just then Pete comes in carrying a flat bundle in a trash bag.

"This yours?"

"Oh yes, thanks Daddy, she was just looking for that," says Terry, taking the bundle. She turns to the woman. "By the way, what's your name?"

"Marika. Marika Hansen."

"I'm Terry Baker, and this is my dad, Pete."

Marika nods. "Are they dry?"

"What?"

"Look inside the bag. Are they dry?"

Carefully, Terry unwinds and opens the package. The portfolio is a little wet at the corners. She looks at Marika for permission to open it, and Marika nods. Terry draws out a map and slowly unfolds it. She doesn't speak for a minute or two, as she studies the map, the birds, the lines connecting avian migratory patterns and human diseases. Then she looks sharply at Marika. Marika raises her eyebrows inquiringly.

"Yes," says Terry, "They're dry." She wants to ask Marika about them, but as soon as she hears the maps are safe, Marika, pale and clearly exhausted, falls asleep.

•

In the spare bedroom, Terry pores over the maps and drawings while Marika dozes in the intense warmth of the comforter, dreaming that Hirsch is speaking to her in Yiddish, as he does sometimes at night when they're tired.

"Make shuffy?" He asks her, smoothing her forehead. It's a tender word meaning "sleepy," and Marika finds it at once erotic and soporific. She smiles now, in her sleep. She sleeps for several hours and wakes to see afternoon sunlight slanting on an unfamiliar wall. Her body feels warm and heavy, her mind open and still.

She hears a rustle of paper and turns her head to see a slender girl, her straight blonde hair partly fallen over her face, studying the maps.

Marika watches her as the background of the scene gradually filters into her mind—she remembers why she is here and, remembering the cold, oily waters of the flood, shivers and draws into herself. She tries to recall the blonde girl's name.

Carefully, the girl rolls up one map and unrolls another. Marika finds herself watching with a strange passivity, waiting to see what the girl will do or say. Finally, she looks up at Marika and sees that she's awake.

"These are very interesting," says the girl. Then she comes over to Marika and gives her a rather professional look.

"How are you doing?" she says, and Marika, seeing herself being searched for symptoms, guesses that the girl is a nurse. She nods a couple of times and then tries out her voice, which feels like it hasn't been used in a long time.

"I'm well, thank you," she says. "A little tired."

"I'd really like to talk to you—" the girl begins, but she is interrupted by another girl with wavy hair carrying a small, sleepy-looking, blue-eyed child.

"Grader's here, Terry," she says. "I've got Kyle packed. How's she doing?"

Terry turns to Marika and speaks gently. "We need to leave the house soon and go to higher ground," she says. "Do you feel strong enough to get up?"

In fact, Marika feels inert, but she nods and slowly begins to stretch her limbs and prepare herself to leave the comforter.

19

Riding in the cab of the grader, Drew Layman, who has recovered almost completely from the symptoms of the virus, wears an expression of solid contentment. He is a man who feels that he is where he is supposed to be, operating a machine he understands, greeted wherever he goes with cries of relief and gratitude.

Occasionally, he gets out of the cab to help someone up. Some people are cheerful, even jovial. Others are nervous and close to tears. Drew himself displays no more emotion than a bus driver driving his route on an ordinary day. The machine ploughing through the dangerous waters, carrying him and his passengers high above the danger, speaks for him.

Pete helps his daughters and Marika into the cab and then swings himself aboard. It's warm inside—there's a small heater down by their feet—and only when Pete feels the warmth does he realize how sore and knotted up his muscles are. He lets out a sigh and relaxes his shoulders.

"Drew," he says, "you're a sight for sore eyes. Let's get this baby movin'."

Once they're underway, Lynn puts Kyle on Marika's lap for a minute while she reaches for his bottle. He still uses the bottle for comfort, though he can use a cup, too. After Lynn takes him back, Marika finds that Kyle is staring at her as he sucks, an unabashed and unwavering stare. Marika stares back for a few minutes, and a small smile plays at the corners of her lips. Suddenly the grader lurches to one side and Kyle, startled, begins to cry, his eyes still on Marika. Lynn hugs him.

"It's okay, Kylie, you're okay," she says.

Kyle's cries subside to whimpers, and he continues to look at Marika, now as if for corroboration. After a minute, Marika fishes in her plastic bag and pulls out the small, tattered volume that she's stowed there along with her maps. She holds it up for Kyle to see, opens it, turns to a story, then looks at Kyle as if to say, "Are you ready?"

"Do you want a story, Kylie? The lady wants to read you a story," Lynn translates unnecessarily, Marika thinks.

Kyle nods once and, to Marika's surprise, allows himself and his bottle to be transferred to her lap where he continues to stare at her, solemnly sucking.

"An intellectual infant," thinks Marika, and this strikes her as comical. Smoothing out the page, she begins to read to the toddler from her book of Hans Christian Andersen tales. Terry, on the other side of her, watches her keenly. Lynn keeps glancing from the book to Kyle. Marika's voice is surprisingly clear over the noise of the engine.

"*Far out at sea,*" she reads, "*the water is as blue as the petals of the loveliest cornflower and as clear as the purest glass, but it is very deep, deeper than any anchor cable can reach. Many church towers would have to be placed on top of each other to stretch from the sea-bed to the surface. Down there the sea-folk live....*"

•

Once they arrive in the emergency shelter at Jasper Elementary School, Pete Baker plants himself in the center of the cafeteria, doggedly focusing on one thing at a time, directing those who have stepped forward to help and fielding the questions and laments of the others. The cots have just arrived, and Bob Atkins is supervising their arrangement along the walls. Noticing an influx of toddlers, Pete directs Lori Layman to put the kerosene lamps and anything else dangerous up out of reach. About a third of the people in the place, he notices, seem to be on cell phones.

Any minute a shipment of water should be coming in huge cans from the milk company in Wilmington, and he'll need to organize the unloading. The supply helicopter, with bread and baby food, will come tomorrow. Then it'll be a question of surveying the land to see who still might be stranded.

A jeep-load of well-heeled weekend fishermen wander in, wanting to know how they can get back to the mainland. When Pete explains that they're cut off, they stand there staring at him a minute like they're contemplating giving him grief. Like maybe it's just a matter of getting better service, or that's how it seems to Pete.

"Sorry for the inconvenience," he almost snaps at them, but veers off into charm at the last minute.

"You boys'll be wondrin' what you can do to help. We're settin' up cots over there. Take off your coats, and stay a while!" Slowly, they move to do his bidding.

Lynn and Terry claim cots, Lynn carrying Kyle and Terry leading Marika, who is still wrapped in Jeanne's comforter. Clutching her bag to her chest, Marika lowers herself onto a cot as soon as it is set up, closing her eyes. But soon she feels a warm pressure on her arm and hears a rustling sound. She opens her eyes to find that Kyle is beside her, pulling on her bag, trying to find an opening. At first, she pulls away, afraid that he'll damage the maps, but he persists, and his small fingers are surprisingly gentle.

"What is it?" she whispers. He looks at her and then resumes trying to open the bag. "The little book? You want to hear more?"

He stops his search and gazes at her, which she takes as an assent. Looking up for his mother, she sees that she is smiling tiredly, approvingly, from her own cot. Marika regards Kyle for a minute, and he stares steadily at her.

Kyle is silent, waiting. She sees that if he knows he is understood he wastes no motion on expression. She smiles approvingly. "Okay," she says. She sits up and draws the book out of the bag. Matter-of-factly, he crawls up onto the cot and settles himself on her lap.

> Do not believe, though, that there is nothing but the
> bare, white sand on the sea bed. No, the most marvel-
> lous trees and plants grow there that have such pliant
> trunks, stems, and leaves that the slightest movement of
> the water causes them to move as if they were alive. All
> the fishes, great and small, slip between their branches,

just as birds up here do in the air. At the very deepest spot lies the sea-king's palace. The walls are of coral and the tall pointed windows of the clearest amber, but the roof is of mussel shells that open and close as the water passes—it looks so lovely, for in each of them lie gleaming pearls, a single one of which would be a prize gem in a queen's crown.

Kyle's cheek grows heavy on Marika's shoulder and he sleeps. Gingerly, she lowers herself back on the cot and, almost instantly, falls asleep herself. From her cot, Lynn looks at them with a mild mixture of jealousy and relief. Terry produces a small flask of whiskey and looking mischievously at Lynn, offers her a sip.

•

Outside, the light is fading and the floodwater, wrapped around the school, stirs in its sleep, its belly full of lost things.

•

The next morning, under a lowering sky, the world stinks. A feeling of foreboding comes over Pete as he smokes a cigarette and looks out at the flooded road. There's just no telling what's down there—dead animals, syringes, antifreeze, pesticides, the contents of flooded septic tanks. In warning people not to drink the water, the official bulletins only spoke of saltwater contamination. But it will soon be obvious to everyone that this water is way dirtier than dirt.

Pete's been through this enough times to remember the tedium of clean-up, the stains and smells that never leave. Of course, you know and say that you're lucky to be alive, but every time, the ache piles up a little more…the ache of lost things.

For a minute, Pete's shoulders slump under a nameless weight. Suddenly he remembers a dream he had last night. He was drawing a bucket up from a well. All around him, thirsty people were waiting expectantly, licking dry lips. The bucket came up empty. Strange dream to have during a flood. Then he hears the sound of the supply helicopter and prepares gratefully to haul heavy boxes. He will use his muscles to the breaking point. He will be of use. Then, after all the meetings and crises and bullshit, have a few beers and with any luck, get some sleep tonight.

•

Dead animals, feces, silt, sand, soil, fertilizer. A dance of glutted molecules. The waters of the flood are a feast for the microbe. The losses of the humans are insignificant compared to the gains of the virus, which will soon enter many more of the humans and see how far it can go. In the lushness of its medium it reproduces with a momentum more orgasmic than orgasm. It expands in a complex, repeating pattern, like a kaleido-scope with no boundaries. It embraces its destiny with a single-minded abandon, ready for the tryst that is the purpose and promise of its life. In the rich, filthy waters of the flood, dinoflagellates arise, awaken and travel from groundwater to well water, from reservoir to faucet, from lips to stomachs to bloodstreams, and become, along with their viral passengers, members of and menaces to society, as yet unrecognized.

•

In her attic bedroom, Jeanne lies on her bed stroking Fred, the tabby cat, and looking out over the flood waters through the dormer window. The tea room downstairs is thigh-deep in mucky water, and Jeanne, looking out at the flood, feels that she's floating above it, floating above everything, floating away. Fred, happy to be high and dry, purrs beside her. High and dry. Jeanne smiles at the phrase. A couple of hours ago, when she realized she was stranded, she smoked a joint. Now she looks out at the swollen gray water and feels that it will rise and rise until it reaches her window, until it pours in, until it engulfs her and Fred and all the bric-a-brac of her life and washes it away. Her feeling about this seems, she notes, to be neutral. It seems to be something she's been waiting for calmly for a while now, like the Queen of Cups on her throne.

She dozes, but she dreams of the room and Fred and the flood just as they are, only perhaps with a few ghosts whispering in the shadows too quietly to hear. And outside, waiting patiently, the end of everything: release from hope and wanting. The nothing it all comes to in the end.

•

In Charlottesville, Don turns on the news and sees footage of Our Lady of the Sea surrounded by water. He recoils as if he's seen someone attack his mother. He watches the brief coverage of the flood. Then, without thinking, he packs a bag, leaves a note for George, the caretaker, to feed Rose, gasses up the car, and drives south. There are checkpoints set up at the beginning of Route 1, but he plays the clergy card, and they let him through with recommendations on how to avoid or negotiate flooded areas.

The police at the checkpoint tell him that most people are holed up at Jasper Elementary, the highest suitable ground, and that gives him a destination. It's only once he's past the checkpoint, driving south on a road deserted except for an occasional piece of heavy equipment, that he begins to wonder what he's doing here. What exactly has he come for?

•

At the shelter, Kenny spots Lynn lying asleep on a cot almost as soon as he comes in, but he can't see Kyle. A jolt of panic slams into his heart. He strides toward Lynn but stops short when he sees Kyle sleeping next to a strange woman, nestled into the crook of her arm. He's annoyed at first to see him with a stranger, but then he sees that she does look vaguely familiar—must be a friend of Lynn's.

Looking at Kyle's peaceful face, he suddenly feels relief take hold of him, making him weak at the knees, so that he has to find a place to sit down. Chairs are scarce, and he finally settles on the floor between the two women's cots, guarding Kyle and watching Jack Brockie ushering Shona through the crowd, his hand on her shoulder protectively, as if she were nine instead of nineteen.

After a while, the hangover and physical exertion catch up with him, and he dozes. What wakes him is a sudden movement from the woman on the cot beside him. Kyle does not wake. Looking at the woman, Kenny sees that she's looking at a man who's apparently just arrived. The man, short and well-muscled, is walking toward the woman with a loving light in his eyes. He stops, looking puzzled, when he sees Kenny.

The woman then notices Kenny for the first time and stares at him, furrowing her brow, looking even more puzzled than the man. When Kenny sees her eyes he remembers her, and after a minute even remembers her name, an unusual one, Maurita, or Markika. Under the eyes of the man and the woman, Kenny feels as if he's awakened into a nightmare of embarrassment.

It's like walking into a lamppost—the first response is anger at the asshole that hit him on the head, then he feels like a double asshole when, a second later, he realizes that he did it to himself.

"Who's the boy?" asks Hirsch.

Marika has forgotten about Kyle, who is nestled so lightly in the crook of her arm that he feels like part of her. She looks down at him now, smiling a little at Kyle and then at Hirsch but is at a loss to explain how she came to be sleeping here with a little boy. The events of the last few hours are all jumbled, as if the flood has swept over her mind as well as over the land. She looks at Hirsch's loving face and feels, shyly, a need to tell him about what happened to her. It seems like a long time since she's seen him.

Kenny stands and, a little awkwardly, points to Kyle. "Mind if I take my boy?"

Marika is startled. "Oh! He's yours?"

Kenny nods and their eyes meet for a strange, disorienting moment. Then Kenny reaches down and gently takes Kyle.

Marika looks to the neighboring cots and sees that the boy's mother is still asleep, but her sister, the medical one, is awake, and staring past Marika at Hirsch.

Following her gaze, Marika looks at Hirsch, who is stretching, and sees that the veins on his arms are faintly outlined in red.

$$20$$

Driving into Jasper on Route 1, Don Cathcart sees Fred prowling around on a roof, and for a disorienting minute thinks that it's Justinian, his graduate school cat. Perhaps because of this he stops the car and though he knows it's a little mad, contemplates a way he might rescue the animal. Jeanne's Tea Room sign and front door are on the ocean side, so, looking from the sound-side, Don doesn't recognize the house, at first.

Fred is angry and frightened now at the inaccessibility of his usual territory. By this time of day he would usually be far down the beach, and he paces back and forth on the roof, tail thrashing with frustration, looking down at the sodden land. As Don lumbers through the waist-high water toward Fred, the cat eyes him narrowly; his orange body is utterly still except for the fur that slowly rises on his neck and along his spine. He continues to stand his ground as Don comes closer, but his tail continues to twitch with ambivalence. Don wants to speak soothingly to him, but he's becoming increasingly alarmed by the height of the water, which almost threatens to sweep his feet out from under him. When he reaches the porch, the water finally picks him up, and he makes a dive for the railing, praying that it's well built. At that moment, Fred, who is normally a cat of stoical silence, lets out a weird sound somewhere between a growl and a wail. Jeanne comes to the upstairs window and sees Don hanging onto the railing, scrambling for a foothold. He gains it for a minute, then loses it, his legs flailing behind him.

"Hello!" calls Jeanne

Don looks up, startled first to see Jeanne and then to recognize her. "Hello," he says.

"Have you come to rescue me?" asks Jeanne. Don looks up at her and lets out a bark of laughter.

"Doesn't seem likely, does it?"

Jeanne smiles too, and then to her surprise, giggles. It feels awfully good to be talking to someone, and suddenly the flood seems like background, a minor annoyance. "Oh, I imagine you'll find a way," she says, leaning out the window, imagining letting down her hair so that he can climb up.

"I appreciate your faith," says Don, and with an effort, he regains his foothold.

"Let me just get a few things," says Jeanne, and she disappears from the window.

Climbing heavily over the railing and onto the porch, Don hopes she's not planning on bringing much and that she's a strong swimmer. Then he hears Fred growl again, and it occurs to him that swimming with an angry cat might not be the easiest thing he's ever done. Beginning to shiver, he wonders if he's bitten off more than he can chew, pretty sure the Lord didn't design him for rescuing damsels in distress. He knocks on the door, waits for a minute, then pushes it open. Just as he comes in, Jeanne comes down the stairs carrying Fred, and both of them stop for a minute, dismayed to see the tea room sodden and stained, a miscellaneous collection of objects—a cup, an envelope, what looks like part of a CD case—bobbing on a small, scummy sea. Don sees that the tea room is a step or two lower than the foyer, which explains why water didn't run out over his feet when he opened the door.

Jeanne remains on the stairs, looking blankly around the tea room. Cassettes, tea bags, an old cordless phone float on the murky water. Something moves near her feet, and Jeanne looks down to see a tarot card floating by, its face turned up to her. At first she's alarmed, but then she realizes it's not from her current deck, which is wrapped in her scarf and safe in her purse. Must be from some previous, discarded, forgotten deck. Peering at the card, she sees that it's the nine of wands. Reversed, obstacles, adversity, calamity. Right-side-up, strength in opposition. Of course, there's no specific reading for a card that's basically surfing.

"Must have fallen behind something," she says aloud, but in her distraction she loosens her hold on Fred, who jumps out of her arms and slips out the open door onto the porch. There he freezes for a minute at the sight of the flood water and lowers himself onto his haunches, tail thrashing, eyes narrowed, facing down the encroaching water. Seeing that the cat won't bolt, Don turns back to Jeanne.

"Got everything?" he asks, relieved to see that she is carrying only two shoulder bags, one full, one seemingly empty.

Jeanne nods, her brown eyes still a little startled.

"How does he feel about being carried?" asks Don, indicating Fred.

"I think we'd better put him in this," says Jeanne, taking off the empty bag and handing it to Don. Seeing that he looks a little hesitant, she adds, "If I get the scruff of his neck he'll be pretty easy to handle. I can do that while you hold the bag."

Don nods, and the two proceed out the door.

"You'd better lock that," he says. "There may be looters."

She looks at him as if she's not quite able to process his statement but meanwhile fumbles in her purse and draws out her keys.

"It's deep right around the porch," says Don. "We may have to swim the first few yards. How are we going to keep him out of the water?"

"I don't think we can," says Jeanne, "but if it's just a few yards…."

Don grins. "I guess we'll find a way to make it up to him," he says.

And with that, bracing themselves, they step off the porch and begin to tread water. Feeling himself lowered, Fred lets out one outraged wail that strikes them both as funny, and they laugh as they swim.

Jeanne has a sudden memory of Humphrey Bogart and Katharine Hepburn swimming away from their bombed-out boat at the end of *The African Queen*, an image which startles her and makes her laugh again. Then her foot strikes the ground and they begin wading, Don holding Fred high above his head.

Fred struggles once or twice and lets out a couple more growls but then seems to give up and fall still.

Before long they are in Don's car. Don reaches into the back and hands Jeanne a towel. Trembling a little, she quickly dries her hair and then wraps the towel around her shoulders. Don turns on the heat, and as they drive slowly down the wet road, Jeanne is overwhelmed by a feeling of warmth and safety, as if the car were a kind of solitary, self-contained little world that nothing could penetrate. She and Don catch each other's eyes and smile shyly, secretively, almost as if they've gotten away with something. And now another movie comes into her head: Marilyn Monroe in *Bus Stop* standing at the bus station on a cold day, wrapping her lover's jacket around her as if it were her lover's arms, as if it were all the home she needs.

After driving for a few minutes, Don starts to say something but then looks over and smiles to see that Jeanne is fast asleep.

•

A smell of wet green beans and square, greasy Salisbury steaks lingers in the cafeteria, partly masked by an overlay of detergent and disinfectant. It is crowded, and there's a loud hum of conversation.

Jeanne and Don pause at the threshold a minute to look around and adjust. There is a sleeping section, full of cots, against the far wall. Near the cots a line of people wait, with towels and toothbrushes, for the bathroom. In one corner there is a children's area, with pillows, toys, and books. A few women and young girls are supervising.

Don scans the crowd for Hirsch but doesn't see him. Jeanne scans for Terry and Lynn, spots Lynn in a corner writing in a journal while Kenny plays nearby with Kyle, but she doesn't see Terry.

They are startled by a voice beside them and turn to see Pete, sitting at a card table with a pile of nametags and some markers. He wears a name-tag with PETE BAKER written in firm capitals.

"Hey folks," he says, with a friendly smile. "Welcome to our little 'Open House.' If y'all will just fill these out and put them on—oh, hey!" he says, seeing that it's Jeanne.

"How are you?" Jeanne asks him, looking softly into his eyes.

"Well, I would say, 'Right as rain,'" says Pete, "but that might not sound too good right now. And how're you folks?"

"Well, we're fine," she says, "but I think Fred here"—she unzips her bag a little, and Fred's nose pokes out comically—"would like to come out. What's your policy on animals?"

"Hey, kitty!" says Pete. "Well, I don't suppose y'all brought a litter box. No, not the easiest thing to carry. Tell you what: for the time being take him into the kitchen, and keep him in the bag. I'll check back with you soon as I get these folks set up."

Jeanne and Don see that a bedraggled family has lined up behind them and move on quickly to make way for them. As they make their way through the crowd to the kitchen, greeting clients and ex-parishioners, Jeanne finds that she is inexplicably filled with a feeling of love for the people around her, as if she is walking through a greenhouse full of beautiful, endangered plants. Glancing at Don, she sees that he's feeling the same way.

When they enter the kitchen, they see Terry, Hirsch, and Marika sitting at a table, talking tensely. The three look up when Jeanne and Don enter, but seem to look at them without seeing them. There is an awkward silence as the two intruders wait to be acknowledged.

Finally Don breaks the silence by holding up Jeanne's bag and saying, "Anyone allergic to cats?"

Terry is the first to snap out of it and respond. "A little," she says. "Why?"

"We've got one in here" says Don. "We're waiting to see if he can be accommodated."

There is another silence.

It is clear that the three have been talking about something more momentous than cats and are struggling to adjust to the narrower scope of the conversation.

"Honey," says Jeanne, rather sharply, "are you all right?"

"Aunt Jeanne!" says Terry. "I'm fine." And she comes forward for an embrace. "Everything okay with you?"

Jeanne nods, continuing to look questioningly at Terry.

"These folks needed a little medical consultation," says Terry, lightly. The other two adjust their expressions on their faces to fit her tone.

"All right," says Don, loath to intrude. "Let's see if we can find a home for this beast."

Once Fred is stowed in a broom closet with a can of tuna and a dish tub full of ripped-up newspaper, Don and Jeanne quietly leave the trio in the kitchen to their conversation. Practiced in discretion, they don't speak to each other of their impressions.

"Thanks for the rescue," Jeanne says, shyly, touching Don's arm and smiling her soft smile.

"Thanks for the company," says Don, marveling at how unembarrassed he feels smiling back at her.

They separate easily and go about choosing their cots, greeting their neighbors, accustoming themselves to these four wide cinder block walls and this high girded ceiling, beyond which a heavy rain is again beginning to fall.

•

"We don't know what it is," says Terry, speaking quietly to Hirsch. "We've seen similar symptoms elsewhere, but we don't know what they lead to. We don't know, for instance, if it's contagious. But because we don't know, I think the best thing to do is to call for a helicopter and fly you over to Elizabeth City or Norfolk. Make sense?"

Hirsch nods calmly. Fear sits at the table with them like a fourth person, a homeless person with bad breath and crazy eyes, behaving himself for the moment.

"Now, the last thing we need out there," Terry says, indicating the cafeteria, "is a rumor of an unknown bug. So we'll have to fabricate a known one, not too serious but contagious, like—I don't know. Measles, maybe. To explain why we're shipping you out."

She gives Hirsch a searching look. "How're you feelin'?"

Hirsch nods several times before answering. "Okay."

"I've got a thermometer in my bag," says Terry. "Let me go get it."

And as she walks to her cot, she mentally replays what she just saw in Hirsch's face: glassy eyes, indicative of fever, slightly reddish rings around the eyes indicative of God-knows-what, and that damn strange rash, if you can call it that, that follows the pattern of the veins. She's never seen that before and neither, apparently, has this Marika lady, in spite of her degree in animal epidemiology and all the thinking and reading she seems to have done about it. But then, Terry never had a chance to finish reading over the Family Wellness Center records before the storm hit. This makes her uneasy. These symptoms could easily slip by someone who wasn't looking for them. Her mind is so full of the symptoms as she reaches under her cot to fetch her bag, that Pete startles her when he taps her on the shoulder.

"Daddy!"

"How you doin', Kitten?" asks Pete fondly.

"I'm fine. How are you holdin' up?" she says, noticing the bags under his eyes, the deepened lines on his forehead.

"Oh, not ready for the scrapyard yet, I guess. Hey, what's that for? Sick kid?"

Terry resists an impulse to hide the thermometer behind her back. Too late now anyway.

"No, it's an adult. Not sure, but it might be meningitis. It may be contagious."

"Think you might need to fly him out? Or is it a her?"

"Him. It's possible. In the meantime, we'll keep him away from the others."

"Well, keep up the good work, Doc, and let me know if you need anything," says Pete.

"You, too, Mr. Mayor," says Terry. Reaching up, she briefly massages Pete's neck. Pete takes a deep breath and rolls his shoulders.

"Thanks, Kitten," he says. "Well, back to the ark."

So that's my story, thinks Terry. Meningitis. She invented it on the spur of the moment, but, considering it as she carries the thermometer back to the kitchen, she concludes that meningitis is a good choice. Not too well known. People know it's serious but don't necessarily know what symptoms might be associated with it. It'll work. She decides to suggest that Hirsch set up his cot in one of the storerooms off the kitchen.

Marika, in the kitchen with Hirsch, keeps her distance from him. The floor needs sweeping, and she has decided, a little absurdly—at home she's not much of a housekeeper—to sweep it.

Without looking, he senses the mindless pleasure she takes in following the long, cleared path of the big industrial broom. He knows her well enough to know that she is struggling with her feelings, wanting to be near him but afraid.

But he stays where he is, leaning against the table, hugging himself and staring into space. He needs his own comfort right now and has none to spare for her.

Eventually, she puts down the broom and folds her arms. She looks at him directly, briefly, then lowers her eyes. As if she has spoken aloud, he can hear her desire for a drink.

•

Outside, the rain is falling on the sodden land and swollen water. It beats on the roof of the cafeteria, breaking the gutters and pouring down the windows, so that people look out as if from inside a waterfall. Radios issue flood warnings, and some in the cafeteria, getting punchy, laugh at the idea of a flooded flood.

The governor declares a state of emergency, shocking some and bringing strange comfort to others who feel both confirmed in their fears and acknowledged by the authorities—almost famous.

In the cafeteria, Jeanne is circulating quietly among the displaced citizens, offering them shoulder rubs. Some of them groan aloud in pleasure at the mere suggestion. In the half-light of morning, dressing under a blanket, Deidre Brockie frowns at the beginnings of a rash on her arm. She puts on a sweater, resolving to wear long sleeves. The microbe, initially rejected by her body, has evolved a completely new "look" since then, and the sentries of her blood now take it for a harmless creature and let it pass.

•

Late that night, Don Cathcart is awakened by a sudden stillness in the cafeteria: the rain has stopped.

Unable to get back to sleep, he gets up and strolls around the edges of the big room, looking down at the sleeping faces and sprawled bodies. Sometimes a bleary, half-dreaming eye looks up at him, and he smiles down into it and passes quietly on.

He is almost beside Marika by the time he sees her, slouching in a window-well, a book, which she is no longer reading, in her lap. She is sitting in a square of moonlight, staring out the dark window and does not acknowledge Don's silent approach, though she seems to sense his presence.

"Rain's stopped," he says, gently. She nods without looking at him.

"Can't sleep," he says, wondering why he's not giving up on conversation.

She looks at him with a wry, measuring smile and then, still without speaking, takes a flask from a hidden pocket and holds it out to him. He chuckles and takes it, inconspicuously wiping it on his sleeve before putting it to his lips and taking a healthy swig.

"Thanks," he says, wiping it again and handing it back to her. "Good idea."

He leans against the wall, waiting for her to speak. He feels that she will and that he is meant to be here to listen. He's been getting this feeling with various people during these long hours in the cafeteria. Nothing can distract him from someone who needs to talk. So different from the old days in his study at Our Lady of the Sea!

They sit for a long time, Marika taking two or three sips of the whiskey to Don's every one. Finally, she looks at him curiously.

"You're a priest?" she says.

Don nods, but says, "Well, I have been. Right now I'm sort of on sabbatical."

Marika nods as if she approves of this idea.

"I was not brought up religiously," she says. Don nods at this familiar disclaimer. Some sort of "but..." usually follows.

"But I have been familiar with death," says Marika, turning her eyes to the window again. "Death of people—close to me."

Another pause, a long one, until Marika finally continues.

"They hold on so—so hard. Far past the point you'd think they would. I wonder why. When they finally do go, it doesn't seem all that bad. Sometimes even good."

Don nods, thinking of deathbeds he's attended. "It's a big change," he says. "People get rattled just moving from one town to another. Change is a hard thing, especially if you're not doing it on purpose. Assuming you really ever do."

Marika nods slightly at this, and they both gaze ahead silently, companionably thinking separate but parallel thoughts. Quietly, outside, the rain begins again.

•

The next morning Terry and Pete spend an hour in an out-of-the-way office with the door closed, Pete on the phone, Terry biting her nails and providing occasional medical information about Hirsch. They decide to have the helicopter land in the west parking lot, which is only slightly flooded and is on the opposite side of the school from the cafeteria.

"With any luck," says Pete, "no one'll know he's going 'til he's gone."

"I think Father Don's a friend of his," says Lynn. "He'll probably notice right away."

Pete nods thoughtfully. "We'll pull him aside and fill him in," he says. "He can help us field enquiries. Lord knows he should be able to be discreet, if anybody can."

•

The helicopter is late and Terry, Hirsch, and Marika wait for it silently in the rain, which is now a mild drizzle. The world has been so wet so long that to Hirsch, in his feverish state, it looks a little as if it's dissolving, the gray-white of the sky running down into the gray-brown of the land.

He's told Terry that there's no one she needs to contact for him—a statement that gives him a pang of sadness—and asked Marika to look in on his house when the floodwaters recede. But she looked at him incredulously, as if it were an inappropriate request. Fine, he thinks, don't love me. Clam up. Whatever. His fever makes him somehow numb, melancholy, and relaxed, all at the same time. What will be will be, a philosophy he's never cared for, feels perfectly natural to him now.

Doris Day singing "Que sera, sera" in spite of finding herself enmeshed in an Alfred Hitchcock Cold War spy movie. Wouldn't like to live in a universe where Alfred Hitchcock was God. But que sera, sera. And what does the bumper sticker say? Shit happens. And then they came out with that other one: Light happens.

By the time the chopping sound of the helicopter becomes audible, Hirsch's sense of time has pretty much disappeared. He could have been waiting for minutes or for months. And it does not particularly surprise him, though it seems a little odd when, after some kind of argument with the pilot, Marika turns to him, and he feels her lips pressing, first on his mouth, and then, repeatedly, on the insides of his forearms, along the lines of the rash.

He feels her touch as if from far away, though the hairs rise on the back of his neck. He watches her as she turns and glares fiercely at the pilot, who shrugs, looking a little spooked and in a gesture of mock gallantry, invites her onto the helicopter.

Some time seems to have passed, and she is buckling Hirsch in, and then he's sitting beside her in the helicopter, watching Marika exchange words with Terry but unable to follow the conversation. He is glad of the solid feel of her body beside him, but thinks, who will take care of my books now? and falls into a reverie of turning page after page of glowing text and illuminated illustrations that far outshine anything in the gray world around him.

•

On the ground, as the helicopter lifts off, Terry stands for a minute in the rain, doubly shaken. When Marika kissed Hirsch's rash it was as shocking as if she'd done something obscene. Terry felt a cry leap to her throat at the wanton risk of life. The woman knew what she was doing. Terry knows that Marika suspects that the disease, or whatever it is, is potentially very serious. The kissing did persuade the pilot to let Marika come along with Hirsch, but mightn't there have been some less dangerous way of persuading him? By the time the two of them got on the helicopter, Hirsch had to be helped aboard.

And that was the second shock. Terry suddenly realized, watching them board in this out-of-the-way parking lot, that she was trying to conceal something that she should perhaps be publicizing: the advent of a serious, possibly contagious disease. If caution and exhaustion kept her from notifying anyone of Drew Layman's symptoms before, what is her excuse now? An urgent feeling of foreboding fills her.

She must go speak to Pete. Immediately.

She finds Pete in conference with Jack in the same little office from which Pete called for the helicopter.

"I think we can recoup some of this with the festival..." Jack is saying, but breaks off when Terry enters the room.

Terry finds herself irritated at the men's patient expressions, as if they are resigned to having to listen to her until she goes away and leaves them to more important things. She realizes that she often feels this way—shut out—when Daddy and Jack Brockie talk, but then she shakes off these thoughts—somewhat inconsequential, given the matter at hand.

"Daddy, can I speak to you alone for a minute?" she says, with a perfunctory nod at Jack.

"Uh—of course," says Pete, seeing her seriousness. The men both get to their feet.

"Catch you later, Pete," says Jack. "Good to see you, Doctor."

"Daddy, we have a problem," says Terry, as soon as the door is shut.

"Meningitis?" says Pete.

"No. I don't know what it is," says Terry, shaking her head.

"You don't know?"

Terry pauses. The facts she does know suddenly seem scattered and inconclusive. Why exactly is she so alarmed? Two isolated incidents of rash and fever that could have been caused by toxins? Hardly an epidemic.

But she is alarmed; alarmed enough not to second-guess herself, not to ascribe her anxiety to the stress of the flood or to discount Marika's oblique warnings because she's not an MD, or to be daunted by Pete's mockery of "Pfiesteria hysteria."

"I don't know, but I think it's serious."

"How do you mean? Something contagious?"

"Well, I'm not sure."

"What are the symptoms?"

"So far a peculiar rash and a fairly high fever."

"Are we talking about something you could die of?"

"I don't know."

Pete nods, looking confused, but trying, Terry is sure, not to look skeptical.

"There's a very strange rash, like nothing I've seen before and a high fever—Daddy, I can't really explain it right now, but this is my professional opinion. I think we need to call in the health authorities. Maybe the Centers for Disease Control."

Pete looks alarmed and is silent for a minute, as if waiting for her to say more. But she presses her lips together, willing him to take her seriously, not to remember how she looked once upon a time, in a diaper and a hair bow. After a minute, he nods slowly and says, "If that's what you think…Okay, I'll call them after lunch."

•

Pete lunches in his office with Jack Brockie, and though Jack does nothing more than slightly furrow his brow when Pete tells him of Terry's request, Pete suddenly feels that he is jeopardizing a whole bunch of plans and a possible bunch of money for what may be an overreaction or even a mistake. After all, Terry's been very stressed out recently, not herself, and as a country GP, she may not be up on the latest diagnoses…. Still without speaking, Pete and Jack stare at each other for a minute, weighing unknown risks against rewards they've been calculating for months. They are attuned to each other now.

Out of their bull sessions and planning sessions a feeling of momentum has arisen, a feeling of seeing farther and potentially going farther than they thought they could. The momentum has been like a return of youth to them, and they're both uneasy at the idea of sacrificing it to something that might never happen. So they stare at each other and reach a wordless agreement so clear that Pete nods as if Jack has said something.

"We've got enough chaos here for now," Pete says. "I don't see this as a red alert. We'll wait a week or two and focus on getting all this muck cleaned up. Ask Terry to monitor the situation; keep us posted."

Jack seems to reflect on this a minute and then says, "Makes sense to me. And I must say, Pete, it's nice to see a cool head prevail."

He lifts his plastic cup as if in a toast and sips the God-awful coffee the Red Cross has provided. Pete appreciates the compliment but does not acknowledge it. He only rolls his shoulders and rubs his tired neck with a tired hand. And the pain in his neck grows more intense later, when Terry looks at him out of Cathy's eyes, with bewilderment and shock, as if she can't have heard him right.

"But why? What point is there in waiting?"

"We've got a lot of people who've been here a long time," says Pete. "Morale is okay now, but…we don't need a panic."

"But do you realize what you're risking?"

"Honey, if you could tell me more…if you knew more…"

This echo of Terry's own doubts makes her blind with fury for a moment, and then she feels suddenly collapsed, without a leg to stand on. If her own father doesn't believe her, what can she expect from the CDC? Tears of frustration spring into her eyes, and this infuriates her even more.

Without a word, she leaves Pete's "office," slamming the door so hard that the window rattles.

Pete winces and rolls his shoulders and head, trying to release the grip of the pain. Aimlessly, he strolls out into the cafeteria, where Jeanne is giving Bob Atkins a massage. She hasn't offered him one, and for a minute, he looks longingly at her wise hands, ironically remembering that he was the first person she'd practiced on. It was his appreciation that had given her the idea to go professional. He'd offered her some money to get started, which she insisted on treating as a loan, sending him regular payments through the mail, with nothing more personal than her signature. Now she smooths Bob's brow, and his face takes on a look of quiet release, as if he's falling asleep. She doesn't look up at Pete. As he watches her, the pain in his neck grows so great that it becomes, in his mind, the main fact about him.

"Gampa, stowwy. Stowwy, Gampa!"

Pete feels a tug on his pant leg and turns to see Kyle holding up a small, slightly ragged book. Kyle is still not a very talkative or eloquent child, but the open intensity of his dark blue-gray eyes tends to make people listen hard to the few, slightly jumbled words that he does say. Pete smiles, and he feels the smile loosening up his neck just a little. He squats down beside Kyle and squints at the spine of the little book: *Fairy Tales of Hans Christian Andersen.*

"Yup," he says, "Story sounds good. Let's find a place."

He takes Kyle's hand and walks him over to the children's area, where he lowers himself into a child-sized chair. Kyle stands behind him, and points in the book where he is to begin. Then he stands behind Pete with his hand on Pete's shoulder, waiting attentively. Pete can't help but smile at his seriousness. He fetches his reading glasses from his pocket and peers at the small writing.

"What's this story about?" he asks.

"Withuth," says Kyle, promptly.

"Withuth?" echoes Pete.

Kyle nods and, for further clarification, adds, "Keep n Kaw."

"Mm-hm!" says Pete, trying to appear better informed than he feels. "Shall I start here?"

"Stawt heeh," Kyle gravely echoes.

Pete begins. "*The wizard who had no name looked through the magnifying glass. It actually appeared like a whole town, where all the inhabitants ran about naked!*"

Pete breaks off and looks at Kyle, wondering if this is the right thing to be reading to him, but Kyle's rapt, dreamy expression prevents him from protesting. Perhaps the boy is really just listening to the sounds of the words, content not to know the meaning of all of them. He seems to remember Cathy pointing out that Lynn did something similar a thousand years ago. He resumes reading.

"*It was terrible—*oh, hello."

Deidre Brockie has entered the play area, carrying a checklist for Pete to sign. Awkwardly, he hauls himself to his feet, checks over the list, which is of supplies to request from the Red Cross, and takes the pen Deidre offers him. He signs the list, and then handing back the pen, he sees, as her sleeve rides up, red lines, like tiny rivers on a map, outlining the veins of her wrist. Looking up at her, he sees that her eyes are unfocused, her hair disheveled, and there are small beads of sweat on her forehead.

"Thanks," he says. "You doin' okay?"

"Just fine," says Deidre. Her eyes are glassy. "Enjoy your story!" she says, and walks away.

Pete looks after her until Kyle pulls on his shirt and says, "Moe stowwy, Gampa."

Pete sits and reads.

> It was terrible, but still more terrible to see how the one knocked and pushed the other, bit each other, and threw one another about. What was undermost should be topmost, and what was topmost should be undermost!
>
> "It is quite amusing!" said the wizard.
>
> "Yes; but what do you think it is?" asked Creep-and-Crawl. "Can you figure it out?"
>
> "It is very easy to see," said the other. "It is Copenhagen or some great city, they all resemble each other. A great city it is, that's sure!"
>
> "It's ditch-water!" said Creep-and-Crawl.

Pete comes to a decision and gets to his feet. "Come on, buddy, let's go find your mama."

And, in spite of his neck, he sweeps Kyle up into his arms, holding him tightly, and strides with him across the cafeteria.

When he finds Lynn, she is talking to Terry, and both girls look startled to see him. He can tell they've been talking about him, but he is in crisis mode and can't be bothered thinking about it.

"Mama, I think you may need to take this boy to the changing room," he says to Lynn. He feels Kyle's steady gaze on him, but the child doesn't protest. Pete, still carrying Kyle, walks with Lynn to the bathroom. Terry watches as they linger outside the bathroom, talking for quite a while. Lynn seems disturbed by something. Then, hurriedly, she takes Kyle from Pete and carries him over to Terry.

"Can you watch him for a minute?" she says. "Here," she says as she fishes in her pocket. "He likes this book. Maybe you can read him a story."

Then Lynn turns on her heel, and she and Pete disappear into the kitchen. Terry glares after them for a moment and then opens the book to a story called "The Wind." She reads:

> When the wind sweeps across the grass, the field has a ripple like a pond, and when it sweeps across the corn the field waves to and fro like a high sea. That is called the wind's dance; but the wind does not dance only, he also tells stories; and how loudly he can sing out of his deep chest, and how different it sounds in the treetops in the forest, and through the loopholes and clefts and cracks in walls! Do you see how the wind drives the clouds up yonder, like a frightened flock of sheep? Do you hear how the wind howls down here through the open valley, like a watchman blowing his horn? With wonderful tones he whistles and screams down the chimney and into the fireplace. The fire crackles and flares up, and shines far into

the room, and the little place is warm and snug, and it is pleasant to sit there listening to the sounds. Let the wind speak, for he knows plenty of stories and fairy tales, many more than are known to any of us. Just hear what the wind can tell.

Huh—uh—ush! Roar along! That is the chorus of the song.

Terry cocks her head to one side and falls into a reverie, staring into space and absently stroking the top of Kyle's head. The words of the story have mesmerized him too, and he leans against her, sucking his thumb, watching an imaginary firelight flicker on the cinderblock wall.

In the kitchen, Lynn folds her arms and plants her feet. "Well, Daddy, is there an epidemic or isn't there? And if there isn't, why do you want to send us away?"

Pete glares at his daughter for a minute and then drops his eyes. After a moment, he speaks in a low, stern voice.

"I am concerned enough to protect my family, which I do on my own responsibility. I am not sufficiently convinced of the danger to risk public panic in a time of crisis." He looks at her.

Two pairs of blue eyes stare intently at each other. Lynn's are the first to drop.

•

The next day they stand in the western parking lot, waiting for the supply helicopter. Lynn wears a black oilcloth jacket. She is pale and a little haggard. She spent last night packing and talking to Terry. She feels rushed, torn, frightened, and resentful. She finds herself arguing with Pete even as she longs for a helicopter to come out of the sky and carry Kyle away from what she now can't help seeing as contaminated ground.

"But Daddy, if there is going to be trouble, I don't want to leave—I want to do something!" she hears herself saying, a gust of wind blowing the words out of her mouth. "I want to help!"

"Raise your child," he thunders.

She stares at him and folds her arms, her mouth tight, looking, he recognizes, just like his.

He takes her gently by the arm and says "I'm gonna tell you something. I…I—" He sits down and wipes his hand across his brow and face. He suddenly has a sad, crumpled look that Lynn doesn't recall having seen before.

It scares her. There is a long pause, during which Lynn, to her horror, sees a tear sliding haltingly down his cheek.

Finally, he says, "You can't do anything more important than take care of him."

Then he buries his face in his hands. After a while he speaks, his voice muffled and distorted.

"I'm sorry," he says.

Lynn puts her hand on his shoulder, wanting and yet frightened to see his face. "Daddy, it's all right," she says. "You don't—I mean, you—"

Then there is a roar from the sky and the helicopter descends suddenly, like some thunderous apparition.

Pete leaps to his feet and runs under the whirring blades to talk to the pilot. He runs quickly, it seems to Lynn, in order to shake off her attempts at exoneration. He shakes hands with the pilot, turning back into the old glad-hander she's used to, saying a few words and then turning to beckon Lynn to the helicopter.

Stunned, Lynn gathers up Kyle and their bags and walks toward the men and the deafening machine, whose noise seems, somehow, to echo her state of mind. They stand for a minute under the whirring blades. Pete kisses her tenderly on the forehead and chucks Kyle gently under the chin, saying a few words to him that Lynn doesn't catch. Then he steps back, and she climbs aboard. There she busies herself getting Kyle settled in, as the pilot seems in a hurry to take off.

As the propeller pulls her into the sky, she closes her eyes, and she doesn't look down at the land until she's far above it. There she sees an unfamiliar pattern of terrain, water covering places that should be land, so that she has a sense of neither knowing where she's going nor where she's leaving. She can just pick out the elementary school, but there is nobody standing in the yard. Pete must have gone in.

Having seen the copter safely lift off, Pete has squared his shoulders and gone into the shelter to look for Kenny. When he steps into the cafeteria, he senses right away that the mood of the crowd has turned some kind of corner. He hears babies crying, hears the contained ferocity of a marital argument somewhere to his left, hears someone drop something and curse as if it's happened too many times. The camaraderie of disaster is souring, and people are turning back into themselves. A weariness and despair washes over Pete so intensely that for a moment he stops in his tracks and feels unable to move a step farther.

These are his neighbors, his friends, his people, and yet he wishes he could be anywhere else.

Lunch is being served, and he spots Kenny in line. He decides to grab a tray and ask Kenny to eat with him in his office. Just like breaking up with a girl, he thinks. Bad news over food. But Jack Brockie waylays him for a minute to talk to some investor on the cell phone.

They retreat into his makeshift office, where he commences verbally slapping this invisible stranger on the back. It's too easy.

•

In the cafeteria, hours later, dinner is ready. Busy on the phone, Pete doesn't hear the slight commotion when Deidre Brockie passes out and falls into the arms of her daughter. Shona, who is carrying a diet Dr. Pepper, staggers and tries to hold Deidre up with one arm, but losing her grip, she lowers herself into a squat so Deidre won't have so far to fall. This lessens the impact, but Deidre is deeply unconscious, and her fall is graceless anyway. She sprawls, her skirt rides up her hips, Dr. Pepper splashes on her face and hair, her mouth sags open.

Shocked by her mother's exposed state, Shona hurriedly puts down her drink and starts to rearrange her, pulling down her skirt, brushing her hair out of her face.

Kenny is ahead of them in line and recoils a little when he turns and sees the mother sprawled on the floor, the daughter leaning over her. He pauses for a second before going to their aid, braced for the dreaded flood of empathy that he's more and more prone to these days. And sure enough it comes.

In spite of the briefness of their encounters, Deidre's whole being seems to cry out to him, his memory of the faint cries of her orgasm, her flat speaking voice and dry wit, her neatness, her smart clothes, her quiet but firm self-loathing, her efficiency, her anger, her cute lean little ass moving under a tight skirt, her expression when she realized he was dating Shona, as if he were confirming things she'd known all her life but was still hoping weren't true.

Kenny reels under the force of this blow. But he's becoming used to these strange bouts of empathy, like chronic waves of nausea, and he fights his way through it to kneel beside the two women.

"What's the matter," he asks. "Is she okay?"

"I have no idea," says Shona. "We were just standing here and all of a sudden—" Then, noticing that a crowd is beginning to form, she raises lost brown eyes to Kenny and says, "Can you make them stand back a little?"

Kenny moves immediately into action. "It's okay folks, just too much stress and forgot to eat. Low blood sugar. Go on about your business, and if someone could fetch Dr. Baker..."

A minute later Pete and Jack, emerging from the "office," see Kenny walk by carrying someone, followed by Terry and Shona. Seeing Shona, Jack looks again and sees familiar calves dangling over Kenny's arm, wearing the green pumps that Deidre bought on her last trip to New York.

As the group passes, Pete sees Terry's tight frown and tense jaw and senses the approach of a bullet that he won't be able to duck. She and the others pass quickly into the kitchen and both men stand, stunned, hearts beating hard, with the dizzy sensation that the ground is slipping from beneath their feet.

In the kitchen, Terry checks Deidre's vital signs and they don't look good. Life is ebbing away. Terry is alarmed, and the more alarmed she becomes, the angrier she gets at her father. Her anger almost blinds and deafens her until she sees Shona's bewildered eyes searching hers, as people's eyes in these circumstances always do, for an admission that this is all a mistake, a misunderstanding, a joke. It takes Terry a minute to blink away her rage and dredge up some gentleness.

"It doesn't look good," she says. "There's not much I can do here but make her a little more comfortable. We need to get her to a hospital."

She doesn't mention that she received her first report on Hirsch from Elizabeth City today, and it wasn't promising. They don't know what the hell it is, but won't admit it, just talk about transferring him to "better facilities" in Norfolk. Nobody wants this hot potato. Where are all the heroic young virus hunters you keep reading about? Seduced away by drug companies, probably.

"All right, let's get her to the hospital," says Shona. "How do we get her there?"

Deidre moans suddenly and makes word-like sounds like someone having a bad dream. Suddenly Shona is aware that Pete and Jack have come in and are standing in the doorway.

"Let's get her there!" Shona says, panic rising in her voice. "What do we do?"

Without looking at Pete, Terry answers "You'll have to ask the mayor about that."

Pete hadn't noticed that Jack was in the room with him, and starts when Jack shouts, "What the hell's going on here? What the hell is there to discuss? We've got someone who needs to be evacuated, let's do it!"

Pete calls the hospital, but the helicopter is off rescuing some stranded flood victims, and there is nothing for anyone to do but wait and, as Terry says, make Deidre as comfortable as possible. Now it's approaching midnight in the kitchen and Shona is still on the floor, holding Deidre's head in her lap. Earlier there was talk of bringing a cot in, but it was decided that it would arouse too much curiosity, and Deidre is now lying on and covered by an assortment of smuggled jackets and blankets.

Shona wears someone's jacket draped on her shoulders. She's not exactly tired but not exactly awake. The cement floor is hard and cold, but she's only intermittently aware of her own stiffness from sitting on it so long. Mostly she's aware of Deidre's hot hand in hers. Deidre is fitfully unconscious. There are dark red rings around her eyes. Shona dozes once and wakes feeling that her hand is like an electrical socket that is connecting Deidre to a vital current, and if she lets go, the current will be interrupted. So she doesn't let go.

People come in and go out. They offer Shona coffee or food, and they urge her to take a break. At one point, Dr. Baker comes in and explains to her gently, as if they're afraid she'll go nuts, that there is a delay and the helicopter won't come for Deidre until morning. But she's not going to go nuts. She doesn't want to move, and she doesn't want her mom to be moved. She wants everything to stay the way it is, with Deidre's chest rising and falling and the current flowing between their hands.

Eventually she surrenders to gravity and fatigue and lies down beside Deidre with someone's jacket under her head. Shortly before dawn she wakes to the sound of her mother's breathing, which has become raspy and painful. She squeezes her hand, and to her surprise, Deidre opens her eyes and looks right at her. They look into each other's eyes for what seems like a long time, and it's as if they've never seen each other before. For a minute, each seems to be waiting for the other to speak, but they don't speak.

In the semi-dark, Shona brings her face closer to her mother's so that their foreheads are touching, and she squeezes her hand again. Deidre's lungs are flooding, and her heart is breaking from lack of oxygen, but she stirs and nestles closer to Shona. The women lie together, one hardly able to breathe, the other hardly daring to, and love each other blindly. No one is the mother, no one is the daughter, but there are ties of blood, for the moment there is breath, and for the moment, a current of love flows powerfully, silently, effortlessly between them. For a moment, there is nothing else.

●

Outside, in the parking lot, Kenny is staring up at the sky. It's a cloudy night and the stars are obscured. A small pale smear of yellow light indicates where the moon must be. He has come out for a cigarette, but he holds it unlit. He can't help staring up at the sky as if Kyle is still up there, though he knows the helicopter must be far away by now. Maybe Kyle is buckled into some child seat in some rented car on his way to Lynn's uncle's farm in Zebulon, near Raleigh, where Pete says he's sending them. He imagines the two of them in that car, driving through the dark amidst all the thousands and thousands of other cars, passing lonely fields and closed gas stations and boarded up churches. It's a big country, and it's a long way. They seem so small. Throwing the cigarette down, Kenny closes his eyes, bows his head, and covers his eyes with his hand. After a while he realizes that he's trying to pray.

21

When the flood waters recede, people shake hands, embrace, exchange thanks and jokes and phone numbers. The ones who have vehicles in the parking lot inspect them carefully, kicking the tires, longing for a car wash, though wincing a little at the thought of all that pounding water. Some say a little prayer before turning the key in the ignition, but most of the vehicles start. Then the people drive them gingerly down the hill and into the muddy town.

Don finds himself increasingly disoriented as he drives by the work of the flood. At one intersection, a half-uprooted street sign leans over the street at a forty-five-degree angle. The name of the street is not visible, and Don is very bothered by the fact that he can't remember it. He's not heading toward Our Lady of the Sea yet, though he dreamed about her—it—last night. Dreamed that there was a hole in the roof and water was pouring in, but then it was light, not water, and he put his hand into it and drew it back not wet, but warm and tingly with a sweet, electric energy.

He's driving now to Hirsch's house to check on it and to pick up some books that Marika has requested. Don has called the hospital daily since Hirsch was taken away, to receive reports from Marika. She describes Hirsch's condition in a detached, clinical way, but her voice seems to Don to be full of rage. Apparently, Hirsch is slipping in and out of coma. He's never been able to talk when Don called.

Hirsch's house is another shock. One side of it is partially caved in, reminding Don of a stroke victim. The porch railings are hanging askew, the window screens are rusted halfway up. And in spite of all he knows about how annihilation can come in the blink of an eye, Don is shocked that all this could have happened so fast just after Hirsch got it all fixed up. It looks like mockery. It seems as if decay was waiting there all along, just behind the paint, the varnish, the shingles, just waiting for a gust of wind to blow away its disguise and reveal it at the core of things.

"In the midst of life..." he mutters, and wrestling with the key in the lock of Hirsch's door, he suddenly feels blind with fatigue. Entering the living-room, he dimly sees Hirsch's couch and lurches toward it, stumbling over a pile of books on the floor. Pausing only to take off his shoes, he lies down and falls into an exhausted sleep, threaded with dreams of people with lost eyes, coming and going in the glaring light of the cafeteria.

He wakes an hour or so later, opens his eyes and stares for a minute before his mind begins to take in what he sees, which is the ruin of Hirsch's library. Books lie all over the floor, askew, open and bloated. Don winces. He knows how this would hurt Hirsch. Reluctantly, he goes over to take a closer look. *Other Inquisitions* by Jorge Luis Borges, *Wuthering Heights*, by Emily Brontë, *Structure and*

History in Greek Mythology and Ritual, by someone named Burkert. All these attempts to describe the indescribable. All these orderly little creations, swamped and stinking.

Don hesitates, puzzled. Should he try to reclaim some of the books? Some of them are beyond repair. And what about mildew? He seems to remember reading that mildew is contagious and spreads from book to book. Is there some way to stop it? Or is Hirsch's whole library beyond repair? Don looks around at the shelves, wondering what he should do. The phrase "beyond repair" echoes in his mind, and he thinks of the many people he talked to in the school cafeteria whose lives, when temporarily suspended by the flood, seemed either in pieces or on the verge of breaking apart, or roughly patched together and in danger of shattering any minute. And then there is this mystery disease that killed Deidre Brockie and is threatening Hirsch, but no one knows why.

Don feels a dark turmoil within himself and covers his face with his hands. Deidre Brockie died two days ago. Hirsch's books are mocked and desecrated by the flood. Is Hirsch, too, ruined beyond repair? Eyes closed, Don sits on the couch and tries to quiet his breathing.

Christ, he muses, had this idea that no one was beyond repair. A radical, dangerous idea that caused people to act in all kinds of foolhardy and self-destructive ways. Don smiles. The tingly feeling from the shaft of light in his dream returns, and he suddenly feels a kind of dizzy excitement at the idea of surrendering his own safety, comfort, ego, life—because nothing can be ruined—and boldly entering the lives of others—because nothing can be ruined—to bring them good things. Or at least to keep them company in pain. The tingly feeling lasts about a minute, and Don, eyes still closed, is engulfed in its light. Then he comes back to ordinary consciousness, and looking around the room, realizes that he still has no idea what to do next. Pick out a couple of undamaged books and take them to Hirsch? Plan his new future life of fearless ministry? And then, someone needs to clean up here before the mold and rot get too far along. What to do? It occurs to him that the Madonna is lying, wrapped carefully in blankets, on the back seat of his car. He decides to consult her.

In the car, he has barely unwound the blanket from around her, has barely glimpsed her beautiful face, when his next step becomes as clear to him as if it were something he knew but just forgot. Obviously, he needs to go to Hirsch, to bring him what he can bring him. Perhaps he can call someone from there—Bob Atkins will know someone—to look in on the house. But see Hirsch first. With surprising calm, he acknowledges the possibility that this lopsided house in front of him may soon—may already—belong to no one. So first things first. Don's sitting in the car with the door open and quickly wraps up the Madonna, stows her, and runs into the house to pick up a couple of clean books. Pulling out of the driveway, he notices that the sun has emerged from behind the clouds, and he smiles in greeting.

•

Jeanne is thinking of Don as she looks around at her own jumbled house. In spite of the daunting mess in front of her, she smiles, remembering Don clambering clumsily over her porch railing and the two of them swimming with the wailing Fred in tow. A lot has happened since then. Ignoring the chaos, she hoists her bag higher on her shoulder and climbs the stairs to her attic bedroom, which is relatively undamaged. The one thing she longed for during her exile was to meditate in her own room, with her own little altar and the sunlight falling on the floor in just the way it does.

She decides to do that first, before anything else, and, slipping her bag off her shoulder, settles down in the lotus position on her turquoise meditation pillow, breathing quietly. After a few false starts, her mind begins to slow down. As she meditates, the sun outside breaks from behind a cloud and sunlight pours in the window. She sees the light from inside her eyelids—touches it—swims in it—tastes it—swallows it. It swallows her. Gears of thought stop grinding and fall silent. The silence of the room grows ripe and sweet. Time drifts like a water flower, blooming quietly, opening slowly, blooming at the speed of blooming.

When she wakes, the sun is in a different place. Her saliva has stopped flowing, but her mouth is not dry. She's not sure that her heart has been beating. She is warm and calm and can't remember why anything might have been worrying her. It's a long time before she feels like moving. The dampness of the house smells strangely good to her—calm and fertile. When she moves she stands slowly, stretches, and gently unwinds Cathy's scarf from the tarot deck.

22

Terry decides to go over Pete's head and call the CDC. They turn her down at first—not enough fatalities to warrant an investigation—but then they mention that someone who works for them vacations on the Outer Banks and isn't currently on assignment. When they say his name, Terry realizes that he is the father of a high school girl she tutored for a few years in college to make extra money. She never met him, but remembers that he was a single father and that he wrote her a grateful letter when his daughter's interest in biology was rekindled.

And so it is that a week later, epidemiologist Ed Shapiro drives into town with Terry's phone number in his pocket. He has been warned about the flooding, so he's prepared for the fact that he will not be seeing the town of Jasper at its best. Traffic on Route 1 was delayed several times as road crews pushed the sand dunes back where they wanted them. In Jasper, where he's arranged to meet Dr. Baker, many gutters are still running and many others are broken, water pouring violently through the breach and onto the ground.

A couple of restaurants have posted cheery signs, "WE ARE OPEN," and there is a certain amount of hard recovery work being done, but lost-looking people still wander around with armfuls of miscellaneous possessions, and a sodden, moldy smell lingers around houses and parked cars. To Ed, that kind of smell signals a bacteria festival. E-coli, salmonella, tetanus, hepatitis, malaria, doing their victory dances, likely to the tune of "Happy Days Are Here Again."

Waiting in the Bluebird, Terry chews nervously on her straw, which yields a faint taste of plastic and root beer. She looks at her notes, which she's been trying to make organized and clear. The name, "Ed Shapiro," is written at the top of the first page, and she's waiting at the Bluebird to meet him. She's very glad he's coming. When he walks in and looks around, she knows right away it's him, and she's even gladder that he's come.

For his part, Ed Shapiro, when he walks into the cafe, meets the eyes of a slight, blonde girl, and he can't figure out her expression. She's looking at him as if he's just told her something very surprising. Her lips are parted and her brown eyes are wide and bright. He's been running over in his mind the various reactions that the people here might have to him, but this was not one that he anticipated. Then her expression changes, as if she's recognized him, though he's pretty sure they've never met. And then she walks over to him and asks timidly, "Dr. Shapiro?"

"Yes," he says.

"Hi," she says, holding out her hand, "I'm Terry Baker."

"Dr. Baker!" he says, unable to keep a note of surprised delight out of his voice. She blushes as he shakes her hand, and he feels his own face growing warm. How very strange. They take a table, and in spite of its being her territory, he offers to buy her coffee, and she accepts. Bringing it to her, he feels a spurt of pleasure when their eyes meet. Then they get situated, get out notebooks and pens and settle down to work.

After about half an hour, he has a rough picture of the situation—one case non-fatal to her knowledge (Drew Layman), two cases definitely and swiftly fatal (Barry Anderson and Deidre Brockie), and one man (Alan Hirsch) comatose in Norfolk with the same symptoms. No fresh fatalities or suspicious symptoms since she made her report. He outlines the next few steps of his procedure, the interviews, questionnaires, and examination of relevant sites. Then it seems natural for them to have dinner together.

They take her car, which is small and modest, with a pile of papers in the back seat and a thin layer of sand on the floor. She suggests The Sandpiper Inn, where the dead lady worked, but he decides on the way there just to relax and have dinner and not try to set up any interviews. Better to let them see his friendly face, drop a few compliments, leave a big tip so they'll be pleased to see him next time. And involuntarily he sneaks a glance at Terry. In profile she looks very young, with her fine bones and straight hair. Suddenly she glances at him and smiles shyly. The worry lines in her forehead are becoming to her. Her brown eyes are bright and curious and—what is the word—nourishing, somehow. Riding beside her in the sunny car, Ed feels a momentary disorientation. What town is this? What car is this? What body is this he's riding in, filled with unfamiliar, exhilarating lightness?

HIGH TIDE

23

Shortly after the flood waters subside, a strange, warm breeze begins to blow on the coast, from Norfolk down to Hatteras. People pace and promenade on piers and beaches, feeling that something is coming, something is changing. It's as if they can feel time passing through them, through and away. They feel it on their bodies and relax and awaken to it as their pores open and their blood quickens a little. But then they realize it's December, and they tense up again, suspecting some sort of trick. This can't be right, wrapping Christmas presents on the porch, in shorts.

An old man comes into The Cove one afternoon, looking very uneasy, has a few beers and ends up bending the bartender's ear about the weather. "Warm December, full cemetery," says the old man, "that's what they used to say when I was a boy."

Ed Shapiro, who is sitting nearby, takes out a small notebook and jots this down, along with the place and time he heard it. Then he goes out onto the deck, where Terry is standing at the railing with a beer. He joins her there, smiling at the sunny sea and breathing deeply. Don't get this kind of air much in Atlanta. He feels the kind of euphoria that often follows insufficient sleep. He and Terry were up late last-night compiling data, kissing, crying. They agreed that they shouldn't go too fast, that circumstances have thrown them together, that they live too many miles apart. Then they embraced and kissed again and again and again. He found during one embrace that his neck was wet with tears, and heard Terry saying softly, "The thing is, it's already going too fast."

"I know," he agreed, speaking into her hair, and for a while he was too scared to kiss her or look at her.

He held her in his arms and grew dizzy with contradictory sensations—that he knew every fiber of her being and that he didn't know her at all—that she was precious and delicate, that she was dangerous and powerful, that he'd been hungering for years for just this moment, that he was too old for this crap anymore. But he went on holding her and, feeling her tremble a little, he found himself stroking her hair, saying, "Sh-sh-sh, it'll be all right, it'll be okay…"

•

After a week of bailing, wet-vacuuming, de-molding and disinfecting, The Sandpiper is open again. Shona is working the evening shift. Every now and then she remembers that Deidre is dead and stands still, waiting for it to sink in, waiting to grieve, but mostly she just keeps moving, on automatic pilot. There's been plenty to do after the flood, and "Jacky-boy" seems too overwhelmed even to hire extra help.

There's been no conversation between them except what's practical or logistical, even when they arranged and attended Deidre's funeral and funeral reception. Shona has the feeling that Jack is just putting one foot in front of another, like she is. She hasn't heard from Barry since the day after the Hallowe'en party. He'd spent the night at The Sandpiper, but, according to Deidre, who was up early drinking Bloody Marys the next morning, he'd left before 8:00 a.m. when he heard that his parents were coming, even though he was very sick, taking a cab back to his place. Now he's not working at The Cove any more, but no one knows why, and his cell phone number isn't working. She's half worried and half pissed, because she could use someone to talk to and someone to cuddle, and Barry was good at both. Kenny has stopped coming around.

Shona is more than ready to knock off work when Terry Baker comes in with a big, balding dark-eyed guy she's never seen before. It surprises Shona to realize, after a few minutes, that Terry's attracted to this old guy. Terry keeps smiling and blushing, and even laughs once or twice, throwing her head back. She and Terry have had drinks a couple of times now at Dan's Pub over in Hatteras, getting tipsy on margaritas and talking about dead mothers.

This guy with Terry is polite and funny when he orders, but she still can't get what Terry sees in him. Gradually, she admits that he has a really nice smile. And he does have those dark eyes—the kind some dark-eyed people have that seem to get deeper and deeper, so that if you look at them too long you feel like you might fall into them. Maybe he's not so bad. And Shona allows herself a moment of satisfaction to think that Terry might be dating. She's seemed a little lonely and…uptight to Shona. Maybe this'll do her good.

Suddenly Shona becomes aware that Jack is sitting in an out-of-the-way booth, staring at her. His posture has changed since Mom died. He slumps now. Shona tries to be patient with her dad, but he's really been getting on her nerves. In fact, lately she can barely stand the sight of him, and she's lost her temper at him a couple of times for no real reason. Then she hates herself for being a shallow, unsympathetic bitch. Then she immediately wants to go shopping (but there's no one to go with) or have sex (but Kenny's avoiding her) and then she feels guilty for that, so she smokes pot and watches old movies—*All About Eve, Breakfast at Tiffany's, A Hard Day's Night*—and stops feeling like shit for a while, until the screen goes blank. She watched *Meet Me in St. Louis* and realized that Christmas is coming in a few weeks, and the thought makes her want to throw herself into the sea.

Now, behind the bar, pouring red wine for Ed, she tears up a little but brushes it away. Again, she wishes she could talk to Barry. But, she thinks, that's probably what I deserve for not sticking with him when he got sick. Suddenly, she remembers how Deidre took care of Barry when he passed out at the Hallowe'en party, taking his temperature and putting cool washcloths on his forehead.

After Ed and Terry have finished their lunch but before she brings them the bill, Shona sits down unceremoniously at their table and says, "Hey, Terry, can I ask you something?"

"Sure," says Terry, a little startled.

"Is it possible that what Mom died of was contagious?"

Ed and Terry are silent so long and look at each other so meaningfully that Shona, looking from one to the other, says, "What? What is it?"

Finally, Terry clears her throat and says, "Shona, this is Dr. Ed Shapiro from the CDC. He's come to investigate just that question."

"Oh!" says Shona.

"I wasn't going to ask you quite so abruptly," says Ed, but I wonder if you and your father would be willing to talk to me about your mother's illness and answer a few questions."

"Oh!" says Shona.

"Not right now," says Ed. "I'd be glad to set up an appointment when it's convenient for you."

Shona looks at her watch. "I'll be off in an hour," she says. "Can you hang around that long?"

Ed looks at Terry, who shrugs her assent. "We'll be here," says Ed. "Thank you, Miss—"

"Oh, this is Shona Brockie," says Terry.

Shona shakes hands with Ed and, seeing him smile, once again finds herself happy for Terry.

"See you in an hour," she says. "Yell if you need anything."

They watch her walk away.

"Sometimes it happens that way," says Ed. "She doesn't seem to be panicking?"

"No," says Terry, "I don't think she's the type."

"Good," says Ed. "Now, where was I?"

"Meetings," says Terry.

"Oh yes—the health department people first and then city officials and anyone local who might be helpful. But meanwhile, you and I and the team are going to need to speculate wildly about what might be causing this thing and at the same time, prevent the general public from speculating wildly."

"We're going to speculate wildly?" asks Terry.

"Oh yes," says Ed. "This is a wild creature. Wild speculation is the only way to understand it. Well—the right kind of wild speculation. We may hear people asserting with great certainty that Russians or Chinese or space aliens are bombarding us with mutant organisms, that our own government has lost control of its biological weapons or even that they're intentionally conducting experiments on unsuspecting citizens."

"Oh, but surely only crazy people—"

"Oh, but wait; think about it. How much less 'crazy' do scientific accounts of viruses seem when you think about it? For instance: are they alive or not? They propagate, so they're alive, right? Well, they propagate, but they don't grow!"

Ed leans forward for emphasis and repeats, "They don't grow!"

Terry thinks he's acting a little like a scientist in an early scene from a horror movie, but she has to admit, it is for some reason a creepy image. Things that never change, only reproduce. A vision of the kitchen at FasterBurger's kitchen pops into her mind, from when she worked there in the summers during high school. All those completely identical patties, parading past, on their way to conquer the world....

"Some say," continues Ed, "that viruses are rogue genetic material. Instead of reproducing by division, or by intersection of eggs and sperm, they're using our bodies. And the reason our bodies' defenses don't work well against them is that we can't recognize them as 'other.' They seem too much like part of us."

"They propagate but don't grow," murmurs Terry, still stuck on that idea. "Talk about the 'unexamined life'!"

"Oh, but they definitely think their lives are worth living," says Ed. "In fact, that's all they think, if you can call it thinking. They want to live. The ones that infect us do it because they can't live without us. We are their world."

24

In Norfolk, between visits to Hirsch in the hospital, Marika follows a regular schedule: get up around noon, breakfast at a greasy spoon with a Danish cook near the motel, eating toast and listening to his accent as he calls out the orders. Visiting hours at the hospital are two to six. After making inquiries of the nurses and, if he happens by, the doctor—just letting them know she's watching and she's not stupid—she usually reads.

When visiting hours are over, she walks along the nearby docks in a pea-coat and knit hat, scowling at the sea and passing sailors. At eight or so she hits the bars. She drinks and plays pool till whenever, witheringly rejecting passes, not wanting to be touched even by so much as a handshake or a friendly look. Back to the motel. Sometimes the cab ride wakes her up, and she has to take a hot shower to help her sleep, waking up the next morning with her hair tangled and matted.

The goal of her evenings is to get worn out enough and drunk enough to sleep without dreaming. She also has to try to remember to eat dinner, or she can't sleep or sleeps too lightly and dreams tease the edges of her mind, roiling dreams full of scummy water with unknown forms—animals, seaweed, men—twisting here and there just below the surface. Then back to the hospital the next day. Sometimes she runs into Hirsch's priest friend, Cathcart.

•

As a priest, Don Cathcart has been in quite a few hospital rooms in his day, with quite a few people. He has been surprised, over the years, at how differently people, especially women, behave. The men are mostly lost—capable only of disjointed small-talk, absurdly grateful to be assigned any practical task, particularly one that will take them out of the room for a bit to fetch someone or something.

But the women—some of them seem unable to stop playing hostess. Doggedly, they keep conversation going about things that are unspeakable—which often rules out what's been going on in the room they're in—determined to offer food and drink, sometimes napkins, and, on one occasion, even moist towelettes. Others well up in tears as soon as they see Don, embrace him passionately, and speak through a continual flow of tears with fervent gratitude and desperate optimism.

Marika, on the other hand, makes no effort to greet him when he enters Hirsch's room, but glares at him numbly.

To Don it seems as if she's thinking "What's the point of you coming here? There's nothing you can do. Nothing I can do. Nothing to be done but sit here in this trap and wait."

And in fact she has the tense, unfocused look of a prisoner. Her clothes are wrinkled, her hair is tangled, and her blue eyes have an empty, wintery look. Empty, that is, except for what strikes Don as a fine, clean rage. So they skip the greetings.

"How is he?" asks Don. "Has he—"

"He's opened his eyes twice when I've been here," says Marika

"And did he—?"

"Did he know me? I think so. But—" There is a long silence, during which Don senses a struggle within her.

This woman has strong feelings and doesn't want them. She is struggling to believe she has a choice in the matter. Don knows better than to try to get her to release her emotions or confront them or accept them or any of the other things people recommend doing with them nowadays. She'll have to deal with them somehow, but only she will be able to figure out how. From the look of her, it won't be easy. But now he waits, respecting her struggle.

Her tone is level and dry when she says, "Maybe I just imagined that he did."

Don nods. Then, with his mysterious new lack of shyness, he meets her eyes and says, "You seem angry."

Marika flashes him a blue look and a tight little smile but doesn't reply.

Don looks at Hirsch hooked up to tubes, his chest barely rising and falling, his face expressionless, and feels anger rising in his own chest. Where is Hirsch now? Where are their conversations, where is their friendship and all the things they had yet to learn about each other? Then he imagines how terrible this must be for Marika, who's known Hirsch more briefly, but so much more intensely. He resolves to see more of her, and after a dry leave-taking, he goes to the tiny hospital chapel to pray for her. Hirsch he leaves to God, who, he assumes, is hovering anxiously over his unconscious friend, preparing in His own time, either to take his life or restore it.

•

A soft warm breeze. The residents of Jasper feel it in the tender places of their bodies. It sighs, they sigh back. Their bodies relent a little, let down their guard. The breeze is gentle. It comes and goes. When it's still, people forget about it. They perspire a little, and when it comes again they appreciate it all the more. Their clothing stirs, brushing against their skin, awakening it. They notice the clouds above them—scattered, drifting, diaphanous, playing with the light. They lean their heads back and notice the way the clouds unwind in slow, sensuous spirals. They feel free to look at them as long as they like. They feel they are becoming like the clouds—soft and easily moved. Gently, calmly, sweetly, they unfurl.

•

But in the world of smaller things—grasshoppers, beetles, mosquitoes, microbes—the unusual warmth is speeding things up. Breeding has accelerated. More creatures are being born faster. Some accelerate faster than others. Some swarm wildly, while others, who normally would have been eating them by now, are still working on getting born. So the microworld goes a little out of whack. Then the coots and swans and ducks and geese, who feed on tiny things, face yet another change in the rhythm of their lives. Some creatures grow hungry. Some, including the microbes now living in Hirsch's bloodstream and lungs, thrive and get fat.

25

Lynn is getting used to the routine of living in exile on Uncle Roy's farm in Zebulon. Every morning, she heads out to feed the pigs. She's taken this chore over from Uncle Roy since his arthritis flared up a few weeks ago, though he was reluctant to surrender it. Aunt Sally is happy to play with Kyle while Lynn is out. This morning, Lynn's mood lifts as she slips out the door and takes the back path toward the hog run, the rising sun in her eyes. She smiles, remembering how carefully Uncle Roy drilled her in the steps of counting the pigs, what to notice, what not to leave out, what to be careful of, which ones were likely to do what. There are twenty-seven in all, and Uncle Roy has trained them to come to him by feeding them cast-off too-small eggs from the henhouse.

They come now without eggs, even to her, just on the off-chance. Uncle Roy runs a free-range farm, and the pigs mostly occupy some scrub woods at the farm's southern edge. Pigs, Lynn has learned, are naturally woodland creatures. Also they're quieter than she'd imagined before meeting them. She reaches the half-frozen stream before they appear, beginning with one large group of eight, picking their way through tree roots, sniffing the ground.

They travel in a close group, often rubbing against and clambering gently over one another. Every now and then they let out a quiet, satisfied grunt, a sound that Lynn has come to think of as polite small talk. Sometimes there's a brief, snorting skirmish and two pigs part. Every now and then, one of them gets spooked for no apparent reason and breaks into a run, followed by several others. Lynn has become used to their ways and finds it relaxing to sit and watch them. There's something about their quiet togetherness and the way they take it for granted that soothes her. Surrounded by their smooth, busy bodies, she finds that her thoughts subside, her sense of self pleasantly loosened and replaced with a simple sense of "us." This feeling of togetherness is a balm for her homesickness, which, though she never speaks of it, is a little sore place inside her.

Kenny has been sending Kyle little postcards with pictures of animals on them—a crab, a bluefish, a pelican. On the back will be a simple, instructive message, such as:

THESE CRITTERS ARE PRETTY STRANGE. THEY LIVE ON THE BEACH. THEY WALK SIDEWAYS AND BURY THEMSELVES IN THE SAND. MAYBE WE'LL CATCH ONE WHEN YOU GET BACK. THEY LIKE TO PINCH, SO WE'LL HAVE TO BE CAREFUL.

Lynn has helped Kyle pick out postcards of pigs, cows, horses, and chickens to send back to his father. She draws a line down the middle and writes the address on the right and then Kyle draws whatever he wants to on the left. Usually it's a collection of circles with lines beneath them. Kyle explains their identities, saying, "Mama,

Dada, Gampa…" Once he attempted a dog, which consisted of another circle with five lines beneath it and an enormous smile, not something that showed up in his drawings of his family. He said the dog's name was Bluey, and Kenny has sent messages to Bluey in subsequent cards. Pete calls and sometimes asks to talk to Kyle, but neither of them is much good on the phone.

Lynn treads carefully, stepping from the field into the pigs' wood. A pretty little stream runs through it. The quiet of the place seems Eden-like to Lynn, and she has brought a journal with her. She sits for some time in the morning quiet of the place. She gazes at the water, following its curves and eddies as it rolls over rocks and around tree roots with a gentle gurgling sound that seems to enrich the silence rather than break it.

She opens her journal and writes:

> Thinking about all the waters of the earth, about water itself, this one element that lives in so many places, how it beats against the rocks of Newfoundland, runs through the gutters of Belfast, sucks down detritus in the Amazon and Alabama Rivers, carries junks on the Yangtze, sits in puddles on a red dirt road in Georgia, shifts in a New Zealand Glacier, collects in clouds over St. Petersburg and St. Croix, rises in the mouth of a hungry dog, spills from the eyes of a grieving woman. And it is all one. It is all the same water.

After writing, Lynn feels moved, as if the stream is flowing through her too, and she sits for a long time with the journal open as the sun climbs higher, and its light begins to play on the water.

Then she awakens from her trance and looking around, finds that several pigs are lying quite near her in the dappled shade. She smiles, overtaken again by the sense of "us" that she feels around them. She carries this feeling back to the house, where she washes her hands and kisses Kyle's warm cheek to waken him.

•

In Jasper, in the back room of The Sandpiper, Pete and Jack drink. Pete clinks the ice in his glass, staring contentedly down at the golden liquid. He considers himself a complete convert to whiskey, and Jack's been muttering lately about introducing him to the delights of vodka and gin. The two talk about drinking even more than they drink, which is quite a damn bit. Jack has even started to go on about "fine wine." Pete thinks he'll draw the line at all that sniffing and gargling, but he can't be sure. These days he seems to have forgotten why he ever wanted a backbone.

One thing they never talk about is Deidre, but as far as Pete is concerned she's usually sitting there with them as they drink. As is Cathy. After all these years he's finally accepted the fact that she's never going to leave him. Today he finds himself telling Jack about it.

"They say that nuclear fallout has a half-life," he tells him. "Lasts for a hundred years, a thousand years. Well, I have a half-wife. That's what she is. Little Cathy. My little half-wife. God bless her."

Jack stares at him with intense embarrassment, but Pete, having gone this far, refuses to stop.

"To Cathy," he shouts, waving his whiskey in the general direction of the empty Sandpiper dining room. "My little half-wife," he repeats, mercilessly, clinking Jack's glass.

"You're a maniac," says Jack, clinking glasses with him nonetheless.

"Yup," says Pete, confidently, "and you're a son-of-a-bitch.'

Jack nods wearily. "Yeah," he says, "I've been meaning to do something about that."

Then he lowers his head to the table and, apparently, passes out. This is the first time Pete has ever out-drunk him, if only by a couple of sips. Not, perhaps, as Cathy points out, his greatest accomplishment. Then she reminds him—lightly, 'cause she never was a nag—that he should probably sober up and make it an early night on account of the press conference about the virus and then the big hoo-hah "banquet" thing tomorrow night.

He hoists himself to his feet and is about to leave when he catches sight of Jack sprawled on the table. Looking at him, he remembers how young Jack is—might be fifteen years between them. Without knowing why, he dips three fingers in some ice water and runs them across Jack's forehead. Poor clueless bastard. He dips his fingers again and does his own forehead for good measure. Then home for a snooze. The hoohah thing tomorrow is a stand-in for the aborted "Maritime Christmas Festival" that he and Jack were planning before the flood. Bands, vendors, pirate costumes, the whole nine yards. But the flood put a crimp in their style, and when Jack realized it was too well-publicized to be comfortably canceled, he tweaked it into a party at The Sandpiper to honor "heroes of the flood," with some of the money going to flood restoration. Smart cookie. But Pete can't shake a strange combination of apathy and foreboding. He takes a belt of whiskey and waits eagerly for the warm numbness that follows.

In the Chamber of Commerce conference room the next morning, he tries to refrain from wincing at the reporters' flash bulbs.

"Man that's bright," he says to Ed Shapiro in an undertone. "Can't they come up with some kind of dimmer technology?"

Ed grins, but Pete notices that Ed doesn't refer any of the reporters' questions to him, so he musters his energy to concentrate and bring what he can to the situation—not be a weak link. By the time Ed has filled them in, he has formulated a statement.

After greeting the reporters and thanking each of them by name for coming, he says, "I've lived here all my life, and during that time I've seen Bankers go through a lot of ups and downs—storms, recessions, hard times—and I have every confidence that we deal with whatever's thrown at us. We welcome the assistance of Mr. Shapiro and the Centers for Disease Control, and we will cooperate fully with whatever measures are necessary to contain and fight this disease. I know my neighbors, and I can assure you all that cool heads will prevail. We will now take questions."

•

Later that evening, when the Maritime Christmas Banquet Honoring Heroes of the Flood is about to begin, Shona sits on the Sandpiper's deck, resting up after back-to-back double shifts over the weekend. She is wearing a gauzy green summer dress. It's a little too chilly for it, so she's also wearing Kenny's jacket, which hangs on her like a coat.

Kenny is beside her, staring out to sea. The flood-benefit party hasn't started yet, but a few other couples are milling around. Kenny is apparently thinking hard about something. Shona kind of wishes it was her. She can't stand Daddy fussing over her, but she kind of wishes someone would.

As if he's read her thoughts, Kenny turns to her, putting a friendly hand on her shoulder and says, "How're you doin', kid?"

Better than nothing, thinks Shona. She feels lost, like a little stray cat, but she lifts her chin bravely and replies, "I'm okay. How you doin'?"

"I miss my son," says Kenny, without missing a beat, as if he's been longing to say it. Shona is surprised and says nothing. "And I expect you miss your mom," says Kenny, looking right at her. Again Shona can't speak. It seems like there are all kinds of things to say—there's a script for this situation, but she doesn't have it or can't read it, and here she is on the spot, tongue-tied.

"This virus thing—whatever it is—I guess they'll come up with a name for it soon," says Kenny. "Pretty scary, huh?"

Shona nods. There's some kind of pressure building up inside her. Now it's she who's looking out to sea—far, far out. She wishes Kenny would shut up and put his arms around her. Or she wishes she could fly. "If I had wings, like Noah's dove…" the words of one of Barry's favorite songs cross her mind and she is filled with silent, desperate longing.

Last week, Barry's parents called Jack to ask about the circumstances surrounding Barry's death. That was when Shona found out he died. His parents didn't even know about her. No one else told her about Barry, either, not even Terry. Shona sips her drink, wondering when this terrible numbness will pass.

•

Farther down the railing Ed and Terry are sharing a beer. Terry, looking out at the scudding blue waves, seems to be wilting a little. Ed knows that it's because she is blaming herself for the two virus-related deaths, thinking she should have acted faster.

"It's not your fault," he says, "and you standing there thinking so is just a waste of time. Believe me, I know what I'm talking about."

After a minute she nods and, turning her head, smiles up at him. And he sees that she does. Believe him. She turns her body to him and allows him to embrace her, and the breeze curves around their bodies, caressing them briefly and moving on.

Nearby, Don Cathcart sips red wine and gazes out at the sound. Beside him, Marika downs a neat whiskey. Neither of them is in a festive mood, and though Don convinced her (and himself) to come to the party as a "mental health break" and a respite from Hirsch's hospital room, they both feel they have come for the liquor, and neither of them has spoken much except to take each other's drink orders.

Then, suddenly, Marika looks up from her empty glass and says, "They should look in the estuaries."

"For the source of the disease?" asks Don.

Marika nods. "Estuaries are where most things around here are born and grow—insects, crustaceans, fish, algae, microbes. It—they—are probably hanging in there somewhere, though finding them may not be easy."

Don nods, somewhat stunned. Then Marika begins very clearly to espouse a theory of her own, involving water, microbes, animal vectors and something called a dinoflagellate. Don can't follow it all.

"I heard a rumor that someone's here from the Center for Disease Control," he says, "checking things out. Maybe you should talk to him."

Marika says nothing to that, but he can see that she is interested, that she is considering it. For a moment she loses the closed look of someone who's merely enduring the time that's passing, and he sees that there is in her a gaunt kind of beauty. A strange woman, but he has no qualms about her ability to haunt the hospital and look after the unconscious Hirsch.

He is snapped out of his reverie by Jack Brockie announcing that dinner is served. Don is dreading the speeches of congratulations and the necessity of laughing at jokes and forming facial expressions that he hopes approximate correct responses to conversation. To his relief and pleasure, he is seated by Jeanne Dubovsky. He feels comfortable with her. After the speeches, they chat easily until the dessert dishes are cleared away. The thump-thump-thump of the dance band can be heard from out on the deck. Jeanne looks pensive for a minute and then broaches the topic.

"This disease—have you heard of anyone else coming down with it?" asks Jeanne.

"No, but I know quite a few who are worried about it," says Don. "Word's definitely gotten out." Jeanne smiles at him, raising an eyebrow, and he adds, "You're the only person I told about it before the press conference."

"Oh!" says Jeanne. And then, after a small pause, "Why?"

There is another pause, as Don sorts this out. "Well, as I suppose you know, you're easy to talk to, a quality I always wish I had more of.

And also…" He shifts his stance to indicate a slight shift of subject. "When we were all in the cafeteria during the flood…when we were trapped with each other, 'twenty-four-seven,' as the kids say—"

He breaks off, searching for words, and tries another tack. "I'm really a very shy person, which is one reason, maybe the main reason, that I left the church. I don't know. Anyway, the point is, there in the cafeteria I seemed to have some kind of awakening. It was as if my shyness disappeared, and suddenly I was able to be with people in the way I'd always wanted to be, and even help a few of them without getting in my own way."

He looks at Jeanne and sees that she is listening closely and seems to understand, so he continues. "I have to tell you," he says, "it was such a relief! It was as if I'd been in prison all my life, and one morning I woke up and the door was just standing open, and I was free." He closes his eyes for a minute, and when he opens them they are moist. "Do you know what I mean?" he asks Jeanne.

She nods. Her eyes are wide—with fear? With joy? He can't tell.

"What I mean is that it seemed to me that you might have been feeling something similar." Don looked at her.

"Oh yes," says Jeanne. They sit quietly for a few minutes. Then Jeanne speaks. "I remember once, when I was in massage school in Wilmington, I was sitting on a park bench on this little square across from the school, and a lady came and sat down next to me. She tried to strike up a conversation—I don't even remember what she said—something fairly ordinary—and she was clean and not raggedy or anything, but you could tell she wasn't quite right. Her—what do they call it?—her 'affect' was, I don't know, I guess she had some kind of mental illness, though not scary or anything. But I guess I was startled, because I got up and left before I finished my lunch. She had just sat down. I saw her face, and she was crushed. And as I walked away, I felt drained. I felt exhausted, just exhausted. Every time I've thought of it, from that day to this, I feel exhausted. But in the cafeteria, during the flood, I felt wonderful. I massaged people and talked to them and listened to them and ran errands. It didn't matter who they were or what they looked like or what was going on with them. I never seemed to get tired. It's like there was no room there for barriers, and once they were down you realized what a lot of energy went into keeping them up. But now that things are getting back to normal, I find they're all going up again. It's like they just build themselves. I mean, I'm alone, and—I don't know." She shrugs and rubs some condensation from her wine glass.

"But it doesn't have to go away!" says Don excitedly. "It doesn't, don't you see? We were granted a shift in perception, a glimpse of the truth. Well, we can't stay face-to-face with the truth all the time, that's just not the way we're made. But once we've seen it, we can keep following the path that led us there. We can keep moving on the assumption that the bottom line is still the same—I don't think I'm putting this very well."

"It hasn't left you, has it?"

"What?"

"That feeling from the cafeteria. You still have it."

"Yes, I do. I've been blessed."

"But how does all this answer the question of why you told me about the...disease...or whatever it is?"

Don looks straight at her for a moment, as if hoping she'll give him the answer to this question. "I'm not sure, actually," he says. "I don't know."

After a brief silence, they laugh a little and pass on to review the banquet and gossip about the people they met during the flood. At one point, Don catches sight of a clock and is startled to realize that they have been talking for two and a half hours. She is nursing the same glass of wine she had when they started talking and, remarkably, so is he.

•

And still the strange, warm breeze blows all up and down the Banks, an unexpected but persuasive visitor, quickening the blood like a gentle touch, in all kinds of veins. In the morning, at the Pea Island Sanctuary, it ruffles the down of the tired swans, and they shake themselves a little and preen, stirred out of their poised melancholy for a moment. Some of them look around in that flat, sharp way of birds. Some females wrap their wings a little more tightly around their young. A few bend their necks to look for food in the water, but there isn't any. There were fewer places to rest on the way here, and the swans are weary.

And now that they're here it's been harder to gather their strength because there's so little to eat. Some days the water seems almost lifeless. Bits of detritus twist in the lazy current, pieces of things that once were alive, occasionally fooling a desperate bird into swooping down for them. The swans do not have the strength for flight, and, after acknowledging the warm breeze by coming alive for a moment, tossing their heads or cocking them to one side, they sink back into uneasy dormancy.

As they do, the microbe unfurls in the warming waters, blooming luxuriantly. It's different now from the creature that was born of the union of swan and pig muck. It's been through several generations of evolution, dying by the millions, evolving by the trillions, learning the behaviors, the weaknesses, the attractions, the codes of its newest, most succulent host. It knows how to attack and how to retreat. It's more complicated now, more nimble, more adaptable. It understands us better.

•

The next day, in his motel room in Jasper, Ed checks and cross-checks surveys. The most crucial one is from the only person who seems to have contracted the disease and recovered, a builder named Drew Layman. He will interview Layman and his wife tomorrow. See if he'll consent to donate some blood to the cause.

Ed has made tactful overtures to the families of the two dead victims, the middle-aged hotelkeeper, Deidre Brockie, and the young bartender, Barry Anderson. Can I dig up your loved one and take some of his blood? Medicine worse than the cure. But the boy's father seemed to understand that this is war. His wife, though, and Deidre Brockie's husband, were dazed and mute, like refugees.

Anyway, this Drew Layman: First attack occurred while he was fishing. Rapidly forming rash, disorientation, mild dizziness. Then fatigue and low-grade fever, headache, irritability, some memory loss, mostly neurological symptoms. The high fever and respiratory symptoms that killed the other two didn't show up in him. This was good luck, finding a survivor so soon. The advantage of working in a small place. Not clear whether the one in the hospital, Alan Hirsch, will survive.

Ed leans back and closes his eyes, trying to allow the facts he knows to arrange themselves into a rough sketch of this creature he's preparing to hunt. There's not much of a picture yet—he hasn't been here long enough or talked to enough people. And everything should become clearer when the blood people get involved. But he has to try every day to visualize as much of the picture as he can. It's a kind of spiritual discipline, like drawing a herd of antelope on a cave wall in preparation for encountering them in the wild.

His mind wanders to other microbes he's read about or stalked. This wandering is okay at first. It provides a context, and comparison can help to define the current prey. But eventually these other images will have to fall away so that he can focus, without comparisons or assumptions or distractions, on the thing itself.

A knock on the door startles him. Answering it, he sees a slight, disheveled woman with tangled hair and keen blue eyes. They stare at each other for a few seconds, and then she says,

"Marika Hansen."

Ed nods, awaiting clarification. This is a strange lady. She wears an interrupted expression, as if it's her train of thought, not his, that is being derailed by this sudden encounter. But one can see at a glance that she's intelligent. So he waits.

"I'm Marika Hansen," she says, trying again. "I tried to call, but—"

"I turn off the phone when I'm working," says Ed, without rancor.

"Yes, well, it's about your work that I've come," says Marika. "I'm a—friend of Alan Hirsch, the man who's in the hospital in—Dr. Baker suggested that I—show you some work I've done that may be relevant to this virus."

"Ah yes, of course, Father Cathcart mentioned you might be calling," says Ed. "Please come in."

She comes in, and he sees that she's carrying a large portfolio under her arm. "Please sit down," says Ed.

She does so, leaning the portfolio carefully against a wall.

"Can I get you anything?" he asks.

"No thank you," says Marika, her eyes roaming to the pile of papers on his desk.

"Well, first," says Ed, extracting some paper from an accordion file, "I'd like to ask you to fill out this survey." He puts it in front of her with a sharp new pencil. "There are some multiple choice, some short-answer questions, and a place for further comments," he says, "but I'll be wanting to discuss it with you in detail and ask some more questions verbally, so—"

He sees that she has already looked over the survey, nodded as if in approval, and has begun filling it out. An odd bird, he thinks, but apparently not one for wasting time. That's good.

Quietly, he goes back to his work. He decides against another press conference and instead sends out a press release on the measures being taken, emphasizing the efficiency and professionalism of the medical community and the way that Bankers have always been "resistant to panic."

•

The next morning, Drew Layman reads in his paper:

> While this is as yet an unknown virus and we have
> not ruled out some degree of contagion, there is no

need for alarm. We recommend taking ordinary precautions, such as frequent hand-washing. We will keep the public informed with up-to-date information as we receive it. Jasper is fortunate and in good hands with its own health-care community as well as support from the North Carolina Department of Health and Human Services and the Centers for Disease Control.

Drew nods, reassured, and checks his arms again, as he does every hour or two, to see if the rash has returned. He has been tired and irritable lately, but as he tells Kenny when they meet for a beer, who hasn't? And they joke about the "Middle-Age Virus—MAV."

Marika also reads the press release. She smiles grimly and tosses the paper into the nearest trash can.

•

Meanwhile, Terry is hunched over the computer, emailing doctors up and down the Eastern Seaboard who may or may not be encountering symptoms of the "Outer Banks Virus," as they call it when it needs to be named. She and Ed have come up with an informal checklist of criteria for whether someone's got it or not. The vein rash, fever, irritability, semiconsciousness, respiratory distress, respiratory failure....

Sometimes these days Terry is oppressed with a heavy feeling of suspense, like the feeling right before a big storm, when dark clouds seem to suck up all the air. Pushing herself back from the computer, Terry stares into space, remembering when she was twelve and came down with meningitis. The weakness, the pain, the fever, the delirium—all those were shocking and frightening. The body's betrayal.

But when she woke up in the hospital, it was being alone, or among indifferent strangers, that truly terrified her.

It angered her that no one had mentioned it to her during her medical training—this primal fear of being dropped from the flock, deserted by the herd. But then there it is, and there's almost nothing a busy doctor can really do about it. Only loved ones can help. That's the worst thing about being sick, and a doctor can't fix it.

Terry slumps in her chair disconsolately. But then she remembers what Ed said when they discussed "the compassion thing"—the problem of dealing with sick, scared people without being sucked in or burnt out. And Ed had said—what was it? Don't beat yourself up. If you do, you're going to take your feeling of powerlessness out on the patient. Guilt makes people cold and irritable. You get preoccupied with yourself, and if a chance arises to relieve the patient's alienation in some small way—and these chances do come along every now and then—you'll miss it.

•

In Arlington, Barry's father, Jay, signs more papers, and Barry's body is exhumed and trucked to the hospital in Norfolk. Barry's mother, Sally, tells her support group about the exhumation, and there is a long, stunned silence before one of her fellow bereaved parents rises to embrace her, followed by one or two others.

At the hospital, a pathologist begins to take apart the beautiful, staggeringly complicated body in which Barry once lived. She makes an incision from the throat to the pubic bone and opens up his body—or the body, as it's being called now—to take out the vital organs and weigh them. The lungs are heavy—too heavy—but the heart is light.

<h1 style="text-align:center">26</h1>

It's a pretty big house," says Don, "and there have never been enough people in it." He and Jeanne are drinking coffee in the Bluebird. It's afternoon, and a golden light streams in on the white walls.

"I've talked with my sister, who owns the house with me, and she likes the idea. Actually, she doesn't care one way or the other, but it comes to the same thing for our purposes."

Jeanne raises her eyebrows, and Don raises a hand as if to slow himself down.

"Getting ahead of myself, aren't I? Let me back up. I've told you my idea about a spiritually oriented hospice for people of all different faiths?"

"Yeah, it's a great idea."

"Well, I feel…. What I'm trying to say is that I'd like you to be involved. I'd like you to come and work for me."

"To do massage?"

"Well, that'd be great, but it'd be more than that. You'd coordinate various kinds of—I guess they call them 'alternative therapies.' You know, all that stuff with smells and sounds and—hell, I don't know, pyramids. If people want it."

Jeanne smiles, and he sees that there are tears in her eyes. "I'm honored, Don, I really am, but—" she shakes her head.

"There'd be a salary, of course," says Don. "I know you'd have to relocate, and maybe that's something you don't want to do, but I'd be happy to help you find a place, or if you want to live there at the hospice—" He breaks off.

Jeanne is still shaking her head and a couple of tears have spilled out and are making their way down her cheeks. Slowly, she rolls up her sleeves. Don sees that there are faint red lines on the white skin of wrists and forearms, following the pattern of her veins.

●

The next morning, the hospital calls Don to say that Hirsch has died. Don asks to speak to Marika, but they say that she's gone and has referred them to him on matters of what to do with the body and belongings. Don has talked to Ed Shapiro and knows he'll want an autopsy.

He still has a gnawing, hollow feeling in his stomach from his conversation the day before with Jeanne. He spent the evening in prayer, first with her and then at home in his bedroom in front of the Madonna, clutching his rosary. Tomorrow he'll take her to the hospital and make the arrangements about Hirsch. First, though, he has to try to find Hirsch's lawyer; see if there are any next-of-kin, maybe call the ex-wife. He decides to skip prayer this morning. He can hash this out with God later. Rapidly, he makes a to-do list and picks up the phone. He tries calling Marika's number at the motel, but finds that she has checked out.

Driving to Norfolk, Don thinks about Hirsch. Where is Hirsch now? Right now, he thinks, Hirsch is a hole in my heart, and Jeanne is another one. These holes are spreading like corrosion, or like those holes in the skins of the fish that that Marika lady told him about. He can feel them eating away at him. But no time to patch them up now, if indeed patching is what's called for. There are other things to be done.

Jeanne has elected to take her own car to Norfolk so she can visit a healing arts center before she reports to the hospital. She has warned Don that she might not do everything the doctors tell her to do. He has no problem with that. He doesn't imagine they'll have much to tell her. He has made his phone calls for Hirsch and is driving at night, planning on staying at a motel and being at the hospital first thing in the morning. As he approaches Norfolk, Don feels his throat and shoulders tightening as a sense of chaos begins to encroach upon him. He presses down on the accelerator and speeds on.

•

That night, Marika stands on the beach alone, letting the waves wash up over her feet. She hasn't taken off her shoes. A path of moonlight glitters on the water, and she stares at it, mesmerized. It looks so beautifully cool, so unearthly bright, like something you'd only imagine, something from a fairy tale. Two silver waves come in, falling short of her feet. Then two converge upon her and drench her jeans almost up to the knees. When the water recedes, her jeans feel heavy and her feet sink in the sand up to the ankles. The sea is inhaling her. She knows the tide will go out soon. Maybe she can finally, finally go out with it now. An American phrase comes into her mind: "He asked her out." The sea's been asking her out for so long now. Very persistent. Hirsch wouldn't like it. But Hirsch isn't here, is he?

●

Kenny never walks on the beach at night. He's never really understood why people do that, and it spooks him a little, all those sounds all around but barely being able to see. That soft, uneasy foothold. This walk was Drew's idea—Drew gets these ideas since he got well. Sometimes he seems to enjoy things stone cold sober that would bore Kenny even with a skinful. But he's known Drew a long time, and he's glad to see him well. Plus, he's had the urge lately to just do different things or to do things differently. Like breaking up with the kid, Shona, as much for her sake as for his own. She's a knockout, and he could have gone on sleeping with her; once, he wouldn't have been able to stop. But she's so confused, and there's no way being screwed by some clueless middle-aged jock who's just passing through is going to be much help to her, no matter what she thinks.

"What's that?" says Drew.

"What?" asks Kenny, looking where Drew's looking, out to sea. Something's splashing around out there. The sound of the splashing is covered up by the roar of the sea, but every splash looks like an explosion of moonlight. What is it? No fish would thrash like that unless it was caught or beached.

"My God, Kenny, somebody's out there in trouble," says Drew. As soon as he says it, Kenny thinks that he makes out the shape of a hand, an arm emerging from the spray.

"Oh man, you're right," he says, and then he gets hit by a shot of adrenaline so powerful that it feels like joy, and he finds himself kicking off his shoes and running into the water. Faintly, he hears Drew call "Kenny!" behind him as he plunges into a wave. He swims hard and it feels wonderful, as if he's been released from a straitjacket. Whenever he comes up for air he checks the horizon for that explosion of moonlight, and it's always right there ahead of him. Someone is fighting for life, and it's been a long time since Kenny's been in a good fight.

He finds that he's fighting both the sea and the woman. At first she clings to him, but then she seems to wake up and begins to pull away. He manages to pin her arms and pull her on top of him, kicking lustily toward shore. She squirms and writhes so violently that sometimes they almost turn over, but he finds that he can prevail over her struggles through a strange combination of surrender and resistance. He exerts himself only when absolutely necessary and otherwise submits to making a strange, zigzagging motion through the water (which, thank God, is calm) in the general direction of land. His muscles become exhausted after a time, but he feels a strange peace and certitude. It is not his time, he feels sure, and therefore, while they are locked in this embrace, it cannot be hers. After what seems like several lifetimes, he finds himself lying on hard sand, breathing painfully, unable to move, aware of voices, sirens and flashing lights in the distance, aware of the woman's body beside him, but not sure whether it's breathing.

•

And so it is that Don, waiting in the Norfolk hospital cafeteria for Jeanne, Hirsch's doctor, and Ed, runs into Kenny. It takes him a minute to register where he knows this fellow from, but then he remembers him—big, handsome blond fellow, did some heavy lifting at Jasper Elementary during the flood, had an ex-wife there and a little boy, and his name is—wait a minute—Kevin. No, Kenny. Almost exhausted from the effort of rooting the name out of his psyche, Don greets him heartily.

"What brings you here?" he asks, as they shake hands.

"Well, I came on a helicopter with a half-drowned woman," says Kenny.

Don notes Kenny's exhilaration and his dishevelment and hazards a guess. "Did you pull somebody out of the water?"

Kenny nods and then shakes his head, remembering. "She wasn't too happy about it either. But it seemed like she'd been trying to stay afloat. Confused, I guess."

"Tourist or local?" asks Don, though he knows there aren't many tourists around near Christmas time anyway, even without rumors of a mystery disease.

"Local," says Kenny. "You may know her, Father. Name's Marika something."

"Marika?"

"Yeah, you know her?"

"I see. Yes. What room is she in? Never mind, I can ask at the front desk."

Kenny waits for Father Cathcart to say how terrible or what was she doing there, or something sympathetic. But the priest's gaze has turned inward and he looks, Kenny could swear, almost angry.

"Anyway," he says, "I figured I'd just hang around and see how she's doing. I didn't know anybody to call. Doc said her lungs were pretty messed up."

Don nods. He tries to formulate a response, but then he catches sight of Jeanne at the door, carrying the shoulder bag she carried when they waded away from her house during the flood. She's looking around for him.

He starts to raise his hand to greet her when a voice at his elbow says, "Mr. Cathcart?"

Don turns. A young doctor—he looks about thirteen to Don—holds out his hand. "Hi, I'm Dr. West," he says.

Don takes his hand, but his face remains blank.

"Alan Hirsch's doctor?" says the thirteen-year-old, as if he's not quite sure himself.

"Oh, of course," says Don. Could you excuse me just a minute?" And he turns back to where Jeanne was, but she's not there. He turns to Kenny.

"Did you see that lady that came in a second ago? Did you see where she went?"

"No," says Kenny. "I didn't see anyone come in."

Don pauses, puzzled.

"We can step into a conference room if you like," says the doctor at his elbow, helpfully.

"Oh, yes, fine," says Don. "Good to see you," he says to Kenny, shaking his hand.

Then he follows the doctor, saying a quick prayer on the way. Just a way of touching base until he can get to the chapel later and find out why he is so angry at a half-drowned woman.

But by the time he's done getting Hirsch out and Jeanne in, it is much later, and he proceeds to Marika's room without thinking, without stopping at the chapel, simply because she is next on his list. He is not surprised to find her unconscious and on a respirator, but he is surprised to find himself lingering and a little alarmed to hear himself talking.

"I identified Hirsch's body," he says. "It was definitely him. I mean. It was his body. And then I turned Jeanne's body—I mean Jeanne—over to—I don't know. God knows who. People who don't know a hell of a lot more about what she's got than I do. Probably less than you do.... So. You made a mess of your lungs, eh? That strikes me—I have to say, that strikes me as a very strange thing to do at this particular time. Why don't you just wait to get sick? You think Death needs help? You think it needs help? It's winning! This is a war, Godammit, and we're losing! Just who the hell do you think you are to be—"

Don doesn't realize that he's yelling until he feels a hand on his shoulder.

"Easy there, Father," Kenny says, looking a little amused and a little scared. "You'll have the nurses down on us."

Don glares at him. He wants to argue with him, wake him up, tell him a thing or two. What the hell's wrong with everybody?

The only way he can restrain himself is by remembering the next item on his list, which is to find Jeanne's niece Terry, who came with

Ed Shapiro and was whisked away by some administrator and, Don thinks, still doesn't know that her aunt is here. Everything is happening so fast.

Then he remembers the empty hospital chapel with its five little panes of stained glass over wall sconces and its wall hanging of the Holy Spirit descending as a dove. His anger still feels heavy and scorching within him, like a hot coal, but he is calm enough at least to speak to Kenny.

"Go on in," he says, "I was just leaving." And he almost does, but then pauses and makes himself turn around to say, "Hey, good job out there."

Kenny smiles bashfully and lowers his head. Don escapes, the sucking sound of Marika's respirator receding behind him.

•

The dove on the chapel's wall-hanging swoops downward against a turbulent background of purples and grays and indigos which becomes calmer as the eye travels higher, resolving itself into lavender, pale gold and finally white. The Holy Spirit, a white bird in a bruised sky. Don closes his eyes.

> O Lord, my God, my Savior,
> By day and night I cry to you.
> Let my prayer enter into your presence;
> Incline your ear to my lamentation.
> For I am full of trouble;
> My life is at the brink of the grave.
> I am counted among those who go down to the Pit;
> I have become like one who has no strength;

Lost among the dead,
Like the slain who lie in the grave,
Whom you remember no more,
For they are cut off from your hand.

Don kneels in silence, knees and hips aching. His chest feels heavy inside. He feels as if something heavy and square is inside it, something impenetrable with sharp corners. He can't move with this thing inside him. He's too angry to move.

People are taken away before we can learn how to love them. We barely have time to see them. There's not enough time. It's all very well for you to incline your ear, Lord, but then what do we ask for? More time? More love? A clue? A magic potion?

The face of his mother rises in his mind, glassy-eyed in her last hours. Mother, now I know what I might have done. At least now I would say something to you. You died for years and no one said anything. You probably felt more alone with your family than when you were by yourself. A clue might have helped, there, Lord. And now here I am, so much wiser, and all that's happening is that things are going faster. I can't keep up.

Don finds that he's grinding his teeth. The pain in his knees is bordering now on numbness, but he continues to kneel.

My sight has failed me because of trouble,
Lord I have called upon you daily;
I have stretched out my hands to you.
Do you work wonders for the dead?
Will those who have died stand up and give you thanks?

"What do you mean? There has to be a protocol!" says Terry, angrily. She realizes, dimly, that she has literally backed Dr. West into a corner, but she can't seem to help herself. Nervously, the doctor looks around her at Ed, who's preoccupied with some papers.

"Well, of course we'll make her as comfortable as we can—" Dr. West ventures.

Terry lets out a loud, exasperated groan, turns from the cowering doctor and strikes her forehead. "Well, she's not going to be comfortable, is she? She's got—"

At this, Ed raises his eyes questioningly from his papers. He looks at her attentively, as if to see what she's going to say next, and then suddenly, Terry's eyes fill with tears. She turns back to Dr. West.

"I'm sorry I'm being a jerk," she says. "Where's the ladies room?" The doctor points, and she exits briskly.

"She wasn't being a jerk," says the young doctor. "This is very frustrating."

Ed notices that there are dark circles under the boy's eyes and nods gently.

"People are beginning to call with questions," says the doctor. "And of course we have no idea—"

"Well, I can help you with that," says Ed. "There are standard things we can say. As long as you don't condescend and you look like you're working on it, most people are pretty patient. Surprisingly patient, really."

The doctor nods, blankly. "And of course," says Ed, putting a kind hand on his shoulder, "we are working on it, aren't we?"

Dr. West nods again, a little more cheerfully, and excuses himself to continue his rounds. Ed straightens his papers and waits for Terry to come out of the ladies' room where, he knows, she is wrestling, as he is, as almost everyone is, whether they know it or not, with the great Enemy. At His terrible approach beloved ghosts arise, like hairs on a dog's neck.

Terry, weeping in the bathroom, sees once again the mother made of water rising up out of the sea, reaching out her arms to Terry, who stands helpless on the shore. And then nothing. Silence. Mother and child reach out their arms to empty horizons. Why did you leave me? Why are you gone?

•

Lying in her hospital bed, Jeanne has forgotten where she is. It seems that for a long time she's accepted this forgetfulness, but now it's beginning to alarm her. She hears voices nearby but cannot tell where they're coming from or what they're saying.

Gradually, as she puzzles over these distant phenomena, her body makes itself known to her, mostly as a complex of discomforts and pains. Her tongue feels swollen. Heavy weights are pressing on her eyes. Red ants are crawling in her veins.

Automatically, as years of meditation have taught her, she lets her attention rest on these areas of conflict and then, in an orderly fashion, on other parts of her body, one by one, attentively, receptively, compassionately. It is very difficult. Waves of confusion, doubt, fear, and anger assail her. She lets them pass over her, through her.

She lets her attention come to rest on her breathing. It is raspy and labored. She accepts this and continues to attend to it, calmly, affectionately. After a while she falls asleep and has a dream. In her dream she is sitting on an itchy, grassy dune, looking down at the sea. The waves are dark and turgid and seem to ooze onto the beach, making their way slowly toward her until they lick the base of her dune. Then they withdraw, leaving a layer of scum on the sand in their wake. The sky hangs heavy and gray. Her sinuses throb, and there is a smell of sewage in the air.

She is full of the bleak heaviness of knowing that this is it, this is her world, and there is nowhere else to go.

Then the sun breaks through the clouds for a moment, making a golden path on the water from shore to horizon. Jeanne watches the path shimmering, and her spirits lift a little. As if on cue, another cloud moves over the sun, the light withdraws again, and the sky darkens. But Jeanne blinks, because the path on the water does not disappear. Instead, as Jeanne stares, it gradually changes color, to a kind of bright aquamarine, almost turquoise. In a moment, her heart soars as she realizes that what she is seeing is a stream of clean, pure water flowing, for no apparent reason, through the stinking sea. She stares at it, expecting it to fade, but it doesn't. She closes her eyes and opens them again. The stream is still there. Where is it coming from? Suddenly, her chest begins to collapse. She struggles, gasping, and wakes up in bed under fluorescent lights, unable to breath.

Soon the faces of good, tired-looking women in hospital uniforms appear above her. She sees them for a second or two and then is engulfed by darkness.

For a few days afterwards she flickers in and out of consciousness. Once, she wakes to see Pete, Lynn, Terry, and Don Cathcart looking worriedly at her. She remembers her dream and wants to tell them about it, but darkness comes down again. Another time she sees Cathy leaning over her, smiling with gentle reproof.

"Wake up, sis," she says.

27

In Zebulon, North Carolina, at her uncle's farm, where Pete has sent Lynn and Kyle for safekeeping, Lynn has been taking Kyle with her to feed the pigs. He looks forward to it and quickly learned to tell them apart and make up simple names for them. The pigs' nonchalant togetherness continues to comfort Lynn. They have quite matter-of-factly accepted Kyle and Lynn's recurring presence with them, as if the difference in species were nothing to fuss about. The togetherness of the pigs is looser than that of a flock of birds in flight—some pigs sleep or root by themselves, while others travel in loose posses. But the pig that Kyle notices has, indeed, Lynn realizes, been unusually solitary.

"Max sick," says Kyle.

The first time he says it, Lynn says, "Maybe he's just resting."

But the second time he says it, she notices that the pig is lying off by itself, avoided by the others and breathing rapidly. She is briefly reminded of Terry's disturbing email about the Outer Banks disease, but the thought is displaced by a worry: What will it be like for Kyle if the pig dies? He's never seen death before, and they've never talked about it.

The next day, the pig is much worse. It's breathing heavily, and there's a rash on its neck. And two other pigs have taken themselves to solitary corners, preserving what seems to be an unrestful solitude. Lynn hurries to tell Uncle Roy and tries to think of a way to begin letting Kyle know that pigs—and if it comes to that, anybody—can die.

Before long, Lynn and Kyle are standing by the pig pen, watching a dying pig struggling for breath. Lynn takes Kyle's hand.

"He's very sick," she says.

Kyle considers this gravely. "When Max better?" he asks.

"I don't know," says Lynn. And, after a pause, she says, "Kylie, he might not get better."

Kyle looks at her, and she resists the impulse to take him in her arms, knowing that, being Kyle, he will have questions.

"Why?" he asks.

"Well, he might die," says Lynn.

Kyle looks at the pig for a minute. "Gun kill Max?"

It occurs to Lynn that that's the only kind of death Kyle has seen on TV, or the only kind that's registered, anyway.

"Well, no," she says, "he might die of his sickness."

Kyle considers this for a minute. "Max frow up. He better," he says.

"That doesn't always work."

Kyle is silent then, and when Lynn finally succumbs to the urge to kneel down and draw him close, he does not resist and rests in her arms with unusual docility. His cheek against hers is warm, and she imagines that his brain is heating with the effort of trying to orient himself to this puzzling world.

In the evening, before Kyle's bedtime, Lynn looks at an astrology book with him, holding him in her lap. She has always had a secret fascination with astrology, ever since Aunt Jeanne introduced her to it many years ago. The book she's looking at now was a present from Aunt Jeanne for her sixteenth birthday. It's a coffee-table book, with vivid, complex illustrations. Kyle has taken an interest in it, and tonight she's decided to make it their bedtime reading.

They are looking together at an intricate medieval woodcut illustrating the correspondences between the human body and the cosmos. Aries the Ram rules the head; Leo the Lion rules the heart. Aquarius the water carrier, Lynn's sign, rules the blood and, for some reason, the ankles. Kyle is tracing the correspondences with his forefinger, following the lines drawn between sign and organ.

Lynn guesses that, although he is not consciously thinking about the pigs or about death, somewhere in the complex process of building synapses, his young brain is trying to find a place to put those things. He is tired this evening, from the effort of keeping up with his own growth, a force of life that pours through him like a thundering waterfall, so most days, he is rarely still. Now, at rest, he accepts the soothing warmth of his mother's body around him, as he does the air he breathes.

Kyle turns the page to a picture of Aquarius, a bearded man pouring water from a jug balanced on his shoulder. Lynn thinks of the Pamlico River, and the secret places she discovered as a girl along its banks. Then she thinks of Kenny, then Daddy, then Terry. Her mind is in one of its skittish phases and won't light on anything for long, least of all what's going on right here, right now. Which is a shame, because in some other moods, when she's reading with Kyle like this, she has a blissful feeling that this is the only place that matters, and this time is the only time.

Now she kisses Kyle's head and, with the smell of his hair, returns to the present for a moment. But then her eye is caught by the torrent of water flowing from the water carrier's jug, and she thinks again of Jasper Pier back home and of the day the dolphins leaped when Kyle was in her belly, and of her mother, and of all the lost things, all the things lost forever.

She thinks of her lined journal and resolves to write in it every night, instead of just now and then. It would be good to keep some track of the days, of Kyle's changes, of her own thoughts, of anything that might connect the days to each other and give her some sense of direction.

"Book, Mama," says Kyle.

He says this, she knows, because she's been silent and still too long. Now she hugs him and kisses his neck, and he leans back against her, sensing she has returned to him. She doesn't want to let him go and lets him stay up longer than he should, looking at beautiful pictures of imaginary circular universes, some divided into complex geometric patterns of great symmetry, some teeming with scales, twins, bulls, scorpions, maidens, fish, lions and crabs. But she begins to lose circulation in her legs and sees that it's getting late, so, finally, she eases him off her lap and, a little stiffly, gets up.

"I'm going to go and start your bath," she says. Then we can read for a few more minutes while it's running. Okay?" And, kissing his forehead, she walks down the hall and into the bathroom, where she looks blankly in the mirror for a minute, smoothing her brow with the flat of her hand. Then she leans down over the bathtub and turns on the water.

Coming out of the bathroom to check on Kyle, she hears the phone ringing. Answering it, she can tell right away, from the flat, fatigued tone of Terry's voice, that something's wrong.

"Hey, Sis."

"Hey, Terry."

"How are you? How's Kyle?"

"Good," says Lynn. "How's everything up there? You sound tired."

"Well, yes. There's a lot going on up here. This thing is still spreading, and we still don't know what it is—"

"How's Daddy?"

"Well, he's maintaining, but—he seems a little burnt out. The thing is—"

There is a pause, and then the words seem to rush out.

"The thing is, Aunt Jeanne has it. She's in the hospital."

"What?"

"Dad told me not to tell you, but—"

"Oh, that's ridiculous. I'll be there by Monday."

"No—"

"End of discussion, T. My place is with you-all. We'll be fine."

Terry sighs with a mixture of resignation and relief. "Okay. I'll tell Daddy."

Lynn hangs up and immediately begins thinking of what to pack and whether to bring Kyle or let Uncle and Auntie take care of him. The sound of rising water startles her, and she rushes to turn off the faucet before the bathtub overflows.

•

When Jeanne dies, Don hobbles down to the dim chapel. His heart is numb, as if injected with novocaine, but his knees are inflamed and aching. He likes the ache because it's a feeling. He crosses himself and wincing, lowers himself to his knees again.

> But as for me, O Lord, I cry to you for help;
> In the morning my prayer comes before you.
> Your terrors have destroyed me;
> They surround me all day long like a flood;
> They encompass me on every side.
> My friend and my neighbor you have put away from me,
> And darkness is my only companion.

28

In mid-December, Don Cathcart finds himself involved with two very different funerals in very different ways. Neither involves a body—both Hirsch and Jeanne opted for cremation—but he has been asked to speak at Hirsch's funeral, which is being arranged by Hirsch's ex-wife and colleagues, and to officiate at Jeanne Dubovsky's funeral, which is being arranged by the Baker family. He has already decided that he wants to include some kind of pagan symbolism in the Christian ceremony for Jeanne—easy enough—and to offer a testament to friendship at Hirsch's Jewish ceremony. He is researching Jewish and pagan funeral customs and making notes about what made Hirsch and Jeanne the people they were—what made them valuable.

It has struck him in the past, though, how often funeral orations have an evaluative quality, assessing a person's life as if for a catalogue of goods, and he makes a note to speak of what both of them meant to him personally, which he thinks will be more significant to the other mourners as well as to himself.

But when he closes a book and pushes himself back from his desk, he is assailed by an unexpected vision of Hirsch's body, and then Jeanne's, approaching the crematory fire. The fire in the tunnel seems like a wild and ravenous animal. It burns so hot and bright that Cathcart seems to feel the heat of it on his face, and his eyes water. He and the fire glare at each other, and it seems to burn all the words out of his mind. What can he say? What can anyone say in the face of those hungry flames? He closes his laptop, grabs his keys, and heads out for a coffee break.

•

At the Bluebird, Ed and Marika are sitting over coffee and pastries. The windows are open, and the warm breeze makes it feel like it could be almost any season but winter, though it's still December. Ed has brought a written synopsis of the information in Marika's maps.

"This is my version of what you've shown me," he says. "I'd like you to take a look at it, if you will, and tell me if I've understood you correctly."

He hands her a folder containing a few typed pages. As she reads, he leans back and stirs his coffee. It's time to start managing his fatigue, to make sure he doesn't burn out too fast. What he thinks of as the "intake phase"—the gathering of data—must come to a close soon, and he must decide what measures to take. So far, he and Terry have just briefed a few other doctors in the area on what to look for in the way of symptoms, and he's put a quick reporting procedure in place.

No one has reported new symptoms in the last couple of days, and miraculously, he hasn't detected much panic locally, though there was an article in *The Norfolk Sentinel* on an "unknown virus" in the Outer Banks. It would be different, probably, if it were tourist season. Folks who live around here have a somewhat stoic or fatalistic bent, he's noticed. Maybe a result of living with the perennial threat of hurricanes and the ravaging tide of tourists. Hunker down, and get through it. Don't fret about what you can't control. Living by the sea does that, maybe.

"This is it," says Marika, handing back his folder. "You've done well." She grins. "Though I must admit it's a little…chastening? that's the word?—to see years of thought fully expressed in two pages. I suppose mathematicians go through this all the time."

Ed studies her curiously for a minute. She is much thinner than she was before her near-drowning a week or so ago. She looks a little frail and shaky. He's surprised they let her out so soon, but she's clearly got a strong will. The hollows of her face and arms seem to have a bluish tinge, as if her skin has become slightly transparent.

She still has her sharpness, though. She needs it, thinks Ed. Without that she would break down. As, in fact, she may have already done. May, still. But these notes and maps she's shown him are fascinating. And, more remarkably, they may actually be helpful.

"I notice, though," she says, "that in your summary you make no mention of the possibility of adaptation of some of the microbes from fresh water to salt water or vice versa. I tried to indicate that possibility on the charts."

"Yes, I noticed that," says Ed, "but even assuming that's possible, I can't see how it would be relevant to human pathology."

Marika smiles a small and it seems to Ed, condescending smile, as if something she expected had just happened—a predictable disappointment. Ed finds her expression mildly annoying but decides to ignore it.

"Tell me, what brought you to study this?" asks Ed. "And why did you choose this unusual—form—to express your conclusions?"

Marika leans back and looks down at her coffee cup, running a finger idly around its rim.

"Well, I'm a marine biologist, and I'm interested in cross-species transmission. As to the form—you mean why didn't I publish an article in a scientific journal? Well, there are a variety of reasons. I'm…not a fan of… 'Science as Usual'."

"Science as usual?"

"Yes. Everyone working on three tiles of a mosaic and insisting that's the whole picture."

Ed nods. "Have you been following the rise of 'Systems Biology'? That shows some promise as a cure for reductionism."

"Yes. Maybe. But it was always a bit of a strain for me, anyway, the academic discourse. After a while, I noticed that for all my colleagues' accuracy and for all their rigor and for all their seriousness, no one really listened to what they said. Not that I expect to be listened to, either. But I more or less decided that if it's all for nothing anyway, I might as well do it in my own way. Although—"

Here Don Cathcart appears at their table, looming above them, looking pale and strained.

"Hello," he says.

"Hello," says Marika.

"There are no other tables," says Don. "May I join you?" He looks a little dazed, as if he's not really hearing what he's saying.

"Oh, of course," says Marika, and she and Ed move to make room for him.

After a pause, Ed sticks out his hand and says, "Hello, I'm Ed Shapiro."

"Oh, hello," says Don, shaking his hand. "Don Cathcart."

There is another pause, and both men come to realize that Marika is not going to do the usual woman's work of explaining them to each other.

"Are you visiting?" asks Don.

"Um, yes," says Ed.

"Vacation?"

"Well, no, I'm here for the CDC."

Don looks at him blankly for a second and then remembers. "Oh, of course. Yes."

There is a pause, and Ed continues. "Dr. Hansen has been kind enough to share some of her research with me, and I just asked her how she came to be interested in it."

Both men turn listening eyes on Marika. "Oh, well, I'm a marine biologist, and I've seen similar symptoms in seals," she says, tersely. "I've also done some research on algae and viruses that I think may be relevant.

"Well," says Ed, "it's impressive that you ventured far enough out of your field to try to apply your conclusions to humans."

Marika darts a swift blue glance at him.

"I don't know why," she says.

"Pardon?"

"I'm not sure why we should make such a fuss about human life. I mean, what have we done for the planet that our survival should be considered so precious?"

There is a brief, stunned silence after this. Ed steals a glance at Don and notes with surprise that the priest is beside himself with rage, breathing heavily, trying to control it. Marika is gazing down into her coffee cup.

"Well," Ed says finally, "I understand what you mean. But perhaps you have no children. I have a daughter. Among my ethical considerations, protecting my daughter from harm looms pretty large. And my daughter is human. So, even if at times I question the worth of my own life—" Here, Marika darts another glance at him, keen and startled. "I consider human life in general to be of intrinsic value."

Don nods, soothed by Ed's calm. "And for me," he says, "it's God."

The other two look at him with raised eyebrows, but he goes on. "I love God, and I believe he loves us. It's not always easy—"

"Loving us?" asks Marika, sardonically.

"Believing that He does," says Cathcart. He looks down at his coffee and untouched Plug-Ugly, struggling to control himself. After a minute he raises his eyes to Marika.

"So," he says, "this gentleman"— indicating Ed —"loves his daughter. I love God. And you loved Hirsch."

He says these last words furiously, jabbing his finger at Marika as if accusing her of a crime. She leaps to her feet, sways a little, and leaves the restaurant.

"Excuse me," says Don, and, throwing down his napkin, he leaves too. Ed stares after them a minute, then looks at his watch, pulls some papers out of his briefcase and begins to read.

In the parking lot, Don strides after Marika. "Who do you think you are?" he wants to say. "Just who the hell do you think you are?" But he stops short before he reaches her, so suddenly that it feels as if he's run into a wall. "No," a voice says inside him, "what you need to do is apologize."

He stands for a minute to try to catch his breath, but she's walking so fast that he can't afford to wait long. He runs after her and calls her name. She doesn't turn until he touches her arm, and when she does, he sees that her face is wet with tears.

"I'm sorry," he says. "That was—I was—I'm upset. I'm sorry. I've been preparing the eulogy for Hirsch's funeral and…I'm sorry."

Marika nods, biting her lip. They both stand for a minute, lost in the middle of the parking lot. Then Don says, "May I buy you a cup of coffee?"

Marika sniffs several times and wipes her eyes with the flat of her hand.

"Come on," he says. "Let me buy you a cup of coffee." He takes her arm, and she lets him lead her back into the café.

They decide not to disturb Ed, who seems immersed in his papers. As it happens, though, the only free table is next to his, so fragments of their conversation drift in and out of his consciousness as he works.

He notices, discreetly, that Marika's eyes are red, and she looks shaken. Then he finds that he has some difficulty returning to his papers, because Marika's red eyes have summoned up Terry's, which filled up with tears over dinner last-night. They had not been talking about Jeanne, or even about the virus, but Terry was blindsided in the middle of small talk by a wave of grief for her late aunt and her long-dead mother.

She ended up crying herself to sleep in his arms last night, and once she lay quietly, he was assailed by emotions in his turn—bizarre desires to say, "I'll be your mother father brother husband; I'll take care of you if you come away with me."

•

At the next table, Marika and Don talk in low voices.

"It's difficult," says Marika, "to avoid the conclusion that the viruses are some sort of self-regulating mechanism for our species, to prevent us from becoming too—dense."

That kind of talk sets Don's teeth on edge, but he feels he owes her a hearing. "What do you mean?" he says.

"Well, many of the viruses that kill us have lived peacefully alongside us—or even inside us—for years or generations before they become fatal. We don't always know what triggers them, but frequently it seems to result from an aggressive population surge. Or from our encroaching on some relatively untouched area too greedily."

Marika glares at Don as if she herself is such an area and Don is an encroacher. But he is calm now and can ease her back into the flow of conversation.

"So you're saying that we bring it on ourselves, in a way."

"Well, not consciously," says Marika, "It may be some system that we're just one part of, whether we like it or not. Or perhaps it's more like a kind of perennial revolution. Some scientists say that all viruses were once part of our own genes. Their structure is not all that dissimilar. Perhaps every now and then some of them turn against us, or, looking at it another way, we turn against ourselves."

Don nods. He is irresistibly reminded of the story of Lucifer—"I myself am hell…."

"So we carry inside ourselves the seeds of our own destruction," he says. "That seems quite likely to me. But, I believe…." There is a long pause here as he struggles with the familiar old demon of doubt. "I believe that we also carry within us the seeds of our salvation."

He feels very relieved after saying this, both because he has wrestled the demon once more to the ground and also because he is free now to simply make this assertion, boldly, blindly, foolishly, without having to build an argument on it and preach a sermon.

Marika stares at him curiously. He sees that the effect of his listening to her has been that she is now listening to him. After a minute she shrugs and raises her eyebrows, as if to say, I don't see it, but I suppose it's as likely as anything else.

At the next table, Ed, involuntarily eavesdropping, lifts his pen for a minute and stares deeply into space. What, he wonders, would be the seeds of our salvation? Where would they lie? Then his cell phone rings. Quickly, he extracts it from his pocket and puts it to his ear. Two more cases in Norfolk, one down the coast at a hotel on the Emerald Isle and one possible one in Elizabeth City. It's as if the thing is suddenly spreading in all directions.

Don and Marika and the rest of the Bluebird hubbub fade away, as Ed turns his mind back to the virus. The lab boys have promised him pictures, and he's been waiting impatiently for them ever since. He likes to see what he's dealing with. He's developing a gut feeling about this thing. So many of these little epidemics peter out, some without ever being truly caught or categorized. Unclear where they came from or why they disappear. But his gut feeling is that this one is gaining a foothold and won't be going away any time soon. In fact, he's on the verge of being spooked by it. And he would like to get a look at this thing that's spooking him. Or almost spooking him.

From experience, he knows that the spread of these things can depend more upon chance than most people would like to believe. Relatively isolated areas like this would once have been considered low risk—indeed, some of the first vacationers to these shores were escaping a profusion of inland contagion—things like typhoid and TB, which people believed could be avoided by doses of healthy sea air.

Stirring sugar into his coffee, Ed leans back and gazes out the window at the road. Quiet. Not much traffic this morning. He thinks about this salty, windy place where he finds himself. Odd place for a plague to be born. He's been reading about the Outer Banks and how much of its character was formed by its isolation from the Mainland. During the Civil War, it sent men to the Union and the Confederacy or let them stay home without much fuss. Then there's this strange "Old Christmas" they still celebrate, said to be a throwback to a time when the whole western world changed calendars but the Bankers didn't get the word. That was a long time ago, and here they are hanging on to the tradition like barnacles. Strange place. Stubborn insularity and rampant tourism existing side by side. Unusual. Maybe because it's so small and so itself you can almost literally see the old ways disappearing or becoming slicked-up, hollowed-out versions of themselves as you drive from one end of Route 1 to the other. Strange, fascinating, disappearing place. Why would a plague begin here?

Maybe this Marika woman is right. Maybe it has more to do with encroachment than with crowding. After all, AIDS was not born in an overpopulated area but in an area newly encroached upon, a jungle in Africa where the virus had been coexisting relatively peacefully with monkeys. A lonely, faraway place. Soon, Ed reflects, geographical isolation may be a dimly remembered phenomenon. There'll be no more "faraway places." Though other kinds of isolation will most likely continue to flourish.

Leaning forward, he shifts his focus back to the enemy. Thank God; at least he's not dealing with the dreaded "flu-like symptoms" that send everyone who sneezes to the emergency room—but the distribution of cases is puzzling. How are people catching the thing? Is it water-borne? Air-borne? Is there a vector or vectors? Mosquitoes? Some sort of waterbug? Or as Marika Hansen seems to think, waterfowl? Could there be human transmission?

In the lab, he knows, tissue from survivors (Drew and Lori Layman) and autopsied victims (Barry Anderson, Jeanne Dubovsky, Deidre Brockie) is being tested to see if this beastie is related to any beasties we already know, and if so, which ones and how? Knowing what it is might—or might not—help in figuring out how it is transmitted. Viruses can be such clever investors, Ed thinks. Multi-tasking. Diversifying their portfolios. Marika's remark about microbes adapting to saltwater crosses his mind briefly, but even if that kind of adaptation were possible, it seems to Ed only tangentially connected to the matter at hand—to this particular battle.

•

Jeanne Dubovsky's mourners gather on December fifteenth, St. Lucy's Day. From this liturgical coincidence Don has drawn the theme for the ceremony. As the mourners enter, the church is unusually dark. In Don's absence, Father Brookner has had drapes installed on the large windows, and they are drawn. The only light comes from the altar candles, the little light on Cathcart's lectern, and a candle burning in front of a portrait of Jeanne, holding her cat and smiling warmly.

> *Réquiem ætérnam dona eis, Dómine; et lux perpétua lúceat eis.*
> Grant them eternal rest, oh Lord, and may everlasting light shine upon them.

The turnout is small—the Baker family and a few other people whom the family doesn't seem to know. Regular massage clients, perhaps? Odd, muses Don, to think of Jeanne literally touching so many people and yet leading, in her off hours, a solitary life.

As the service proceeds, he remembers how the acoustics of Our Lady of Peace sometimes turn the congregation's responses into a murmuring sound, like a wave coming and going on the shore.

Everyone is saying the words, but their voices are all running together in a quiet hum. The readings over, he takes a deep breath and prepares to deliver the homily. He thought he might never do this again, but, times being what they are…. He turns to face the shadowed faces of the congregation.

"Welcome. We come together today to mourn the passing and celebrate the life of our dear sister-in-law, aunt, and friend, Jeanne Elaine Dubovsky. It so happens that today is the day celebrated by many churches across the world as St. Lucy's Day. This day is typically celebrated with candlelight. One might say that it is the first festival of light leading up to the ancient lighting of the Yule Log. In part, our attraction to candlelight and firelight in December is, of course, a response to the long nights of winter—there is a physical craving for light. But these lights are also a response to the spiritual craving that leads us to call Jesus Christ 'the Light of the World,' the light that dispels the darkness of despair.

"In honor of the spiritual light and of the warmth and light that Jeanne Dubovsky brought into our lives, there will be a brief candle lighting ceremony at the end of this service, which I invite you all to share."

The Paschal candle by Jeanne's portrait flickers in a sudden draft. It is much smaller than the crematory fire, but still contains, in Don's eyes, that fire's ravaging energy, momentarily controlled in the service of the ritual.

The wordless fear of his vision—the bodies approaching the furnace—steals over him, and he is thankful for the ritual script of the Mass, which he could say in his sleep and he suspects, sometimes does.

…Kyrie Eleison. Kyrie Eleison…
…Holy holy holy…
…My soul shall be healed…
…Go in peace…

The Mass moves smoothly, seemingly of its own accord, and then is over. Tenderly, Betty Sue and the altar guild pack away the wafers and wine for next time.

Don nods a signal to Pete Baker to begin the next phase of the ceremony. One by one, the mourners come and light their candles by Jeanne's smiling face. Don sees that Pete steals a glance at the portrait, seemingly in spite of himself, and is visibly smitten with anguish so heavy that he seems to walk back to his pew bowed under the weight of it.

For a minute, Don regrets these theatrics that he's added to the Mass, but the other mourners seem to be more gently moved, looking at the photo with various degrees of love and affection before and after they light the candle, though love is tempered in the faces of Jeanne's nieces with sorrow and regret. He is glad to see the rhythm of the candle lighting is slow, the mood contemplative. And once all the candles are lit, he lights his own and turns to see the congregations' lit candles form a small blaze in the dark of the church.

He can see only parts of the candlelit faces as he turns to the congregation with his own little flame flickering and glances to the walls to see if his last piece of theatre is ready.

"Thank you for coming together to witness the life and death of Jeanne Dubovsky," he says. "On your way out, please place your candles in the holders by the door."

…the rising sun will come to us from heaven
to shine on those living in darkness
and in the shadow of death,
to guide our feet into the path of peace…

On this cue, Bob and Betty Sue open the drapes and the sunlight comes flooding in. The light from outside reduces the candles to relative insignificance, which was Don's plan. There is Another Light.

But this last illumination is apparently too much for Pete Baker, who suddenly collapses helplessly into loud sobbing, curling himself against the light as if he can't bear it. After a shocked pause, his daughters move to comfort him. A few of the others stop by to pat him on the shoulder before proceeding to the door to blow out their candles and deposit them in their holders. Others pass the grieving family with eyes averted, embarrassed. Don stands discreetly apart in case he is needed. Having brought on this deluge, his role is now that of a mute witness as Pete's sobs continue to slash through the peace of the sunlit church.

•

For the next week, Pete spends most of his time in bed. During the day, his bedroom door stays closed. He comes out for an occasional meal, but rarely finishes it, giving Lynn a weak smile before retreating to his room again. Occasionally, Lynn gets up to get Kyle a drink of water and finds Pete in the kitchen, staring at a glass of milk or a beer. She doesn't know what to say, and he says nothing.

29

On December twenty-fourth, there is a sudden cold snap. Lynn takes Kyle with her to buy Christmas baking ingredients. It's so cold that she wants to run across the parking lot to the doors of the grocery store, but Kyle, a small bundle with feet and mittens walking beside her, makes that impossible. He does not complain of the cold.

Lynn has observed a certain stoicism or detachment in her son's personality, even at his tender age. The times he's cried are rare enough to be remembered: after a blow to the head from a sharp cupboard door, or when he had to go to bed before finishing a jigsaw puzzle. Right now, Lynn knows, he's admiring the steam of his breath in the cold air—a phenomenon he's only recently discovered.

Once inside the store they pause for a second, adjusting to the shock of being inside. Lynn wrestles a shopping cart out of the line of folded carts, hoists Kyle into it, and fumbles for her grocery list.

"Wass dat?"

"Cinnamon."

"Simmanim?"

"Yes."

"Wass dat?"

"It's a spice."

"Pice?"

"Yes. It makes things yummier."

"Yum!"

"Yum."

"Wass dat?"

"Walnuts."

"Why?"

"Why what?"

"Der name Wall Nut?"

"Um…well, that's just their name."

"Dat where dey grow?"

"Is what where they grow—Oh, you mean on walls? No. I don't know how they got that name. They grow on trees."

"Yeah."

As Kyle digests this information, Lynn is amazed at all the things she doesn't know, just concerning the contents of one shelf in one aisle of the grocery store. "Okay," she says, consulting her list, "now we need golden raisins."

"Get toy?"

"Here? No, it's a grocery store."

"Golden!" says Kyle insistently.

"What are—oh, you mean, can you buy toys with golden raisins? No. They're not money, they're food."

"No golden?"

"Well, there's a metal gold and a color gold. These raisins are the color gold—sort of—but they're not metal. We wouldn't put metal in our fruitcake would we?"

Kyle nods, considering this. "Too hard," he says.

"Yes, too hard," agrees Lynn. He hasn't had time yet, she reflects, to develop a sense of humor. Too busy sorting things out. When he finds out it can't actually all be sorted out, then the humor will kick in.

Back at home, they take the groceries into the kitchen, Kyle carefully carrying a plastic container of sprinkles for Christmas cookies. Lynn is flooded by mixed responses to the familiar old room with the big pine table—she still thinks of it as Mama's kitchen table—by the window looking out on the sound. She is relieved to be back home, though part of her is always wondering when and if she and Kyle will ever have their own place. This is better for him now, though—being surrounded by family.

She is worried about Terry, who is working too hard, and Pete, so faded since Jeanne's funeral. Kenny called, delighted, when he found out they were back in town and immediately wanted to know when he could see Kyle.

Lynn feels guilty about not inviting Kenny for Christmas dinner, but all this is overwhelming enough as it is.

"We start?" asks Kyle.

"Well," says Lynn, "we can start making cookies today."

"Kyle help?"

"You bet! It'll be fun. It's Christmas Eve, and you can stay up as late as you like."

Lynn takes the brightly colored container of sprinkles from Kyle, puts it in the cupboard and then pretends to put him in the cupboard too, which makes him shriek with laughter.

•

On Christmas morning, Lynn wakes while it's still dark, remembers where she is, and finds herself crying. She is not prepared for these tears, and they hurt coming out. She doesn't get up, and the tears flow sideways onto the pillow. She wishes she had been more forgiving toward Aunt Jeanne. She sees now that Jeanne was just a lonely woman doing the best she could. And now it's too late.

Lynn breathes hard with the effort of staying silent and not waking Kyle in his little cot on the other side of the room. It still feels very wrong that she was not with Jeanne when she was conscious and able to say goodbye.

Another burst of heaving sobs that make her ribs ache with the effort of making no noise, and then suddenly she's calm.

In fact, she feels oddly exhilarated, remembering that she and Kyle are making Christmas dinner and the fridge and pantry are full of everything they will need for the feast. She will make this celebration work, and distract them all from all their worries for a little while. The thought gives her a lift and gets her out of bed.

She pads into the kitchen in her slippers and puts on a big pot of coffee, and then, going to look at Kyle and seeing that he is fast asleep, she takes a shower. She has told him that he can help her make dinner, and as she's showering, she runs through the things that he might be able to help her with—washing vegetables, putting cookies on a plate, what else?

As to presents, she has already suggested that since everyone's been so busy, they could all just give each other IOUs, and last night she passed out Christmas cards so they could all write their IOUs to each other, though she suspects there will be some actual wrapped presents for Kyle. Terry is bringing Ed, the man from the CDC, so that'll make five.

After her shower, still in her bathrobe, Lynn pours a cup of coffee and takes several sips before Pete comes in, sniffing exaggeratedly.

"Good smells already!" he says.

"Can I get you a cup?" says Lynn

"No, no, you stay where you are," says Pete.

He pours himself a cup and sits with her at the table, blinking sleepily and running his hand over his brow, trying to wake up.

After a few sips, he smiles at her fondly. "You know," he says, "I should be mad at you for coming back, but I can't muster it. It's good to see you."

"Good to see you, too, Daddy," says Lynn.

They are still smiling when Kyle comes in, rubbing his eyes.

"Well hey there, sleepyhead," says Pete. "I was beginning to think you were going to sleep through Christmas."

"I'm growing," says Kyle.

Pete and Lynn laugh.

"Yes, son, yes you are," says Pete.

•

Presents come first, and then a long and satisfying dinner. When they adjourn to the living room for coffee and a ritual viewing of *How The Grinch Stole Christmas*, Pete quickly falls asleep in his chair. He looks contented, though, which is good. He's been sleeping most of the time since Jeanne's funeral, hidden away in his room, silent and expressionless when he comes out for meals. Today he gave Kyle an IOU for one thousand stories, though, which Lynn views as a good sign.

Kyle wanted to redeem the coupon right away, but Lynn was able to divert him with a jigsaw puzzle. As they work on the puzzle, Ed and Terry look on, helping occasionally, serving each other cup after cup of coffee. Lynn realizes that they probably have hours of work still ahead of them, and, sure enough, they leave early, Terry hugging everyone and Ed shaking hands, just as Cindy Lou Who asks why Santa is stealing her Christmas tree. But Lynn feels they have been able to relax a bit, and they all agree to meet at the Bluebird for a day-after-Christmas brunch.

Later, lying on the floor among crumpled Christmas wrapping, full of roast beef and potatoes, and still helping Kyle with his puzzle, Lynn catches sight of Mama's old Nativity scene on a shelf near the tree. That place and time of ultimate togetherness, frozen in an eternal, warm enchantment. Mama, Baby, Daddy. She feels a pang of melancholy, but it's hard to do major angst with a belly so full of food. And after all, Daddy is dozing in his chair and Kyle is next to Lynn on the floor, puzzling, quietly aware that bedtime has been suspended. At the moment, Lynn feels no need to suffer, or in fact to move. After all, the nativity scene itself was just a moment. The kings went home, the sun came up, Joseph went to work. That golden light was perfect, and then passed into memory.

Eventually, Lynn puts Kyle to bed and comes back to the kitchen to do the dishes, but instead, she sits down at the kitchen table, puts her head on her hands and falls into a deep sleep.

Pete comes in and smiles. Kid really knocked herself out to give everyone a good Christmas. Cathy would have done that. He does the dishes himself, but she still doesn't waken until he shakes her a little and says, "Bedtime, Princess. Merry Christmas."

•

Abuzz with after-dinner coffee, Ed goes home and stays up all night in his hotel room puzzling over the source of the virus. The water supply comes, he has learned, from a deep lens of fresh water under the Jasper Woods. It would be difficult, though not impossible, to contaminate from inland—from the sound, for instance, which is the most likely source. The Jasper Woods aquifer is uphill of the waters all around it, but apparently contamination does happen sometimes in times of repeated heavy rain—nor'easters, for example, or hurricanes. So it can happen, and contamination can last as long as four months—long enough, perhaps, for some significant mutating and spreading of opportunistic organisms, for instance, hungry microbes, an ambitious virus.

And then there are Marika's maps—the role of waterfowl, the question of whether their migration patterns, which turn out to be less predictable than he thought, are corresponding in any way to the spread of the disease. Too soon to tell, probably, and there may be asymptomatic cases—haven't isolated the virus yet, so can't test for it. Marika Hansen sent him an article about genetic engineering of marine algae to produce animal feed and biofuels. Out of courtesy he read it, but is not sure how to respond. What is she getting at? Is she a crackpot, or does she see something he doesn't? Either way, he doesn't see how it's relevant to this particular hunt, and right now he has no time for anything that isn't relevant.

Exhausted, he closes his eyes and leans back in his chair. He feels dizzy with the effort of tracking patterns, on maps and charts and graphs and in his mind. He almost nods off, but jerks himself awake. No time for sleep right now. But he has been working long hours for the last few days, and he feels muddled and bogged down. Shaking himself a bit, he stares at a picture of the microbe, taken from an autopsy sample that the biologists in Atlanta have sent.

It is strikingly beautiful, symmetrical and flower-like, a flower composed of thousands of flowers just like itself. What is with this thing? How can it be waterborne and have no intestinal symptoms? If it's not waterborne, how exactly is it getting around? Is it related to the dinoflagellate blooms that have been on the increase in these parts? If so, is it seasonal? Will it have a peak season, like influenza? And how will it evolve? A couple of people have recovered from it. Is it getting smarter or weaker or both?

Ed stares at it with a predatory intensity. "Hello," he says. He has the uncanny feeling that it is waiting for him to make a move.

30

Next morning, when Pete calls, "Rise and shine!" Lynn is jolted out of a profound sleep. "Brunch in twenty minutes, honey," says Pete. "I'm just going to go shave."

She falls back asleep. When she wakes again, she sees Pete standing over her.

"Hey, are you all right? You're not usually a slug-a-bed."

Lynn sits up, but feels weak and dizzy.

"I don't know, Dad," she says, frowning. "I feel weird."

"Well, you worked your ass off yesterday, and you did just move back and all. How about I just take the truck, and you take your time and come in the car when you're ready?"

Lynn nods and lies back down.

"Tell you what," says Pete, "I'll even take Kyle."

Already asleep again, Lynn doesn't hear him.

•

The day is fair but windy. The Bluebird is busy and the Bakers and Ed have to wait in line before they can get a table. The family chats and fusses over Kyle, but Ed is silent and preoccupied. The Christmas lights around the counter are still lit.

"No hurry," says Marcy, as she wipes the counter. "I'll have 'em down by Valentine's Day. Or St. Paddy's Day. Definitely by Easter."

Terry looks around the café. There has been, it seems to her, a strange feeling around the town lately. The expressions on some peoples' faces have startled her—pale and haggard, as if with worry or grief. Oppressed, furtive, even suspicious. Avoiding people at the grocery store whom they once would have greeted or even embraced. The town is changing. There's no panic, but a lot of people look worried. She glances at Pete, who's also looking around, and she sees that he sees it, too.

Once they are seated, Ed says to Terry, in an undertone, "Three in Chapel Hill, two in Richmond, one in Charlottesville."

Terry nods. That's twelve. "Anything from the pathologists?"

Ed shakes his head.

Inhaling deeply, Terry squares her shoulders for a minute and stares out the window.

"Where's Lynn?" asks Ed.

"Sleeping in," says Terry. "She'll come in a bit."

Suddenly the door bangs open, blown by a willful gust out of the hand of Kenny, who looks surprised and then sheepish. He checks around the room a little tiredly until his eye lights on Kyle, and then his face is transfigured with happiness. Nevertheless, he restrains himself from rushing, and instead walks slowly up to where the boy sits in a child seat between Terry and Ed and waits to catch his eye.

When he does, he says, "Hey Kyle, remember me?" but the words are not out before Kyle holds up his arms to be picked up and yells, "Dada!"

Kenny lifts him gently out of his seat.

"Where's Lynn?" he asks Terry, who is smiling in spite of herself.

"Catching up on sleep," says Terry.

"Y'all waiting to order? Mind if we just go for a little walk? I'll bring him back in five minutes."

"Sure," says Terry, and Kenny strides out into the morning sunlight with Kyle looking happily back over his shoulder. Five minutes later, they return, and Kenny deposits him back in his chair.

"Here," says Ed, standing and offering his chair to Kenny. "I'll just move one over."

"Well thanks," says Kenny. "I sure appreciate it. I just came in for a cup of coffee, but I guess it's my lucky day! I'm Kenny Peterson, by the way."

He sticks out his hand to shake, but realizes that he's given the man his sales greeting, and he can see Ed's friendly smile wavering. Turn down the volume, he thinks, as he takes the seat beside Kyle.

"You're from the CDC, right?" he asks, quietly.

"Right," says Ed, a little less wary.

"I'm—I'm not a medical person or anything," he says, glancing at Terry, "but I'm—I've lived here all my life, and I just want to say, if you need anything done—I mean, you know, grunt-work, whatever—I'm—I'd like to help."

Looking up at him, Terry finds herself unable to contain a sudden irritation. "Have you ever done that kind of thing before?" she asks, sharply.

Kenny wavers for a second, but he looks at her steadily and says, "No, but I think I'm ready. And I'm good in a crisis."

Well, that's true, thinks Terry.

"No, I'm sorry, I think you'd better just go," says a hard voice from the counter behind their table.

The three look back in surprise. It's Marcy's voice. Her tone of barely controlled panic, as much as its slightly raised volume, causes everyone to turn toward the counter, where she is standing behind the register with her arms folded, looking upset. She is talking to Lori Layman, who is standing at the counter, holding out some money.

"I'm sorry," she says again, shaking her head, "I can't risk touching your money."

Lori turns away from the counter and walks toward the door, tears in her eyes, blind with embarrassment. Everyone watches in stunned silence, including Ed, who catches sight of red, vein-shaped marks on her wrists and forearms. Quickly and quietly, he gets to his feet.

"I'll go calm her down" he says to Terry, who has seen the marks too. "Let's nip this in the bud."

Terry glances at Marcy.

"I'll explain it to her," says Ed.

Explain what, thinks Terry—what is it that we know, exactly? But she knows what he means. He's going to convince Marcy and Lori not to panic. She's seen Ed do this before, and has always been startled and amused to see how good he is at it. He seems to proceed on the assumption that facts are relatively unimportant (the reverse of what he usually thinks), and what matters is looking someone in the eye and speaking with quiet authority. It almost always works.

"How do you catch this thing, anyway?" asks Kenny.

Ed stands up. "We don't know yet," he says, looking at Kenny with a hint of challenge in his expression.

"Okay," says Kenny.

Ed walks out after Lori, past the morning newspaper in its rack, the main headline reading "Quiet Christmas on the Banks," a smaller headline reading, "Killer Virus?"

A waitress comes to the Bakers' table, taking her pencil from behind her ear. "What'll it be, folks?"

Terry looks around "Uh…what do y'all think? Pancakes all around?"

"Suits me," says Kenny. "How about you, son?"

"Yes!" says Kyle.

Ed is gone with Lori for about twenty minutes, and when he comes back, he remains quiet and preoccupied, eating and drinking automatically.

He waits until everyone has had their fill of pancakes, the dishes have been cleared and the coffee served, before he begins.

"Folks, I want to thank you for including me in your Christmas. This has been my best for quite a while, in spite of the—circumstances that brought me here. Y'all are a wonderful family, and I'm glad I met you. Now, speaking of circumstances, I have an announcement to make. You'll be hearing about this a lot, but I thought I might as well start here and give y'all a heads-up. There have been enough cases of this mystery illness—we're calling it the Outer Banks Virus right now, for lack of a better name—and it's been spreading fast enough that we're going to need to take some precautions."

"Are you talking about a quarantine?" asks Pete.

"Partial quarantine for some, full quarantine for others. For most of the town we'll put the same kind of procedures into effect that you might use during a big snowstorm—closing places of public congregation like schools, non-essential stores, and so forth. So it'll be like 'snow days' without the snow.

"We're also encouraging people to wear masks. You might notice a few people have started that already. Now there is a group that we know for sure has been exposed to the virus, and that's the people who were holed up in the shelter during the storm and flooding that I understand happened in November. Those people will go into quarantine."

He pauses a minute to let this sink in.

"So that's us!" says Kenny.

"That's right," says Ed.

There is a silence at the table. Ed looks around the Bluebird, where they are having breakfast, at the patrons companionably eating, chatting and reading newspapers in the morning sunlight.

"I won't lie; this is going to be a big change for Jasper," he says. "I'm counting on you and people like you to act in the best interest of the community. It's just a matter of time before we contain the virus, and I have no doubt that we will pull through this together. Also, I welcome any suggestions, especially from you, Pete, and obviously from Terry, on the best way to get the word out. I am hoping I can count on you to be leaders in the quarantine headquarters, which will most likely be the same school where you all holed up during the recent flooding. Any questions?"

"Yeah, I have one," says Pete. "Do you CDC fellows really have your ducks in a row?"

Ed can't help but grin at the question, but he nods. "If we don't, we will very soon. This is what we're trained to do. Any more questions?"

Terry shakes her head, but Ed notices that her hands actually tighten on the arms of her chair as if she's in an accelerating vehicle.

"Very soon you're all going to be plenty busy," says Ed. "So get good rest. Think about basic essentials to be packed for the move to the quarantine locations. Explain the situation to your families, your friends—as many people as you have time to contact. Some people listen better to people they know. And here's something important: If you see anybody start to panic, look 'em in the eye, pat 'em on the shoulder, whatever it takes to calm them down. Imagination can be a good thing, but…not always."

•

That night, Terry and Ed heat up a frozen pizza at her house for dinner. They are silent with exhaustion.

Terry sighs. "I don't know," she says. "Sometimes it seems like if a virus is smart enough, it's gonna get us. There's not much we can do."

Ed nods as if this has occurred to him. "Yes, well, that depends on a lot of things. Partly it depends on how flexible we can be. Generally it takes a huge threat to effect any substantive change in group behavior. A lot of people had to die before we started washing our hands as a matter of routine. And some things we may not be able to change: our desire to grow and expand, our need to huddle together, our difficulty believing that people we don't know are real, our inability to imagine our own deaths until they sit right down in our laps. Then there are genetic factors—who our parents had sex with. And then, always, there's the unknown."

They fall into an uneasy silence, Ed deep in thought. After a minute, Terry asks "Where do you think this thing is coming from, anyway?"

"I'm pretty sure it starts in water," says Ed.

"Pretty sure?" says Terry.

"Yes. I just don't know how, or how it gets from there into humans. Or what to do about it. Yet. But it may be transmissible between humans, and I do know what to do about that."

Terry nods and going to a cupboard, brings out two surgical masks and unwraps them from their plastic wrap. She puts them on the table between them and then looks wryly at Ed.

"Give me a kiss," she says.

They kiss for some time, and then put on the masks.

"Okay, here we go," says Ed. "Not too scary, eh?"

Terry shrugs. He squeezes her hand.

After he leaves, Terry prepares to move to the quarantine center. Once she's all packed, she falls into a kind of fearful reverie. There's a chance this thing could still just peter out. Or it could suddenly gain momentum and turn into a full-blown plague, like cholera or TB or AIDS. Or worse. Something with the versatility of AIDS. and the virulence of the 1918 flu epidemic that plowed down men, women, and children like a tank. That story of a woman who got on a streetcar feeling fine and was dead by the time she reached her destination. Marie Curie's mother afraid to kiss her because of TB. Other young mothers coughing their lungs out beside children with nowhere else to go. Plague victims abandoned when alive and left unburied when dead. AIDS patients abandoned by their lovers and families, dying homeless.

She is haunted by words that Ed showed her in a book about a plague that visited the Algonquin Indians at the Plymouth Colony:

> In the end, they were not able to help one another;
> no, not to make a fire, nor to fetch a little water to drink,
> nor any to bury the dead.

31

rew Layman's energy has never come back completely since he was sick, but he's trucking along. Lori is still sick, though. The rash has disappeared, and no new symptoms have come up—no coughing and not much of a fever—but her energy is gone and she feels the cold keenly. She spends most of her time bundled up on the couch watching television. It's been a rainy week, and Drew, who has been out in the garage working on the truck, comes in for a lunch break. Taking off his boots in the foyer, he sees that Lori's watching *Gone With the Wind* on the old movie channel, and it's the scene where Scarlett decides to make the drapes into a dress. He knows this is her favorite scene and smiles at his wife, once so rosy and busy, now pale and swathed in sweaters and blankets. He's kind of been enjoying taking care of her for once.

Then suddenly a man's voice issues from the TV "—state of quarantine…" it says, "snow day…if you think you have been exposed to the virus, call…or log onto…no need for alarm, but we must be careful to—"

Drew enters the room, and he and Lori look at each other, bewildered, and then at the screen, where Ed speaks slowly and calmly amid a whir of cameras.

•

At the Bluebird, Marcy frowns at the small TV set above the counter.

"Shit," she says, and then the microwave signals that the hamburger buns are thawed. "Shit," she says again, and begins rummaging around for paper and markers to make a sign: CLOSED UNTIL FURTHER NOTICE. SORRY FOR THE INCONVENIENCE.

As she's rummaging, she considers whether she feels she's been sufficiently exposed to warrant joining the quarantine. If she doesn't go will they come and get her? Can they do that? And who are "they," anyway?

•

Shona is on the beach with Fred the cat. It is her day off, and she feels lonely, but she doesn't want to see anyone, which she knows doesn't make sense. Fred has curled up nearby and is allowing himself to be petted. This is just right, she decides, and prepares to settle down for a nice long sit. She even considers turning off her phone, but just then she feels it vibrate. Automatically, she pulls it out of her pocket.

A text from Dad: "There's a quarantine. We have to shut down and move to the school." Squinting, she says aloud: "What?" She texts back "huh?"

And the message comes back: "Quarantine. Come home."

•

At Ed's request and under Terry's supervision, Don Cathcart has teamed up with his successor, Father Brookner, and other local clergy, to call every number in their congregation directories and tell whomever they reach about the mock snow day, to calm them and encourage them to comply. The first thing everyone asks about is groceries, and he is able to assure them that grocery stores will be open, though for shorter hours, and the required masks will be available at the door. There will be no need, he emphasizes, to stock up as they do before a normal snow day.

Pete and Jack do their best to contact locals who have traveled elsewhere for Christmas and encourage them to extend their stay and to keep visitors in Jasper, so as to minimize coming and going. The health department provides as much information as it can about those who may have been exposed. Ed and Pete supervise the distribution of masks at the grocery store, the pharmacy, the clinic, and even the post office. More and more people go about their business with their faces covered, and fewer and fewer shake hands or embrace.

•

Meanwhile, the town of Jasper adapts to its invisible blizzard. No one goes to school or to church. Realtors' offices and the bars and restaurants lie idle. The grocery stores are full of masked and gloved figures, nodding awkwardly to each other and hurrying home. The sunlight moves silently across the empty tables of the Bluebird. At The Cove and The Sandpiper, the curtains are closed, and cockroaches and millipedes begin to venture out from behind the walls. In the trinket shops along Route 1, the shell necklaces, coffee mugs, T-shirts, postcards, sunglasses, packs of gum, baseball caps, lighthouse key chains, beach towels, and souvenir placemats all quietly gather dust. Cut off from each other, the people of Jasper, in and out of quarantine, fall asleep in the light of their televisions and nestle into their dreams. All public gatherings have been cancelled, but in their sleep the Jasperites have parties—large, convivial gatherings of the living and the dead.

•

There is a long line at the quarantine center the next morning. People are masked and quiet, clutching quickly-assembled possessions—pillows, towels, suitcases full of clothes and toiletries, laptops, teddy bears, a few books. In spite of the determined good cheer of the people checking them in—including Pete Baker and Kenny Peterson—it is difficult for the quarantiners to avoid a feeling of uneasy displacement and depersonalization, even a whiff of concentration camp.

Pete sees that the mood under quarantine is quite different from the time they all gathered here during the flood. Then this place was a refuge, plain and simple. This time—well, it's kind of like taking refuge in the lion's mouth. Here they all are, with their masks and their fears, bundled together but afraid to get too close to each other.

His neighbors, he finds, are responding by being passive and quiet, moving like sleepwalkers. They do what they're told, but it seems they're "not all there"—they've put themselves on hold.

The exception is the children's corner, where mothers and children are very clingy with each other. This morning Pete saw a little girl with a troubled expression lift a mask from her mother's face for a moment, as if to make sure it was still her mother. The mother held her breath, smiled tenderly, then quickly pulled the mask back on.

•

When Lynn arrives, leading Kyle by the hand, Pete is shocked at how tired she looks. There are deep circles under her eyes, and she looks pale and dazed.

"You all right?" he asks her, in an undertone. Kenny walks over, looking worried.

She looks at them for a minute before answering. "I gotta admit, Dad. I feel pretty shitty," she says.

"Go see Terry," he says, "Right now. I'll take Kyle."

"Or I can take him," says Kenny.

"No," says Lynn. "You guys have to check people in."

"I can watch him," says a voice behind Lynn, and she turns to find that Marika is standing behind her, carrying a rucksack. She recognizes the keen blue eyes over her mask.

Marika crouches down to talk to Kyle. "I brought my little book," she says. "Do you remember my little book?"

Kyle stares for a minute, over his child-sized mask, his own eyes grayer and darker than Marika's, more open, but equally intense, and then nods.

"Would you like to hear it again?"

"Moe book, pease," says Kyle, and Lynn, though barely conscious, smiles with pride at her son's good manners.

Marika leads Kyle to the children's area, which is marked off by a screen. As soon as the two are out of sight, Lynn sinks to the floor, her fall broken at the last minute by Kenny, who lunges forward to catch her.

"The infirmary is that way," says Pete, indicating with his head, and Kenny carries her quickly through the door. Instinctively, he moves as quietly as possible, to avoid giving onlookers time to panic. Pete quietly asks Jack Brockie, who is standing nearby, to take his place at the check-in desk, and then he follows Kenny.

The room where they bring her is still in the process of being turned from a classroom into an infirmary. As Pete enters, he sees that Terry is on duty. He looks at her apprehensively, but after one stricken glance at Lynn and one at him, she immediately becomes professional.

"Okay, I've got it, thanks," she says. "I'll do an examination. You guys go over to that sink by the door and wash your hands. Then go on—come back in an hour for an update."

The two men are unable to move at first, both gazing at Lynn as if expecting her to do something. Terry waits.

Finally, Pete says, "Okay. Anything you need—"

"Thanks," says Terry, opening the door. She pats Pete's shoulder as he leaves, squeezing it before closing the door after him.

As soon as they are gone, she puts on gloves, carefully unbuttons the sleeves of Lynn's blouse and rolls them up. There it is, the strange, vein-shaped rash. Terry takes a deep breath in and out and begins the examination: Pulse, temperature, blood pressure. Fever is beginning to take hold, and a small film of perspiration appears on Lynn's forehead.

There is a knock on the door and it opens, admitting a man from the health department wheeling in some equipment on a trolley.

"Respirator's here," he says. "Whoa, you got someone already? I'll just set up over here."

Terry nods, staring at Lynn. She feels a distant sense of panic, but it is largely drowned out by a loud voice in her mind saying, quite clearly, "This can't happen." She tears herself away from the bedside and is preparing to draw her sister's blood for analysis just as Ed walks in. His head snaps back when he sees Lynn in the bed, and he goes to Terry, who is examining a needle, and puts his hands on her shoulders.

"Are you all right?" he says.

And it is then that she begins to shake. She tries to stop, and is frustrated to find that she can't.

"Okay," says Ed. "It's my shift now. Here's what I want you to do. Go and sit down and get a cup of coffee. I'll set things up here and then come check on you. Okay? You're going to be fine. You're having a natural reaction, and it will pass."

Terry nods several times, tries to speak and then walks into the small antechamber where the coffee is perking. She watches it drip down into the pot, works to steady her breathing, and gradually feels the shaking subside.

In the infirmary, Ed works on drawing Lynn's blood, pushing the needle into the oddly marked vein, and his mind travels many channels simultaneously—the doctor channel, the scientist channel, the public health worker channel and the boyfriend channel. The scientist channel is the dominant one. The microbe has been isolated. He has sent various samples to Norfolk and has been nagging the lab there regularly for results. Blood is being drawn from Drew and Lori

Layman, the only known survivors of the disease. The race is on. For a minute, he pictures Lynn's face beaming over the Christmas dinner, but he puts it out of his mind. If he can find a way to fight this thing, it will be too late for her. He just has to hope that whatever's winning in the Laymans' bodies will take up arms in hers.

For the next few days, Lynn's fever lingers, but doesn't rise beyond safe levels. Her breathing periodically becomes ragged, but always quiets itself. She is not responsive to speech, but she sometimes starts very slightly when blood is drawn, and Terry is convinced that Lynn feels it when Terry holds her hand and soothes her brow.

Terry and Ed alternate shifts between Lynn and the Laymans, the other two residents of the deeper level of quarantine. Meanwhile, Marika and Kenny take turns taking care of Kyle, with Pete pitching in occasionally. Marika reads to the child whenever she can.

Kenny wakes him up and gets him dressed in the morning and undresses and tucks him in at night, sleeping nearby in case Kyle wakes, and spends most of the rest of his time in the cafeteria kitchen, where he unloads huge boxes of supplies and stacks them in the storeroom on an orderly plan laid out by Jack Brockie, who is supervising the kitchen.

The company that delivered the cafeteria food has just kept on delivering, so that everyone is drinking milk out of little cardboard cartons and eating tater tots and canned string beans off indented plastic trays. Pete is in charge of coffee, which the catering company is now supplying in much greater amounts than it did when school was in session, and Kenny and Marcy supervise a platoon of busboys and dishwashers for clean-up.

Don Cathcart makes sure the old and infirm are served. Meals are served in shifts, servers masked and gloved, diners unmasked but sitting with at least one chair between them.

Out of his cafeteria manager office, Jack does a discreet business in illicit booze, which he thought to bring with him and is rationing out in moderation, with a generous mark-up. Marika is his best customer, but she never appears to be slowed down or hung over, working long hours in the lab and reading to Kyle at least once a day.

Her lab work consists of meticulous processing, packing and mailing of samples to Norfolk for analysis and keeping careful records in a data tracking program. Ed and Marika work quickly, but Marika sometimes suspects that the lab at Norfolk doesn't share their sense of urgency, judging from the slowness of its responses and apparent reluctance to cut through any of the massive red tape that seems to coil around Ed's feet. Red tape is Ed's department, and she sees him sighing over paperwork late into the night, the circles under his eyes a little darker each day.

The infirmary is behind a window that was once used for observation and evaluation of students being considered for speech or occupational therapy. Pete comes to look through the window in the evening when he knows Terry is off duty. He wants to see Lynn, but he doesn't want Terry to see him seeing her. He notices that Lynn is thinner, and it looks like Terry has brushed her sister's hair, which brings tears to his eyes.

Fortunately, Lynn doesn't look much like Cathy, which makes it almost bearable to see her in the hospital bed. He wills her to live. He knows that his will is not enough. He should pray. But can he pray? No. He's too angry.

About to turn away, Pete notices Lynn's eyes moving under her eyelids. Do people in a coma dream?

•

For the legions of the microbe, Lynn's body is a haven. She is the difference, for them, between life and death. Once inside her, they convince her body to make more of them. Their mission is to change her in a fundamental way, so that their genetic destiny becomes hers. They are just trying to survive. They don't know that they are harming the body that is their host, but they are. They don't know that they are trying to alter the course of human evolution, but that is what they are doing. So far, Lynn's antibodies do not recognize the new intruder, so they cannot defend her against it. They are on the alert, but not for this enemy.

3 2

A few days into the quarantine, in a little corner of the children's area, Marika reads to Kyle while a few other children nap nearby. When she pulls the ragged little book out of her bag, she feels an odd sense of reverence and excitement, which she knows she's catching from Kyle, though she has a vague memory of feeling the same emotions when Moder read to her all those long years ago. They have been reading "Thumbelina," and are approaching the ending, when Thumbelina, engaged to the horribly respectable mole, finds a bird almost dead from the cold—a bird whose song she remembers from earlier days—and wraps it up in leaves and moss.

The next night she again stole out to see him. He was alive, but very weak; he could only open his eyes for a moment to look at Thumbelina…. "Thank you, pretty little child," said the sick swallow. "I have been so nicely warmed that I shall soon regain my strength and be able to fly about again in the warm sunshine."

Marika stops suddenly, with a lump in her throat. She pauses so long that Kyle turns around in her lap and looks at her.

"Da end?" he asks.

"For now," Marika manages to say. "The end for now."

And the two sit silently for a minute, still under the spell of the story, breathing together under their masks.

•

On the third day of Lynn's semi-coma, Ed convinces Terry to switch patients and take a shift with Drew and Lori Layman, the other residents of the deeper level of quarantine. Their beds are set up in the school librarian's office.

Terry has been having difficulty sleeping and feels faded and almost dizzy when she knocks on their door, but as soon as she enters, she feels, with relief, her doctor identity establishing itself and lending her its strength. When Terry comes in, Lori is reading from an old Bible that looks to Terry like its cover is wrapped in wallpaper. Drew is listening to the radio. Lori is in bed, but Drew is up and dressed.

Terry tries to make sure that she's talking to them, Drew and Lori, the people she's known for years, and not just to the virus that may or may not be inside them.

"Good morning, folks," she says. "How're y'all holding up?"

They look at her for a minute, over their masks, before they speak, as if they've forgotten, briefly, how to answer a question.

"Hey, Terry," says Lori, closing her book but keeping her place.

"How're you?" asks Drew, reflexively.

"All right," says Terry. "A few funny dreams, sleeping in my old third-grade classroom. Remember Mrs. Mackey?"

They nod their heads, and she can see that they're smiling now—it's pretty easy to tell, from the eyes, even with the masks on.

"Man, she hated me," says Drew

"That's 'cause you would never sit still, Drew," says Terry.

"Nothing much changed there," says Lori.

"Okay y'all," says Terry. "You ready for the questions?"

She's carrying a list of symptoms to ask them about just in case she forgets any, though that doesn't seem likely at this point. Before starting the list, she takes their temperatures. Drew's is normal, Lori's a little elevated.

"Okay," she says. "Any rashes?"

Each day, Terry and Ed draw blood from husband and wife, hoping to identify the intruder partly by categorizing the defenses that their bodies have marshaled against it. Lynn's blood, too, has been sent off for analysis but results are slow in coming. Right now, Lori seems sicker than her husband. She has an apathetic air and is sleeping a lot. Drew is energetic enough to be restless, occasionally calling Kenny, who is busy working in the kitchen, taking care of Kyle, and filling him in on the latest sports news.

While Terry talks to the couple, Ed checks Lynn's vitals. He is aware that he is gentler with Terry's beautiful sister than he might be with another patient, though, apart from an occasional flicker of the eyelids, Lynn has shown no signs of consciousness. She continues to run a fever, which spikes in the evenings and becomes almost normal in the mornings. No problems with the IV drip or dehydration. After the check, Ed pauses for a moment before returning to the lab and gazes at Lynn. On the outside, her body is still and her face blank. Inside, though, he knows, is a raging conflict. If he is to have any impact on this conflict, he must do it by walking away from this battleground and shutting himself in the lab. While he tabulates data, fighting a shadow war, defeat or victory for Lynn will take place here, on that bed, and he can do little more than observe.

•

A few more days into the quarantine, Marika and Kyle finish "Thumbelina" and sit silently, Kyle on Marika's lap, breathing through their masks. Marika absently muses on the melancholy and silliness of Andersen's fairy tales. A man who never grew up, and who sometimes makes that seem like a good idea. Kyle too seems to be pondering the story, and for a minute, she tries to imagine how it appears to him. How many of the words does he even know? She smiles a small smile.

Trying to imagine her way into his mind is a little like reading a fairy tale—seemingly simple, but full of deep mysteries. She is startled when Kenny opens the door and Kyle suddenly jumps out of her lap. The active part of his day has begun. Inspired by the masks, which remind him of gunfighters' bandanas, Kenny has invented a game of "showdown" that the two play whenever they meet during the day.

"Draw, Pardner," says Kenny, slitting his eyes and walking in a slow, bowlegged saunter.

Kyle mimics Kenny, performing a more wobbly version of the walk, arms crooked at the elbows as if about to draw imaginary guns.

When they meet, Kenny sometimes falls down, clutching himself and saying, "Ya got me!" whereupon Kyle laughs with delight and jumps on him for a mock-wrestling match. Sometimes Kenny says, "Aha! Gotcha!" and scoops Kyle into the air, again to the child's delight.

Marika marvels at how Kenny can give the appearance of roughness, which Kyle seems to love, but which is always gentleness in disguise. It takes a while, though, for Marika to appreciate this, because she has to recover from the feeling Kyle leaves when he jumps out of her lap, a kind of empty ache, surprisingly sharp. She wants a drink, but takes a few deep breaths instead, and stowing the little book in her bag, she goes to check on Lynn before she begins her shift in Ed Shapiro's makeshift lab.

Today Terry is there and stands with Marika, gazing at her sister.

"She's breathing on her own," says Terry, "but only just. We keep thinking we're going to have to hook her up, but she stays just this side of needing it."

The two women stare at Lynn. She is still, but soaked with sweat. Marika can see that Lynn has grown thinner, and she feels a sudden gnawing at her own stomach. Neither she nor Terry speak for a while. Marika herself feels on the verge of tears and makes a date with herself to drink heavily later. This level of anguish about this mother and son—people she barely knows—seems absurd.

When Marika leaves, Terry sits and talks to Lynn.

"Kyle's being so good. He asks about you every day and wants to know the details of how we're taking care of you. Yesterday he asked if he could have an 'Ivy dip.' I guess he thinks it's like an ice cream cone. He gets wiggly sometimes, and then Kenny steps in and tosses him around a bit. They're actually pretty good together. Sometimes Daddy reads him a story, but he's pretty busy supervising. Mostly it's that Marika lady that reads to him. She seems to like it as much as he does, though I wouldn't have pegged her as a kid person. Daddy's learned to make coffee. Prides himself on it. Weird, huh? Ed and I— we're kind of on hold. Co-workers now more than anything."

A huge yawn suddenly takes hold of Terry, and she slumps in her chair. "So tired, sis. I almost wish I could join you." But then she sits up straight in her chair. "But that's not what's going to happen. I'm not joining you, you're joining me. Got it?" She crosses to Lynn's bed, she puts her hand on her sister's heart, to feel it beat, to will more life into her in a kind of energy transfer in which she herself does not believe.

Then Aunt Jeanne flickers into her mind, and then her mother, and she has the odd feeling that she would be sobbing now if she weren't so tired. She focuses again on her hand on her sister's heart. "I don't have much, sis," she says, "but take it anyway. There'll be more tomorrow."

Terry stumbles to her little cot off the quarantine section—she's on call tonight—sinks onto it, and falls asleep with her clothes on. She has the old dream again, but this time it's Aunt Jeanne rising up out of the water and looking silently at Terry as she stands on the shore. Jeanne's expression is sad but patient and a little conspiratorial, as if she's waiting for Terry to join her.

•

Getting ready for bed, Don Cathcart finds himself thinking about the conversation he had with Jeanne Dubovsky after the flood, about the strange feeling of freedom that came over them then. This situation is different, and he is still trying to get his bearings. It's odd to be banded together for protection from an enemy that thrives on togetherness. Being together now is a more difficult and tentative business.

He is still shaky from the loss of Hirsch and Jeanne, and every now and then he begins to tremble and has to sit down suddenly, put his hand over his face and let himself grieve. He's hoping this will pass and that God will show him some way to minister to this uneasy flock.

Tonight he's sitting on his cot, praying, when Marika appears suddenly beside him, offering him her flask of whiskey. Opening his eyes, he chuckles.

"Déjà vu," he says.

"Insomniacs unite," says Marika.

Don looks at her for a moment and then accepts the flask and takes a deep drink. Marika sits beside him, and they both look out over the sleeping bodies in the half-light of the cafeteria.

"Strange bedfellows," says Marika.

Don nods, handing the flask back to her. He feels an odd mixture of resentment and gratitude at this unexpected visit.

"Were you praying?" Marika startles him by asking.

"Yes," he says. Is there mockery in her voice? Cynicism? Envy? Hard to tell. "Well," he says, after a pause, "Partly praying. Partly fretting. Tomorrow's Sunday."

"Ah, yes," says Marika. "Will you be holding services?"

"Yes," says Don. "I'll do something for anyone who wants to come. And I guess I'll offer confession for the Catholics." There is another pause, and then he adds, "I haven't been to confession myself in a while."

Marika is silent, unable to account for the strange feeling of alliance she has with this man, so different from herself. She offers Don the flask again, but he declines.

"How goes the enemy?" he asks.

"You mean the virus?"

"Yes. Any scientific breakthroughs?"

Now it is her turn to wonder about his tone of voice. "Nothing that can be described as a breakthrough," she says. "It's a sort of race, really. It'll be interesting to see who wins."

"Interesting?" says Don. There is anger in his voice.

Marika takes another drink, wondering why his anger makes her feel glad. She can feel the heat of it on her averted face. There is another pause, then Don suddenly says, "Have you read *A Tale of Two Cities*?"

"Charles Dickens? I think so…a long time ago."

"There's a passage in it that I think about often," says Don. "It's about flies walking around the rims of wine glasses. Some flies have fallen in, and the ones that haven't fallen look down at the ones that have as if they were 'elephants, or something as far removed'."

There is a long silence.

Finally, Marika nods several times. "I don't think I'm an elephant. But yes, I remember that passage now," she says. "I remember trying to imagine how one fly could save another fly from drowning. It didn't look good."

Don shakes his head and chuckles sadly. "I have some milk in the fridge in the kitchen," he says. "Perhaps we could sneak in there and warm it up? It used to help my mother sleep."

"Yes," said Marika. "Mine too." She darts a look at Don. "Good idea," she says.

In the kitchen, as they watch the milk heating in the pan, Don says "I wonder what Hirsch would have made of all this."

Marika turns her face away and nods several times. Then she turns back to Don and looks at him directly, as if to say, "I can do this."

"I don't know," she says. "I don't—didn't—know him as well as you did. I never saw him in a group. It was always just the two of us."

Don stares into space for a minute, stirring the milk. "He was very good in groups. Not loud or anything, but…he was one of those people that just seemed to make everybody feel better when he came into the room. Why was that? I don't know. He liked to have a good time. He liked everyone to have a good time. He was an intellectual, of course, but he had almost no—hidden agenda. He just wanted everyone to be happy. I guess that's part of what made him such a good friend."

Marika nods. "Yes," she says. There is a long silence as Don pours the milk into mugs. Marika takes a sip and lets out a small sigh of contentment. "Very good," she says, and then, after a small pause, "I think we were in love."

Don blows on his milk and takes a sip. "Yes," he says. "I'm sorry you lost him."

Marika shakes her head. "No," she says. "Really, it's amazing that it happened at all." That night Marika sleeps well, the taste of warm milk in her mouth.

•

The next morning, though, she wakes up very early, before dawn, from a nightmare in which Lynn has died and Kyle has contracted the disease and lies on a hospital bed, listless and unreachable. In her dream, she walked by the sea to assuage her grief. It was dark and she lurched over the uneven, invisible sand beneath her feet. Slowly, she realized that the sea sounded wrong. The usual rushing momentum of the waves on the shore was quieter, slower, as if the sea were thickening and becoming viscous. Then a foul smell entered her nostrils.

Marika's heart is beating fast when she wakes, but gradually slows as her mind convinces her body of the falseness of her dream. The foul smell, for example, is coming from the kitchen, where Jack and Shona Brockie are boiling hundreds of eggs for breakfast.

But then another worry intrudes itself—another thing that she's been trying not to care about. A new element has been added to her picture of the waterfowl spreading disease through the water, of this vision she has been having of a sea contaminated with contagion. Or rather, not new, but the resurgence of an idea she's had before.

The new element comes from the rush that she's been seeing in the scientific news to manipulate saltwater algae as an alternate source of livestock feed and biofuel. Such a rush! Always such a rush when there's money to be made. Grants are offered, language is inflated, and nobody wants to think about the complexity of the processes they propose to manipulate. And they call this science.

A familiar bitter taste rises in Marika's mouth. She went on the web last night and saw that two major start-ups have declared their intention to begin experiments with algae as an alternate fuel source. She did see one timid article by an ecologist suggesting that not enough attention was being paid to the risks of contamination if genetically modified molecules were to escape containment and, for instance, re-cross the barrier between fresh and salt water. Organisms that had never been able to cross that barrier—viruses, for instance— might piggy-back on genetically engineered organisms, creating a whole new kind of contamination and contagion—one that could travel the oceans of the world, spreading a pandemic more thoroughly than ever before.

Fool, fools, fools! Some damned cowboy is probably doing it right now.

She gives up on sleep and moves quietly to the lab to make coffee and begin her work, feeding yesterday's data into the tracking program. She takes her mask off to do this, alone with her computer in a converted mop closet. She works with grim resignation.

When she's finished with her data entry, she shudders as she puts her mask back on. How she has come to hate the thing! She can't get used to it. It irritates her skin and is a constant reminder of the constriction of her current circumstances, in which everything seems to be getting on her nerves.

She realizes that, before the quarantine, her long periods of solitude—the rambles by the sea, the evenings with her maps—might have been keeping her sane. She misses the waves, the salty air, the seagulls, her own personal coffee pot, as if they were close relatives—her family.

•

As breakfast is being served, Marika spots Don Cathcart sitting alone on a cot in the sleeping area with his face in his hands, apparently praying, and wonders if he is really talking to God or just pretending so people will leave him alone. She tries to stay away from Lynn's bedside, but she finds that she is compelled to check and make sure she is still alive. Looking at the unconscious figure, she feels the knot in her stomach grow harder.

33

The next morning is the last of the year. As usual, Marika downs several cups of coffee and then pushes past her fatigue to work with Ed Shapiro in the lab.

Ed is more silent than usual, but after they've been working for about an hour, he swivels away from his microscope to face her, looking at her until she looks up from her paperwork.

"They want to recall me," he says.

"What?"

"The CDC wants to reassign me."

"But…we need you here!"

"Not enough fatalities for the funds," says Ed drily.

"Well that's—you have to fight it! This could be very serious!"

"Yes, I know. I've told them. It's not their fault. They have to do cost-effectiveness assessments of human suffering."

There is a stunned silence.

Marika gets up and paces around the room. "This is unacceptable!" she says.

Ed nods sadly, and she notices how exhausted he looks.

"Would it help if I wrote a letter?" she asks.

"I don't know," says Ed. "Probably not. Unless you enclose a massive check."

For the first time since Marika has known him, she sees Ed slump a little in his chair, turning inward.

"Take a break," says Marika. "Go for a walk or go call somebody. I'll do your rounds."

He hesitates.

"Go" she says. "I'll wrap up here."

Ed nods. "Okay," he says. "Maybe a breather is in order. Thanks."

Marika prints a set of labels, double-checks them and then turns off the computer. She glances around the lab to see that everything is in its place and then turns off the light, locks the door and goes, clipboard in hand, to check on the quarantine patients. She is deep in thought—so deep that she herself doesn't know what she's thinking—and almost passes the door to Drew and Lori Layman's room before abruptly turning and knocking.

When she enters, gloved and masked, she sees that Drew is out of bed, sitting in a chair next to Lori, who is sleeping. A little CD player in the corner is playing hymns. Drew stands when Marika enters, and turns down the volume of the CD player.

"She likes them," he explains, as if apologizing. He hovers a little as she looks at Lori.

"She just got to sleep," he says. "She's been kinda upset."

"Why?" asks Marika

"Money," says Drew again, almost apologetically. "We don't really know how much all this is costing, and we—we're not insured."

"I'll check," says Marika, "but I'm pretty sure you're not charged for any of this."

"Really?" asks Drew. "Really?" and Marika can see his brow unknotting, his shoulders relaxing. "Wow! That's so—we're still paying for Mom's nursing home and—that's really good news."

Marika looks at Lori over her clipboard. Is she asleep, or is it something deeper? Lori's face is waxen and pale. Rolling up Lori's sleeves, she sees that the rash has returned, though seemingly without the fever. Loath though she is to disturb Ed, she decides to go and consult him and maybe bring him back to help with the examination. "I'll be right back," she says, and steps into the hallway, where she almost trips over something on the floor right by the door.

Looking down, she is astounded to see that it is Kyle, curled up asleep. She has to blink to make sure she's not seeing things. She stares in wonder for a while and then squats down to pick him up, hoping that he'll stay asleep until she can put him in his bed. But his sleep is shallow, and as soon as her hands are under him, his body seems to grow stubbornly heavier, even before he opens his eyes. When he does open them, the two stare at each other for a while, both wondering what's happening, until suddenly Kyle remembers his purpose and stiffens with resolve.

"Kyle want Mama," he says, as if Marika is a genie he has summoned to help him.

Marika sits back on her heels and regards him worriedly. She is speechless. How did the child find his way here? And then she is suddenly filled with a yearning (where did this come from?) to let Kyle have his way. She sees that, stoical though he has been, he can no longer accept the wrongness of this separation from his mother, a wrongness that he feels in his barely knitted bones. In her stunned silence, she finds that she has forgotten all the sensible, adult reasons that he cannot have what he wants. She sits down beside him, and he sits up.

"Kyle help Mama," he insists.

"We can't go in to see her," she says, "but we can help her without seeing her." She puts her arm around the child, who waits for her to explain, which she will do when she has the slightest idea what she means.

"Right now it's time for sleep," she says. "But tomorrow we will think of a way to try to help your mama." She stands up and holds out her hand. Kyle takes it and allows her to walk him back to his little cot beside the snoring Kenny. She tucks him in, and seeing his sleepy blue eyes staring up at her, she can't keep herself from kissing his forehead.

"Good night," she whispers, "see you tomorrow," and his eyelids flutter and close.

Hurriedly, she finds Ed and returns with him to the Laymans' room. When they get there, Drew is just coming out the door, looking very agitated.

"I can't wake her up!" he says.

Ed, Terry, and Marika work through much of the night to save Lori, hooking her up to the same kinds of machines that are sustaining Lynn, but around dawn, Don receives the call to administer last rites, and Lori dies without regaining consciousness. Her defenses against the virus were so weak that she didn't even run much of a fever, and it cut her down swiftly.

•

That night, Don stays in the Laymans' room until Drew falls asleep with the help of sleeping pills provided by Ed. Then Don heads back to the general sleeping area, eases himself into his cot and, after a brief prayer, falls asleep almost immediately with his mask still on. In his dream, it is broad daylight, and the beach at Jasper is full of people, as it is in high summer—sleeping businessmen, families hooked up to their phones, self-conscious young girls in revealing bikinis, teenage boys desperate with desire and boredom, young mothers dizzy with exhaustion, watching their children teasing the waves. The sun bathes them all insistently in light. From the corner of his eye, Don sees a movement out to sea. From the calm blue water a wave is approaching, growing rapidly larger and larger until it looms high over the people on the beach. Then there is a kind of freeze-frame, and everything is still. Don looks around. How tiny all the people suddenly look, how fragile, how utterly beautiful! He yearns not so much to warn them as to wake them up, to make them see their own beauty. His yearning has the force of revelation. Then a wave of deeper sleep flows gently over him and folds his dream back into the depths of his consciousness.

•

Marika wakes suddenly in the middle of the night, and finds she is unable to get back to sleep. She tries another nightcap, tosses and turns, and tries to calm her breathing, all to no avail. Everyone else is asleep, including Don Cathcart, her usual insomniac companion. Her restlessness is almost unbearable.

Rising noiselessly, she lifts the corner of a window shade and sees a full moon staring back at her. This brings her to a quick resolution. She must go for a walk or go mad. She knows where the master key is kept. She recalls that the alarm is disconnected.

Hurrying now, she shoves a small flashlight in one pocket and her mask in another. Holding her breath, she opens the drawer where the key is kept, fits it into the lock, steps outside and eases the door shut behind her.

The parking lot is utterly still, bathed with silver light, and Marika takes a deep breath of the blessed cool night air. She knows exactly how to get from here to the sea, and in fact, one of her favorite places is not far away. Without hesitation, she strides, almost running, toward it.

When she gets to the beach, masses of clouds are passing over the moon. In the dark, the sound of the waves seems to be shushing her like a weary mother. She breathes deeply. The sea is calm, but the tide is high. Marika has visited this spot often at high tide, and each time the ribbon of sand where she stands has been thinner. The sand—this whole shore—is being pushed steadily southward.

Before long, she expects to come one night and find her little cove gone. The thought has always exhilarated her. There is a super-human time scale operating here, in which beaches come and go like clouds on a windy day. Easier to see on a beach like this than in most places, though true everywhere. So liberating compared to the claustrophobic urgency of life with people, where everything insists on mattering so much.

The clouds are thickening and the night is dark. Scanning the black water, Marika sees a faint scintillation, growing brighter. Tiny lights cascade with a beautiful, mesmerizing rhythm. They enter her reverie easily, of a piece with the shushing of the water and the exhilarating tang of the sea breeze. But then the scientist in her awakens. Bioluminescence. Dinoflagellates responding to disturbance from turbulence by dazzling potential predators. Sometimes the display is harmless, but sometimes it signals a toxic algae bloom, dangerous to wildlife and humans.

All the worries and fears that have been assailing Marika return full force. There's been some kind of shift inside her, and she cannot escape those worries, even in a haven like this. What's more, she can't follow lines of thought that lead to ecological disaster or emerging diseases without a painful feeling of anguish, an anguish connected somehow to Kyle and to his unconscious mother.

She curses under her breath. The only place that she can find peace, and now, there's no peace for her here. Her throat constricts, and hot tears course down her cheeks. Head in her hands, she sobs until she is exhausted.

A long time seems to pass until she looks up. The clouds are parting and the beach around her is becoming visible. Looking around, she realizes with disgust that there is a campsite here, littered with beer cans, chicken bones, and cigarette butts. Looking more closely, she sees that something is moving on it, and as the moon emerges from the clouds, she sees that it's a seagull picking tenaciously at the debris. She sits on a nearby dune to watch it.

The bird's concentration never wavers. Its life, Marika feels, is full of purpose. Despair is a luxury it cannot afford. Marika watches it for a long time. When the seagull finally waddles away and begins to preen, she shakes herself, realizing that she's been staring at a pile of garbage. It is the gull, though, that holds her attention. It has such patience, sifting through for something that could be used. Maybe there's something to be said for garbage after all, thinks Marika. After all, who's to say what is wasted? And an unexpected, painful warmth rises inside her, as she realizes: that's what Hirsch would say.

To her astonishment, resolutions begin to form in her mind. She can't let this virus be ignored. She must try to make her research more accessible She must bombard former colleagues, journals, the scientific press, and the CDC with her findings. She must make them listen, even if she has to talk to fools and to look like one herself. She has former colleagues in high places, and she will see whether they can pull strings so that Ed can stay longer. She is filled with a mixture of fear and resolve which merge to create a sense of purpose stronger than any she has felt before.

She turns away from the seagull and peers out to sea. A cloud passes again over the moon, but the phytoplankton continue to blink in the darkness, as if the sea is sending a signal. On the beach, a wave comes in and swirls around the little garbage heap that preoccupied the seagull. The wave withdraws, whispering.

Slowly, Marika stands, brushes the sand from her pants, and walks back to the peopled world.

About the Author

Teacher, author, playwright, and poet Andrea Fisher Rowland (1957-2019) made her home in Charlottesville, Virginia.

Andrea spent her childhood years in New Zealand, and thereafter was a Virginia resident for most of her life. She graduated in English from James Madison University, where hers was the first student-written play—entitled "Fancies"—ever presented on the main stage of campus and for which she won the Norman Lear Award for Comedy Playwriting.

She earned an MA from the University of Virginia with a concentration in Creative Writing, studying with John Casey and Greg Orr. She went on to earn a PhD from the University as well, working with Karen Chase and Edgar Shannon. Her dissertation, *The Supernatural Muse: Representations of the Creative Impulse in the Fiction of Emily Brontë, Charlotte Brontë, and Charles Dickens*, examines the supernatural figures (ghosts, genii, etc.) appearing in those authors' works.

She worked as an Assistant Dean and Director of Studies at the University of Virginia, taught composition and literature at Wake Forest University, and taught introduction to theater at James Madison University. She taught English at Renaissance School in Charlottesville. She directed readings and productions of Shakespeare and other early modern playwrights at Wake Forest and at the University of Virginia.

Throughout the years, while raising her son Liam, she wrote poetry, plays, and fiction, notably her novel *High Tide*. In 2017, an excerpt from *High Tide* was a finalist in the Virginia Festival of the Book Fiction Contest, and her poem, "These Same Fields," won the Writer House / Jefferson Madison Regional Library Poetry Competition. *Artemis Journal* published her poem, "Waikato," in its 2018 collection.

Andrea's poetry collection, *Family Album*, and her novel, *High Tide*, launched in 2019, both from Chenille Books.

Visit www.andreafisherrowland.wordpress.com to learn more about the author, her books, and related news and events.